A Man's Worth

Also by Nikita Lynnette Nichols

None But The Righteous

You can contact the author by e-mail at
kitawrites@comcast.net

A Man's Worth

Nikita Lynnette Nichols

www.urbanchristianonline.net

Urban Books
1199 Straight Path
West Babylon, NY 11704

ISBN-13: 978-1-60162-968-5
ISBN-10: 1-60162-968-0

First Printing September 2008
Printed in the United States of America

10 9 8 7 6 5 4 3 2

Distributed by Kensington Publishing Corp.
Submit Wholesale Orders to:
Kensington Publishing Corp.
C/O Penguin Group (USA) Inc.
Attention: Order Processing
405 Murray Hill Parkway
East Rutherford, NJ 07073-2316
Phone: 1-800-526-0275
Fax: 1-800-227-9604

Dedication

My parents, William and Victoria Nichols, there are no words to express how deep my gratitude and love runs for you. You've been my rock, my base, and my foundation. I dedicate this book to you.

Acknowledgments

Well, Father, you've done it again. You have proven yourself to be the divine wonder that you are. I thank you for your grace. You've walked with me, talked with me and held my hand as I pushed this baby out. You gave me the words and I penned them to paper. I acknowledge you as the author of this book.

Chapter 1

There's something about the way it looks outside that lets you know it's Sunday. For as long as he could remember, Randall Loomis woke up and knew right away that Sunday was here. Maybe it was the way the sun shined, or it could be the way three birds gathered on his bedroom windowsill and sang. It never failed that these little birdies would appear around seven o'clock AM, Sunday after Sunday, to wake him with a praise song of their own.

Finally, Sunday was here. Randall had been living in anticipation since Monday morning for Sunday to come again. Church was his life. It seemed that he was there every time the church doors opened. On Sundays, there was prayer from eight o'clock to eight forty-five AM. From nine o'clock to ten-fifteen, he attended sunday church school. At ten-thirty sharp, morning worship began at Holy Deliverance Baptist Church, located on the corners of Perry Street and Bomer Avenue on the south side of Chicago.

On Monday nights at seven-thirty, there was men's

ministry. Pastor Cordell Bryson always had a church full of brothers, young and old, who were serious about getting right and staying right. On Wednesday nights, Randall had sanctuary choir rehearsal at seven o'clock PM. On Thursday nights, he was there for Bible study.

But there was nothing like Sunday morning worship. Then Randall could lie prostrate in the presence of God and allow the Holy Spirit to minister to him. He loved God, and he loved to go to church. On Sunday afternoons, while driving home from church, Randall's spirit would be so full with the Word of God that he felt about five months pregnant. Being full of joy, peace, and hope made him feel as though he would burst if someone rubbed against him.

Pastor Bryson always gave Randall enough fire to take him through the week. But the days between Sundays had the ability to take their toll on him. Even though Randall was on his knees in God's face every morning before work, someone would say something or something would happen to remind him that Satan still existed. And by Saturday night, his pregnancy was terminated.

But thank God it was Sunday again. As he lay there listening for his alarm clocks to finish their trio and fly away, Randall couldn't wait for what Pastor Bryson was going to feed his soul today. Randall's spirit had been drained during the week, and he was hungry for the Word of God.

When the birdies had finished their song and flown away, Randall looked down and smiled at the sleeping beauty who was lying peacefully on his chest. *Amaryllis, such a beautiful name for such a beautiful face.* He smiled.

* * *

From the moment he saw her two years ago, trying on shoes in Evergreen Park Mall, Randall knew Amaryllis would be his forever. She paced back and forth in that yellow halter dress (that may as well have been painted on) modeling stilettos in the knee-high mirror. He had been on his way out but he stopped in his tracks, giving Amaryllis his full attention.

She slipped off a pair of four-inch black patent leather Cole Haan heels to try on three and a half inch turquoise Stuart Weitzman pumps. Randall got a glimpse of the prettiest feet he'd ever seen on a woman. Her toenails were filed evenly and painted hot pink with a little glitter sprinkled. He could tell this woman was a regular at someone's nail shop. Her skin was the color of light caramel. Her hair, dark brown with deep golden highlights, was parted down the middle and flowed past her shoulders. She had brown eyes that would hypnotize any man. Her nose was small and petite, and she had full lips that were lined just right with a touch of shiny bronze gloss. And God curved her body in all the right places. She was blessed and highly favored with a perfect figure eight frame. Amaryllis was *woman* in every sense of the word.

As Randall watched her sashay across the floor in those three and a half inch turquoise heels, he wanted nothing more than to drink her in. Unbeknownst to Amaryllis, she was like a magnet to Randall. He kept watch of every move she made, like a predator staking out its prey, waiting for just the right moment to pounce. He slowly walked into the shoe store as though in a trance. He knew he was getting closer to her, but he couldn't feel his feet touching the ground. Before Amaryllis knew it, Randall was upon her.

"Excuse me," he said.

Amaryllis was facing the opposite direction and looking down at her feet when she heard his voice and turned around. She exhaled loudly, giving Randall a nasty attitude.

"Yes?"

He looked into her eyes and forgot what he wanted to say. At that moment, he didn't know his own name, address, or social security number. He stood there dumbfounded. He opened his mouth to speak, but no words came forth. Up close, she was even more beautiful. Randall didn't know this woman, but if she told him to rob a bank and bring her all the money, he'd waste no time putting on a black ski mask and heading for the nearest bank.

Amaryllis stood there watching him ogle at her. Already irritated by his presence, she spoke with much attitude. "What is your problem?"

As she spoke, Randall was in awe at the way her lips moved. The dark brown lip liner blended with bronze lip gloss reminded him of a piece of butterscotch candy. He was tempted to lick them. Amaryllis lost patience with him. She turned back around, picked up three shoe boxes, and walked to another mirror.

Unaware of his surroundings or what he was doing, Randall approached her again.

This time, he was less than an inch from her, and she had to step backward to keep him from touching her. Amaryllis was already frustrated because she wanted three pairs of shoes but could only afford to buy two, and she couldn't decide on which two. She looked Randall in his eyes and put her hand on her hip. "Who are you, and what do you want?"

Randall knew she was irritated and probably felt like he was stalking her. Nervously, he uttered the first thing that came to his mind. "My name is Randall, and I'm not crazy."

To Amaryllis, Randall's behavior fit the description of a bonafide psychopath. If a man walked up to a woman and declared that he wasn't crazy, then it usually meant that he was in denial.

"Okay, now that I know your name and that you're not crazy, although I think differently, I'll ask the question again. What do you want?"

"Can I be honest?"

"You can be gone. How about that?" Amaryllis took off the Stuart Weitzman pumps she was modeling and put them in their box. She then grabbed the other two shoe boxes and walked to the cash register. Like a puppy dog on the heels of his master, Randall followed. Already, he had rubbed her the wrong way. He couldn't help the fact that she took his breath away. Obviously, this woman didn't know how beautiful she was. You'd think she would be used to this kind of attention.

The only salesclerk in the shoe store was tending to another customer. Amaryllis stood at the counter trying to decide which two of the three pairs of shoes she would get. In her peripheral vision, she saw Randall walking toward her. She decided that if the nutcase said one more thing to her, she would let him have it.

Her body language told him she didn't want to be bothered, but Randall had to do something to fix the situation. If he could just get her to smile and give him her name, he'd leave her alone.

"Please don't be angry with me. I'm not a stalker, I was just admiring your feet. I was walking by this store and happened to see you trying on shoes, and I couldn't help but notice how pretty your feet are. I wanted to approach you and ask your name, but when you turned around and looked at me, your beauty took my breath away. I was honestly at a loss for words and couldn't speak. I'm sorry if I offended you, that was not my intention."

Amaryllis looked into Randall's eyes and knew that he was sincere. She couldn't help but smile about the compliment he gave her. She let her guard down, but only a little bit.

"That was a beautiful thing to say. Thank you very much."

As Amaryllis was smiling, Randall looked at her dimples. He wanted to say more, but from nowhere, a cat came and stole his tongue. The salesclerk took her place behind the counter and asked Amaryllis if she could help her. Amaryllis gave her two pairs of shoes and held on to the Stuart Weitzman shoebox. "I can only afford these two pair now, and I'll come back for the most expensive pair. Can you hold them for forty-eight hours?"

The clerk stated that because the Stuart Weitzman pumps were discounted, she wasn't permitted to hold them. Amaryllis looked disappointed and Randall saw the sadness in her eyes and stepped in to try and see those dimples again. "Why don't you let me buy the last pair for you? You look as though you really want them, and considering how pretty your feet are, I want you to have them. No strings attached."

"You don't even know my name, so why do you wanna buy shoes for me?"

"Okay, tell me your name."

Another loud exhalation reminded Randall she was irritated by his very presence.

"Why?"

"Because I wanna know what it is."

"Why?"

"Those light blue heels were gorgeous on your feet. I

don't know if it was the color or what, but they really brought out your nail polish. I really want you to have them. Consider them a gift."

Amaryllis looked into Randall's eyes again, wondering what his motive was. "Why are you pressing so hard to buy these shoes for me? You don't know me from Adam."

Randall chuckled at her words. "Believe me. If I saw you standing next to anyone named Adam, I'd definitely know who was Adam and who wasn't."

Amaryllis smiled again and gave the clerk her debit card to pay for the two pairs of shoes she could afford, then she looked at him. "Randall, is it?"

He smiled and nodded.

"Thank you, Randall, for your offer, but I don't think it's a good idea."

The clerk gave Amaryllis her receipt and shoes. Amaryllis turned to walk away when Randall grabbed her lightly by the elbow. "I'm buying these heels. I can take them home and sit them on my dresser and look at them everyday and imagine your pretty little feet in them. Or you can take them with you and enjoy wearing them, which will make me even happier. Either way, I *am* buying these shoes. So, why miss out on a blessing?"

Amaryllis looked down at his hand gripping her elbow then connected her eyes with his. Randall released her.

"Because, Randall, if that's your real name, you call it a blessing when it could very well be a curse. I've been down this road with men before. I know firsthand that when a man wines and dines a woman, he'll pick up the tab at the restaurant, but he'll expect the woman to give him dessert before the date is over. Too many times I've been given gifts only to learn later on that they come with a price after all. So, you can keep those heels, because I know you didn't mean it when you said 'no strings attached.' "

Randall asked the salesclerk for the price of the light blue Stuart Weitzman heels. Amaryllis took note that he didn't flinch at the five-hundred-and-fifty dollar price. She couldn't believe her eyes when Randall withdrew six crisp, newly printed, one hundred dollar bills from his wallet and laid them on top of the counter. He placed his wallet back in his pocket and smiled at Amaryllis. Randall couldn't help himself. He'd had a foot fetish for as long as he could remember. Women with beautiful feet really did it for him.

"Keep the change and do whatever it is that you do to keep your feet so pretty."

One last smile at Amaryllis and Randall left the shoe store. The salesclerk felt she had just witnessed a scene from a fairytale movie. "See, stuff like that never happens to me. You just happened to be in the right place at the right time, and look what happened." The clerk looked down at the shoes, "Are you gonna take these heels?"

"Of course. I ain't no fool," Amaryllis stated, but not so sure about her own answer.

"Humph, I don't know about that. Seems to me you just let your future pass you by."

Amaryllis walked out of the shoe store with her gift and looked all around for Randall. She spotted him looking at tuxedos through a showcase window. She took off her shoes and put on the turquoise Stuart Weitzman heels. She then put the shoes she had been wearing in the box and walked over to him. "Amaryllis Price thanks you."

When Randall turned around, she was already walking away. He looked down at the heels and smiled. He took a pen from his shirt pocket and wrote her name on his palm. He was absolutely sure he didn't know how to spell it correctly. He watched her walk until he couldn't see her anymore. When she had disappeared from his view, he turned to look at the tuxedos again and thought to himself, *A man who findeth a wife, findeth good thing.*

As soon as Randall got home from the mall, he raced to the telephone with a notepad and pen ready when he dialed information. There was only one Amaryllis Price listed in Chicago. The operator gave Randall the number then connected him. It rang four times then Randall heard, "Hello, you've reached the home of Amaryllis Price."

He gently placed the telephone on its receiver and smiled. It was her voice, something Randall would never forget. He sat on the sofa with a satisfied look on his face. There was no way he could call her because he gave his word that he wouldn't bother her again. If Amaryllis had actually answered his call, Randall would've hung up. But not seeing or talking to her again wasn't working for Randall. He wasn't okay with just buying her a pair of shoes, he wanted to give Amaryllis the world, *his* world. Randall was so sure he'd met his Eve that day. He leaned back on the sofa and spoke out loud. "Amaryllis, such a beautiful name for such a beautiful face. How do I make you my wife?"

She wasn't his wife yet, but Randall was still praying on it. It had been almost two years since that day at Evergreen Park Mall, and although Randall did manage to get Amaryllis to fall in love with him, he was no closer to making her his wife today than he was then. He watched her sleeping on his chest. She was purring softly like a kitten. Even as she slept, Randall thought she was breathtaking. He wondered what time she had gotten in from the riverboat casino last night. He hadn't gotten to bed himself until after one o'clock AM, and she still wasn't home. He began to massage her face and she stirred.

"Good morning, precious," he smiled.

Amaryllis yawned and looked up at Randall. "Good morning, Black."

'Black' was the nickname she had given him because according to her, Randall was extra tall, extremely dark, and exceptionally handsome.

"It's Sunday, baby. How about I make you eggs and bacon before church?"

Still lying on his chest with her eyes closed, Amaryllis looked happy and comfortable.

"I'm too tired to go to church today, Black. You go ahead and say a prayer for me."

Randall let out a loud sigh. He was disappointed yet again. In the past two years, he could count on one hand how many times Amaryllis had actually gone to church with him. Either she was too tired or had something else to do. She always promised to go the next Sunday. Amaryllis was not saved and had told Randall many times that she didn't believe in heaven or hell. She insisted that her life was fine without religion but Randall knew the consequences and repercussions of living an unsaved life. Just the mere thought of Amaryllis being left behind after the Rapture terrified him. He felt that if he could get her in the habit of going to church with him at least two Sundays a month, maybe God would send a special word to Amaryllis that would open her heart for Him. "Come on, precious. You promised that you'd go with me today and I was looking forward to it."

"I know, baby, but I got home real late last night and

I'm really tired. You don't want me falling asleep in church, do you?"

Randall exhaled loudly. "Amaryllis, if you can go to the riverboat and gamble all night with your girls, then you can certainly go to church with your man. Where is your priority? And you know I don't like you going to that boat anyway."

Amaryllis opened her eyes and looked at Randall. She didn't like the tone of his voice.

"Who are you? My father? If I say that I don't feel like going to church today, then I don't feel like going." She rolled off of Randall's chest, turned her back to him and pulled the sheets up to her nose.

Randall got out of bed, went into the living room and knelt next to the sofa. He'd been praying for two years for God to save Amaryllis's soul. His lack of judgment, evidenced by inviting Amaryllis to share his home and his bed and not abstaining from sexual relations, had clouded Randall's ability to see the trick of the enemy. He was totally oblivious to see that because of fornication and his love for Amaryllis, he himself had fallen out of the grace of God. Over the past two years, Randall's prayers had gone from asking God to keep, protect, and guide him, to only asking God to save Amaryllis's soul.

After prayer, he went into the kitchen to make breakfast for Amaryllis. He left it on the table covered in saran wrap then took his shower. Once Randall was dressed, he kissed her forehead and left for church . . . alone.

Chapter 2

After Sunday School at Holy Deliverance Baptist Church, there was usually a fifteen-minute break before morning worship began. During this time, a complimentary breakfast was served downstairs in the fellowship hall. This was one of the highlights of Sunday mornings at 'Holy D,' which was what the church was affectionately called by the congregation. Drinking coffee, eating doughnuts, and good conversation helped to set the mood for Pastor Bryson's hooping and hollering.

Cordell Bryson was a handsome young man, twenty-eight to be exact. He was raised in the same church at which he pastored today. Having a father as a deacon and a mother who was president of the usher board for twenty years before she died, Cordell was at church practically every day of his young life. During his adolescence, he studied English, math, and history during the day, and studied scriptures and the Word of God in the evenings. The difference between Cordell and his peers was that he wanted to go to church whenever he

could. He actually looked forward to it. His parents had
known since the moment he was born that God had a
special calling on his life.

Throughout most of his childhood, Cordell didn't
have many friends due to the fact that he was hardly
ever around to play tag or softball. He was a church
boy, as the kids on the block called him. Cordell was
called into his ministry at the age of twenty-three and
preached his first sermon entitled "Hold On To Your
Spiritual Composure."

He told the church about his experience as a child:
being teased because he chose to go to Bible Study
rather than going along with other boys to the park to
play basketball. Although he tried to convince himself
that the name 'church boy' didn't bother him much,
there had been many a day that he wanted to yield to
temptation and drop those school books and prove that
church boys can fight too. In his sermon, he had en-
couraged the church to stay in prayer when the enemy
came upon them to eat of their flesh. The people of God
didn't have to fight for themselves, because the battle
belonged to the Lord. He told the saints to ask themselves, "What would Jesus do in this situation?" The
congregation understood that they must keep their
spiritual composure at all times.

Cordell Bryson was voted in as pastor of 'Holy D' at
the age of twenty-five, shortly after the previous pastor suffered a heart attack and died while preaching in
the pulpit. Cordell thought that the best way to meet
your Maker was while doing His will.

So, for the past three years, he had taken on the
task of head shepherd, though it hadn't always been
easy. Having the responsibility as pastor was sometimes stressful and challenging. Trying to live right,
set a good example, and lead God's people to right-

eousness were just a few of the requirements that could wear a pastor down. And Cordell was no exception. Being single, saved, and young while in the pulpit put him directly in Satan's line of fire.

Within the first three months of Cordell's pastorship, he received a telephone call from a young woman who said she needed counseling because she felt the enemy was attacking her life. Cordell gathered scriptures and holy oil, then off he went to pray for the sister. As he walked up the steps to the front door, he heard soft jazz music coming from the living room window. She must have been watching for him, because the door opened before Cordell had a chance to ring the doorbell. Ruby red lips, burgundy cheeks, and light blue eye shadow greeted him at the door.

What in the . . . ? Cordell immediately apologized to God for this thought. He looked down at what appeared to be his mother's lace curtains draped across this woman's body. On her feet were high-heeled sandals with fur balls on top. At first, he thought he had arrived at the wrong house. He stepped back to look at the address above the door.

"Yes, Cordell, you came to the right place. It's me, Beverly." Her right hand was on her hip, and her left arm reached up to hold the door open.

Cordell saw that her underarm held more hair than his own. If the light blue eye shadow wasn't a turn off, this nappy hair with caked up balls of white deodorant definitely was. Cordell knew that if he stepped one foot in that house, his ministry would be in danger. Not because of what he would do to her, but because of what she would try to do to him.

"Excuse me, sister, you're gonna have to turn off that music and put on some decent clothes if you want me to pray with you. And I would appreciate it if you address me as Pastor Bryson."

"Well then, Pastor Bryson, I didn't call you over here for prayer. I can pray for myself. But I'll tell you what you *can* do for me; how about laying hands on a sister? Let's see if you have the anointing to deliver some sexual healing up in here."

Cordell broke out into a sweat. He had been a pastor for three months and nothing like this had happened yet. He didn't know what to do: to turn around and walk away, or try and persuade her to change her clothes and her life? He knew this woman needed spiritual guidance, however, he also knew that he wasn't the one to counsel her, especially right now.

"Sister, whatever you had in mind for us to do when I got here is not gonna happen. I don't know who you think I am, but I'm not that kind of pastor and I don't appreciate you wasting my time. It's Monday night and I had to find a substitute to lead men's ministry tonight because I thought one of my members was in trouble."

Beverly was insulted by Cordell's words. "What do you mean I'm wasting your time? I see the way you look at me in church. Who are you trying to fool?"

"Sister, I don't know who you are. What are you talking about?"

"I'm talking about the way you greet me, hug me, and smile in my face. What's up with that?"

"I greet, hug, and smile at everybody. I'm sorry if you read more into it and took it to another level."

"Oh, you ain't sorry yet. But you will be when the church finds out how you came to my house to seduce me and wouldn't take no for an answer. I bet you'll be real sorry then."

"Well, sister, if that's what you feel led by God to do, then you go ahead and say what you wanna say. I can't do anything about that."

Beverly slammed the door in Cordell's face. He turned around, walked down the steps and got in his car. After he fastened his seat belt, his head fell backward on the headrest. "No weapon . . ."

Beverly hadn't been to 'Holy D' since. Cordell learned a lesson that day. And from then on, no matter who called him for prayer, man or woman, he always had them meet him at the church. If it was a woman who needed counseling, he would have the church mother sit in on the session.

After Randall was dressed in his choir robe, he went to Pastor Bryson's office and knocked on the door.

"It's open," Pastor said.

Randall opened the door and walked in. Cordell sat at his desk looking over his sermon. When he saw Randall, he smiled and stood to shake his hand. "Good morning, Randall. It's good to see you."

"Praise the Lord, Pastor. It's good to be here. How are you this morning?"

"You know me, Randall. I'm always fired up for the Lord. What brings you in here this morning?"

"Nothing, really. I just wanted to encourage you, that's all. To tell you to be sure and let the Lord use you this morning. I need you to bring forth a good word."

Cordell and Randall were best friends. They were the same age and had grown up together at 'Holy D.' Whenever you saw one, you saw the other—two peas in a pod. When something was bothering one, the other always picked up on it. It was something about the bond they shared. They had always confided in each other about their problems.

Looking into Randall's eyes, Cordell knew that his buddy was troubled. And he also knew that Amaryllis was the reason. Two years ago, when Randall told Cordell that he'd met his wife in Evergreen Park Mall, the first thing Cordell asked him was, "Is she saved?"

Randall ignored the question and proceeded to tell him how beautiful she was. Cordell let him ramble on about Amaryllis's hair, eyes, lips, and feet. He waited patiently for Randall to finish praising her, then he asked him again. "Is she saved?" Cordell looked at Randall and knew that his friend was getting into something that wasn't good.

"Well, is she saved or not, Randall?"

"Man, why do you always have to get into stuff so deep? I just met the girl. We haven't talked about that yet."

"Randall, I'm your best friend. I'm also your pastor. And as your pastor, I suggest you find out if this woman knows God before you get involved with her."

When Randall told him a month later that Amaryllis had moved into his condo with him, Cordell was fit to be tied. "Randall, you can't be serious. You know better than that. Why would you do something so stupid?" Cordell asked his friend.

"Hey, man, all I know is that I love her."

"Then if you love her, you introduce her to God and help her establish a prayer life and relationship with Him. And you pray that God will save her soul. When that happens, then you ask God if she's the woman for you. Then you allow Him to guide your relationship and lead it to marriage, if that's His will. But you don't move a woman in your home and play house. I don't care how much you shout, dance, and pray. If you ain't right with God in every area of your life, He ain't feeling your praise."

"Cordell, I knew you were going to be like this." Randall's voice sounded irritated.

"You're doggone right, I'm going to be like this. What did you expect me to say? 'Congratulations for shacking up with your girlfriend; I hope you two will be very happy together?' Is that what you thought my response would be to something like this?"

"Nah, man, I was just hoping you'd understand how I feel, that's all."

"Randall, I do understand. I'm a man too. But I'm also your pastor, and I'm telling you that you're playing with fire and you're going to get burned. Deep down inside, you know better. We were raised in Bible class and Sunday School together. Whatever I learned, you learned also. You used to be able to recognize the trick of the enemy. What happened?"

"Nothing happened."

"Yes, it did. And since you don't want to admit it, I'll tell you what happened. You saw Amaryllis and fell for her the moment you laid eyes on her. You allowed your flesh to overpower your spirit, man. You became so wrapped up in how she looks on your arm, you lost focus on what's important. Yes, Amaryllis is beautiful, I'll be the first to say that. But beauty is only skin deep. God doesn't look at that. He looks at the soul. You can't even get her to come to church or pray with you. Don't you know that you're worth more than what she's willing to give you? And sometimes, when you come to men's ministry or choir rehearsal, she tells you that you don't have time for her. So, you sacrifice your blessing by hanging in the street with her, doing whatever she wants to do, or sit at home in front of the television. And now you have the gall to move her into your house and share your bed. How is God getting the glory in that?"

"Cordell, I love Amaryllis, and one day, I'm going to

marry her. And besides, she's already moved in. What am I supposed to do?"

"I'll tell you what to do: just as quickly as you moved her in, you move her out."

That had been Cordell's advice to Randall almost two years ago. And as time went on, and Randall and Amaryllis's relationship progressed, it turned out that she wasn't saved, had no intentions of becoming saved, and marriage was definitely not on her agenda.

As Randall stood in Cordell's office, he felt a bit uncomfortable because he knew that Cordell could read him like a book.

"Where's Amaryllis this morning?" Cordell asked. "You said that she would be here today."

Randall didn't hesitate before telling Cordell the absolute truth. Because of their close friendship, Randall wasn't embarrassed. "Yeah, I know, but she was tired. She and her girls went to the riverboat casino last night. She got in late and couldn't get up this morning."

Cordell sat on the corner of his desk and looked at his friend with grief in his eyes.

"You know I love you, right?"

"Yeah, man, and I love you too."

"It's obvious that Amaryllis has no intentions on marrying you, and she has no interest in God whatsoever. You two are unequally yoked. Your relationship will not prosper. It's bound to fail. Even if you do get married, are you prepared to miss out on church because Amaryllis can't understand why you need to be at church Sunday after Sunday? Are you willing to give up the life that God has predestined for you to live for a trophy?"

Randall became more irritated at Cordell's tough love. "Man, Cordell, why you gotta say it like that?"

"Because that's the way it is. I'm not gonna sugar

coat your situation, Randall. It is what it is, which is living in sin."

There was a knock on the door and Cordell opened it to see his father, the head deacon of the church. "Come on, son. It's ten-thirty; time to get started."

Cordell told his father that he'd be out in one minute then he closed the door. "Randall, it hurts me to see you living this way. Do you know that before you told me that Amaryllis had moved in with you, I was considering appointing you to take over the men's ministry on Monday nights? And I couldn't do it because I knew what your life was like outside of this church. How were you gonna minister and teach other men how to live right if you weren't doing it? God is calling for strong men to stand on His word, to do work in the church. You've fallen out of love with The Holy One and in love with Amaryllis, who isn't holy. You can't straddle the fence and serve two masters, Randall. You tell me that you love Amaryllis, but not only are you jeopardizing your soul, but her soul is in jeopardy too. So, if you love her like you say you do, then you'll do the right thing and tell her to move out. I want you to think about that and meditate on it. Now let's go have a great service."

Throughout morning service, Randall's heart was heavy. He glanced around the congregation and saw couples sitting together. Whether they were man and wife, he didn't know. They could be engaged or just starting a relationship, but they were in church, together. Whatever their relationships were, Randall noticed they looked very happy. *I wish Amaryllis was here.* But he knew it would take more than a wish to make her become the woman of God that he knew she could be.

Chapter 3

The aroma hit Randall's nose as soon as the elevator doors opened on the eighth floor. Walking toward his condominium, he knew the smell was coming from his unit. When he walked in the front door, he saw the zigzag lines in the plush carpet, evidence that Amaryllis had vacuumed. The oak wood cocktail table was shining and all the crystal was sparkling.

He saw the dinner table set for one. Everything was in its place from the scented candles to the dozen roses in a vase. In the kitchen, he saw Amaryllis bent over, removing a pan covered with aluminum foil from the oven. She wore a Victoria's Secret pink lace teddy that had arrived just yesterday. It left nothing to his imagination. On the sink sat a boom box blasting music that Randall knew wasn't gospel. Amaryllis had no idea she wasn't alone anymore.

Randall stood in the doorway of the kitchen watching her cook and groove. She placed the pan on top of the stove, turned off the oven, then removed the lid from a pot and stirred mustard and turnip greens. Randall placed his Bible on the kitchen table, walked over to Amaryllis, grabbed her by the waist and pulled her to him. When he touched her, she jumped nervously and dropped the wooden spoon in the pot.

"Black, what did I tell you about sneaking up on me? You know I hate it when you do that," she fussed.

Randall held her tight and buried his face in the crook of her neck. "I'm sorry, Precious. I couldn't help myself. You look so sexy to me. And something smells good. What is it?"

"Well, for being tall." She directed Randall's attention to the pot of greens. "And for being dark." She removed the aluminum foil from the pan and revealed a pork roast. "And for being handsome." She uncovered another pan to show her famous macaroni and cheese. "And for loving me right." She pointed to the counter where a peach cobbler sat covered with saran wrap.

"Thank you so much, Precious. I never have to ask you to do anything for me. You always know what I like."

"Follow me." Amaryllis led Randall out of the kitchen and into the bathroom where a hot bubble bath was waiting. Three aromatherapy candles were lit along the ledge of the Jacuzzi tub. A tall glass of fresh lemonade, sweetened to Randall's liking, sat on a small tray beside the tub. "All of this is for you, Black. I want you to take your clothes off, get in the tub, and relax."

She didn't have to tell him twice. Randall was undressed and leaning back in the tub with his eyes closed in less than one minute. Amaryllis lowered the volume on the radio and Randall listened to her move around in the kitchen. He thought about his conversation with Cordell before church and was seriously considering telling Amaryllis that he'd made a mistake by allowing her to move in with him.

In the eyes of God, Randall knew he wasn't living right, so he would just have to be a man and do the right thing. But a man would have to be crazy to give up a woman like Amaryllis. She cleaned house like a professional maid, cooked like a gourmet chef, and smelled nice all the time. And she was so fine. She was everything he ever wanted in a woman. Who could ask for anything more? She did everything he asked of her, *and* she was fine.

Amaryllis walked in the bathroom and knelt by the tub. She reached across Randall for the soap sponge and lathered it up with liquid soap. Randall looked at his woman and fell in love all over again. She caressed his body with the sponge, and Randall lay there enjoying his bath.

As she moved the sponge over his chest, Randall looked at her mouth. The way she lined her lips with the dark brown liner and made them shine with lip gloss drove him crazy. Randall couldn't give her up. She was too good to him. And she was fine. Surely, God would understand.

When the water started to get cool and Randall's fingers and toes looked wrinkled enough, Amaryllis drained the tub. She helped him stand and dried his body. When Randall stepped out of the tub, she applied cocoa butter lotion over his entire body, even behind his ears. She took the time to massage lotion in between his fingers and toes. She lowered the toilet lid, draped the towel over it, and sat Randall down. She opened the medicine cabinet and took out her nail kit. She knelt before him and carved away any dirt that may have been left beneath his finger and toenails. And if that wasn't enough, she evened out all of his nails with a nail file.

Amaryllis stood Randall up and wrapped him in his black satin robe. "How do you feel, Black?"

"You make me feel like a million bucks."

She took his hand, led him into the dining room, and pulled out his chair. Amaryllis disappeared into the kitchen, returned with his dinner on a plate, and placed it in front of him.

"Where's your plate? Aren't you eating too?" Randall asked her.

"Not right now. It's all about you, boo."

She sat down next to Randall, diced the pork roast into small pieces, and raised a forkful to his mouth.

"You're gonna feed me too?"

"I wouldn't have it any other way," she answered seductively.

Amaryllis guided the fork gently into Randall's mouth. Each time he swallowed, she'd wipe the corners of his mouth with a linen napkin. Again, he looked at his woman and thought what he often thought. *Amaryllis, such a beautiful name for such a beautiful face. How did I make it this long without you? This can't be wrong because everything feels so right. Oh, yes, Lord, you're just gonna have to understand.*

Randall had been so caught up in Amaryllis's beauty that he forgot to take the time to thank God for his food.

"Black, honey, I need some money to make it through the week. I gambled more than I should've last night." Amaryllis believed a sure way to Randall's wallet was definitely through his belly. She was extra careful to wait until she fed him before making this request.

Randall swallowed and looked at her. "Precious, I pay your car note and insurance. I give you money to get your hair and nails done. I remit the balance on all three of your credit cards every month. You live here rent-free. I pay for the telephone, light, and gas. Plus, I give you an allowance of two-hundred and fifty dollars a week. You have a full-time job. What are you doing with your money? The only things I ask you to be responsible for are groceries and gas for your car. And don't think I didn't see those charges from Lord & Taylor and Macy's on *my* Visa statement this month. You're just gonna have to learn how to budget what I give you, because I don't have any more money to give."

Amaryllis stood and straddled Randall in his chair. She grabbed him softly by the ears and licked his entire face.

"How much do you need, Precious?"

Randall walked to the clerk's desk and signed his name in the log-book at five forty-five, Monday morning. She gave him his assignment and told him that his train was already on the platform and scheduled to go into service at six o'clock.

Randall took his job as a motorman for the Chicago Transit Authority seriously. He was very dependable when it came to getting Chicagoans to work on time. He enjoyed driving the train from Ninety-fifth Street through the Loop, all the way to the north side of the city, then back again. He thought the red line was the best line to work on because he got to see so much.

The Windy City was one of the greatest cities in North America, and Randall felt blessed to live in it. As he boarded the train and headed to the motorman's cab, he greeted a young black male who was seated on the train. He looked to be about fifteen or sixteen years old. Randall couldn't help but notice his dingy white shirt and soiled gym shoes.

"Good morning, young brother," Randall greeted.

The young man looked as though he didn't want to be bothered. "What's so good about it?"

"The simple fact that God woke you up this morning is a good thing."

The young man sat slouched in his seat with his arms folded across his chest. His facial expression revealed that he was probably angry at the world. "Yeah, well, tell it to someone who cares, 'cause I ain't feelin' that right now."

"What's your name?"

"Brandon. Why?"

Randall extended his hand to him. "My name is Randall. It's nice to meet you, Brandon."

Brandon hesitated a moment before he took Randall's hand and shook it.

"Do you have a church home, Brandon?"

He frowned like he didn't understand the question. "A what?"

"Do you go to church?"

"Nah, man, I ain't tryin' to be down with that. I work two jobs to help my momma out with my brother and two sisters. So, by the time Sunday comes, all I wanna do is chill. You know what I'm sayin'?"

"Yeah, man, I feel you. But who do you think blessed you with those two jobs?"

Brandon made a smacking noise with his lips and looked at Randall. "Come on, man, I don't feel like being preached at. It's too early in the morning for all that ying yang. You know what I'm sayin'?"

Randall saw the train was getting crowded with passengers. He sat down in the empty seat next to Brandon. "I ain't trying to preach to you, my man. I'm just trying to get you to see where your blessings come from, that's all."

"Man, what blessings? What are you talkin' about? My momma is on welfare. She smokes dope all day long, and right now, she's pregnant by some dude who smacks her around. And because she smoked dope while carrying my baby sister, Eboni, she was born half crazy. I'm out here at sixteen years old, unable to go to school, 'cause I gotta work two jobs to keep my family together just so the DFACS won't split us up. And all five of us share a dirty mattress on the floor in a one-bedroom apartment. So, what blessings are you talking about? Seems like God skipped over my neighborhood when He was dishing out blessings."

Randall looked at his watch and saw that the train was scheduled to leave in two minutes. "Look, Brandon, I gotta get ready to take this train out, but I wanna finish our conversation. Where do you live?"

"In a dump; I just told you that. Why?"

"Because I would like to come by and meet your family and take you and your little brother to my church tonight for men's night."

"Man, didn't I say that I ain't tryin' to be down with no preachin'?"

"Men's night isn't about that. We get together, men of all ages, and share our problems and our success stories. We pray together and put our heads on one accord and try to help each other out. We talk about everything from sports, broken homes, jobs, and even relationships. We encourage each other to speak out and say whatever is on our minds."

"Ain't y'all got no girls at this church?"

Randall chuckled. "Yeah, there are plenty of women. But if you want to see them, you've gotta come to Sunday morning worship or Bible Study and choir rehearsal on Wednesday and Thursday nights. Monday nights are strictly for the fellas. There is no one there to point a finger at you. We are all there to fellowship, lift each other up, and encourage one another to stay strong when times get tough. Sometimes our discussions are so good, we lose track of time and before we know it, it's time to go home. And on the nights that we have some time left, we all walk around the corner to Brainerd Park and shoot some hoops. I think you and your little brother would enjoy it if you give it a chance."

"I don't know, man, but I'll think about it. If I do come, it'll just be me. My brother is only four. But I have to make sure everybody's bathed and fed before I do anything, 'cause Moms ain't there half the time."

"Hey, man, that's cool. It's nice to see that you're committed to your family and ain't afraid of responsibility. There are a lot of young brothers out here who could learn a lesson from you."

"I'm just doing what needs to be done for my peeps. They look to me for everything. You know what I'm sayin'?"

"I'm down with that." Randall wrote his home and cellular numbers on a piece of paper. From his wallet, he gave Brandon the church's business card. He stood up and shook Brandon's hand again.

"Brandon, my man, it was good talking to you. And if you decide to come tonight, call me and I'll come by and pick you up."

"Nah, man, you ain't gotta do that. This church ain't too far from my house, and we ain't got a phone anyway. I am gonna try and make it, but I ain't makin' no promises though, 'cause usually when I get home from work, I gotta play momma."

"Okay, that sounds cool. If not tonight, then maybe next week. We meet every Monday."

Brandon's stop was downtown at Van Buren Street. When he exited the train, he walked to the motorman's window. Randall slid it open.

"You never said what time I'm supposed to be there tonight," Brandon stated.

Randall's grin could have taken the place of the sun. "Seven o'clock, and don't forget we may have time to shoot some hoops."

The conversation with Brandon made Randall's morning. He really hoped that Brandon would show up that night. Of all the young men he recruited to come to men's night, not one of them had strayed away. Once they came out and saw what it was about, they looked forward to coming every week. The hard part was getting them there.

As Randall exited the train back at Ninety-Fifth Street, his cellular phone rang.

"This is Randall."

"Hey, Black. How are you doing, honey?"

"Hey yourself, Precious. I'm great now that I hear your voice. How is work going?"

Amaryllis was an administrative assistant at a law firm in the Loop. "It's going okay. I've got three briefs that need to be typed before lunch. These lawyers around here must think I'm a super woman. I called to tell you that we're going to my mother's tonight for dinner. Her sister, Aunt Bessie, is visiting from Georgia."

"Precious, you know I gotta be at church on Monday evenings. I've got men's ministry tonight. Can we go by there tomorrow?"

"No, Black. Dinner is tonight, not tomorrow. And I already told Aunt Bessie that we'd be there, and she's looking forward to meeting you."

"Amaryllis, you can't spring this on me at the last minute. Especially when I just met a young man and invited him to meet me at church tonight. How would it look if I don't show up?"

Amaryllis's voice raised a pitch higher and Randall could see her neck rotating. "Black, you go to church every Sunday, sometimes twice on Sundays. Then you go on Mondays, Wednesdays, and Thursdays while I sit at home doing nothing. I get tired of coming home to an empty house. I cook for you, clean for you, and wash and iron your clothes. I even give you sex when I don't feel like it. And what do I get in return? All I get is 'Come and go to church with me.'"

"Amaryllis, please don't go there. Any other night would be perfect. I just can't disappoint this young man. I get the feeling that he really needs me to help make a difference in his life."

"Oh, so you'd rather disappoint me instead, right? Look, I need you too, Black, and I'm getting sick of being put on the back burner. Now I gotta call my momma and tell her that we'll miss another family engagement because you gotta go to church."

Amaryllis slammed down the phone in Randall's face. On his lunch break, he thought about what she had said. Everything she had said was true. She kept the house just the way he liked it. He always had a clean pair of boxers to put on in the mornings and she kept his belly full. Even through her headaches, she was submissive. Plus, she was finer than fine. Missing one Monday night wouldn't be bad. On his cellular phone, he dialed the church.

"Holy Deliverance, how may I help you?" the church secretary answered.

"Wanda, it's Randall. How's it going?"

"Hey, Randall, what's up with you?"

"Everything's cool. Is Pastor Bryson around?"

"Yes, he's here. Hold on a second."

Amaryllis and Cordell were like oil and water; they

just didn't mix. Randall could only imagine what Cordell would say when he told him that he was going to be with Amaryllis instead of coming to men's night.

"Randall, my man, what's happening?" Cordell asked when he got to the phone.

"Ain't nothing much going on. I need you to do something for me tonight."

"Sure, what is it?"

"I met a young man on the train this morning and invited him to come out tonight. His name is Brandon, and he's sixteen years old. But something just came up with Amaryllis and I won't be able to make it out to the church tonight. I need you to keep an eye out for him and treat him good. If he shows up, tell him that I'm sorry I couldn't meet him and maybe I'll see him on the train tomorrow."

"Okay, he's in good hands here, you know that. If you don't mind me asking, what has Amaryllis got you doing tonight?"

"Her aunt is in town from Georgia and the family is getting together at her mother's house for some grub."

"For how long will Amaryllis's aunt be in town?"

"I think she's here for the whole week. Why?"

"I was just wondering if you could see her aunt another time. If you've invited a young man to be your guest tonight, you should be the one to greet him."

"Cordell, I tried to get out of this dinner thing, but Amaryllis went off about me not spending enough time with her. She feels that I'm neglecting her when I go to church while she sits at home."

"Randall, Amaryllis sits at home because she wants to, and that's only if she's not out gambling."

"She's calmed down a lot. She doesn't gamble as much as she used to."

"And that makes it all right? If she decides that she's too lonely on Sunday mornings and wants you to sit at home with her, would that be all right too?"

"Nah, man, that ain't gonna happen; 'cause I'm too strong for that."

"Are you sure about that, Randall?"

"What's that supposed to mean?"

"Just think about the conversation we had yesterday. I told you that you and Amaryllis are unequally yoked. And when you're unequally yoked with a mate, they start to feel that you're spending too much time at church. Now listen to me, Randall, and hear me good. You canceling out tonight is just the beginning, and if you're not careful, you'll start second guessing yourself about going to church altogether."

"Cordell, I hear what you're saying, but I don't see it that way. This is just my way of pacifying Amaryllis. She just needs attention, that's all."

"What she needs is Jesus."

"Whatever, man. I'm out." Randall disconnected the call. He wasn't in the mood for another one of Cordell's 'Amaryllis Is No Good' sermons.

Chapter 4

Brandon held two part time jobs. He had to drop out of high school as a freshman to support his family, so he couldn't be hired anywhere as a full-time employee until the age of eighteen. From seven o'clock AM to eleven o'clock AM, he delivered urgent letters and packages via bicycle throughout the Loop for an express delivery company. From twelve o'clock PM to four o'clock PM, he cleaned bathrooms and emptied garbage cans in a ten-story office building next to the express delivery company.

Brandon liked his morning job, especially riding around downtown Chicago. Going from office to office with urgent mail kept his adrenaline flowing. But being a janitor was not what he wanted to do to earn a living. He could tolerate emptying small garbage cans, but he felt that cleaning up behind grown folks was beneath him. The way some adults left the bathrooms was a shame. If they could flush their toilets at home, why couldn't they flush the toilets at work? And after they dried their hands, why couldn't they throw the paper napkins in the garbage can instead of leaving them on top of the sinks?

For the life of him, Brandon couldn't figure out why women had to advertise that their "friend" was visiting. Why should he have to plunge toilets stuffed with things that are too big to fit through the pipes? And the men's bathroom was no better. If men couldn't aim straight into the toilet, then they should sit down. Even if they missed the target a little bit, did they have to go upside the wall?

At the end of the day, Brandon punched his time card and left the building. On his way out, the maintenance manager asked if he could speak with him in his office. When Brandon sat down across from him, he saw a white letter-sized envelope with his name written across the front, lying on the desk.

"Brandon, I want you to know that for the past year that you've been here, I've heard nothing but great comments regarding your work. You are always on time and the bathrooms are spotless at the end of the day," his manager stated.

Brandon smiled and looked at the white envelope again. Thank God he was finally getting the raise he deserved. Maybe now he could afford to get those Air Force One's he'd been wanting for the past two months. "Thank you, Mr. Cramden. I always try and do my best around here," Brandon said proudly.

"And it shows. It's not often that we get someone who is committed to doing a perfect job like you, which is why I'm sorry to say that I have to let you go."

Brandon's heart skipped two beats. Did he just get fired for doing a great job? Was this some kind of office humor? He looked around the office for the hidden camera. When he didn't see a small flashing red light anywhere, he looked at his boss.

"Oh, you got jokes today. Okay, Mr. Cramden, you got me. You got me real good. I get it, this is "Play a Joke on Brandon Day", right? That was a good one. Who put you up to this?"

"I'm sorry, Brandon, but it's no joke. We've been privatized, which means that a lot of jobs are being cut so that someone else can be hired to take the place of those who appear to be making too much money."

"Mr. Cramden, I don't mean to sound disrespectful, but I don't get but seven lousy dollars an hour for cleaning this building, so what are you sayin'?"

"I'm saying that someone will be hired to take your place for $5.50 an hour."

"You can't do this to me. What about my family at home? If I don't feed them, they won't get fed." Losing his job was not an option.

"How many kids do you have?"

"I have a brother and two sisters who depend on me for everything. And if I can't take care of them, the government will take them and split us up."

"Where are your parents?"

"I don't know who my father is and my mother is probably somewhere suckin' on a glass pipe. I'm all that my family has, Mr. Cramden. I will take the job for five-fifty an hour. I don't care how much it pays. Please don't take food out my family's mouth."

Mr. Cramden's heart went out to Brandon. "Brandon, I had no idea that you were carrying this load on your shoulders. Your attitude around here is as if nothing bothers you."

"I can't let my feelings and problems stop me from doing what I gotta do for my family. I got a five-year-old sister who has special needs. The doctors say that she will never be in her right mind. But she's my heart. Everyday on the way home, I stop at the corner store and get her favorite candy, Mike and Ike's. She loves those. When I walk in the door, her whole face lights up because she knows that I got her a treat. Giving her that box of candy every day makes it worthwhile for me to go home. You know what I'm sayin'? I'm the daddy for three kids. You can't take my job from me."

Even though Mr. Cramden was a middle class white man, he could relate to Brandon's situation. He too had been forced to drop out of school to help his mother support himself and his younger brother.

"Brandon, I'm sorry, son. I can certainly relate to your situation. I was there in your shoes myself. But the company has already hired their own people. I'll tell you what I can do, I'll submit your name to the lead manager and give you a great recommendation. Hopefully they'll consider hiring you. I'll do all I can to try and make that happen."

"But you can't guarantee me nothing, right?"

"No, Brandon, I can't. I have a check for you for the past two weeks and two weeks severance pay. Hopefully, you can find work soon."

Brandon's whole world just fell apart. "Man, I can't go home and face my family as a failure. How do I explain to my baby sister there ain't no more Mike and Ike's?"

Mr. Cramden stood up, reached in his pocket and pulled out two twenty-dollar bills.

"Brandon, I know this is not nearly a fraction of what you need to provide for your family, but I want you to take this forty bucks and use it for whatever you need."

He gave Brandon the white envelope and shook his hand. "Again, Brandon, I'm sorry."

Brandon took the envelope and the cash and put them in his pocket. "Thanks, Mr. Cramden."

"Keep your head up. Everything will work out for you."

As Brandon was leaving Mr. Cramden's office, he turned around to face him. "I guess you can't guarantee that either, can you?"

Mr. Cramden didn't answer him. He watched Brandon leave his office with nothing to look forward to.

Riding on the train heading toward the south side, Brandon couldn't wait to get home and wash the stench of the day from his body. He was depressed. What was he going to do? How was he going to keep the government from tearing his family apart?

When he got to the corner store he asked the clerk how much a whole carton of Mike and Ike's cost. A carton of twenty boxes, at fifty cents each, cost ten dollars.

"Give me four cartons."

It was just about ten minutes 'til seven when Brandon entered his building. He could hear his neighbor, Mrs. Beasley, banging on the door to their apartment, calling for his mother. He ran up the three flights of stairs, two at a time, almost dropping his sister's treats. "What's wrong, Mrs. Beasley?"

"Oh, Brandon, thank God you're home. Family Services came and took the kids away today. I was cooking in the kitchen this morning when I heard the kids and Vera screaming. When I opened my door, I saw two cops and a lady carrying the kids downstairs. The kids were kicking and screaming, so I asked the lady what was going on and she said that someone had called the Department of Family and Children Services and reported that the kids were living in an unsafe environment. I asked if I could keep them until you got home, and she said that after seeing the apartment, she had no choice but to take them away. She left her card with me and said for you to call her. After they left, I tried to calm Vera down. I sat with her for a couple of hours, then I had to go down the street to check on Mrs. Hall. I told Vera that I would be back soon, but I've been banging on this door for over an hour."

Brandon dropped the candy boxes. He unlocked the door and rushed into the apartment. There was his mother lying unconscious on the living room floor. A pool of blood was running from beneath her legs. Next to her was a straightened wire hanger.

Her bra was the only piece of clothing she wore. On her right arm, Brandon saw a piece of rubber tube tied into a knot. A used hypodermic needle lay next to her arm.

When Mrs. Beasley saw Vera, she screamed to the top of her lungs. "Oh my God, Vera! Vera! Oh, my God!"

Brandon ran over to his mother. He lifted her head and shook her. "Ma, wake up. Please wake up."

Mrs. Beasley ran across the hall to her apartment and called an ambulance. She came back with a bed sheet to cover Vera from the waist down. Brandon untied the rubber on her arm. He took it and the needle and threw them across the room.

"Why, Ma? Why it gotta be like this? I was doing the best I could." Brandon felt his whole world falling apart.

Mrs. Beasley felt for a pulse then let her head fall to her chest. "I can't feel a pulse, Brandon."

He sat down on the floor, pulled his mother onto his lap, wrapped his arms around her neck, and rocked her back and forth. He bowed his head next to hers and cried.

"We could've made it, Ma. Why you let them take the kids? Why you let them take my kids? They were my kids, Ma. *My* kids." Tears dripped from Brandon's chin. This was the last thing he needed.

When she heard the ambulance's siren, Mrs. Beasley went downstairs to escort the paramedics up to the correct apartment. When they entered, they rushed over to Vera to resuscitate her. They tried to take Vera from Brandon's arms, but he held on to her, crying and moaning.

"Son, you've gotta let her go. Let us do our job," a paramedic said.

They worked on Vera for fifteen minutes before pronouncing her dead. Certain that they'd done all they could, one paramedic pulled the bed sheet over Vera's face and looked at Brandon. "I'm sorry, son, she's gone. We couldn't bring her back."

Brandon yelled and snatched the sheet from Vera's face. He straddled his mother's waist and began pumping her chest as hard as he could. "Come on, Ma, fight. Breathe. Wake up."

The paramedics grabbed Brandon and pulled him off of his mother. "Son, we've done all we can. She's gone," one paramedic stated remorsefully.

Brandon sat on the floor and cried as he watched his mother's body being carried away.

"We're taking her to Saint Bernard Hospital. Do you want to come along?" another paramedic asked.

"No. Just leave me alone."

They took Vera away and Mrs. Beasley went over to Brandon and pulled him into her arms. "I'm so sorry, Brandon. I shouldn't have left her alone. I knew she was upset about the kids, and I should've stayed with her."

Brandon jumped up and ran from the apartment, down the stairs, and out of the building. He had lost one of his jobs, had his family taken away from him, and found his mother dead—all in the same day. His life was over. His sole purpose for living had been snatched away.

He was walking nowhere in particular, just walking. He found himself on the doorsteps of Holy Deliverance Baptist Church. He walked in and saw a group of men and boys sitting in the sanctuary talking and laughing. Cordell was facing the door and saw Brandon standing in the vestibule watching them. He walked to Brandon and saw the look on his face. "Are you all right, son?"

Brandon was choked up and could hardly speak. He had forgotten the name of the man he was supposed to meet here. He reached in his pocket and pulled out a piece of paper.

"Is Randall here?" Brandon asked.

"You must be Brandon, I was expecting you. I'm Pastor Bryson and I'm sorry Randall couldn't be here tonight, but he wants you to come in and fellowship anyway, and he says that maybe he'll see you on the train tomorrow."

Brandon fell to his knees. He put his face in his hands and started crying again. "Ain't nothing going right for me today. I might as well be dead."

Cordell knelt down to him. "What's troubling you, son? What happened?"

Three men came out of the sanctuary to see if Cordell needed any help.

"Help me get him to my office," Cordell requested of the three men.

The men carried Brandon downstairs and sat him in a chair. Cordell told the men to leave Brandon alone with him. After they left, he looked at Brandon. "Son, I can see that you're hurting, but I can't help if you don't open up and talk to me."

"I need to talk to Randall," Brandon stated.

"Well, as I said, Randall can't be here tonight."

"I'll only talk to Randall."

Cordell looked at his watch. "It's a quarter 'til eight; maybe he's still at home." He picked up the telephone and dialed Randall's home number. When the answering machine picked up, he hung up and dialed his cellular phone. Randall's voicemail picked up after three rings and Cordell left a message. "Randall, this is Cordell. I have an emergency here at the church. I'm here with Brandon, the young man you called about, and he's deeply troubled, but he will only talk to you. It's urgent that you call me as soon as you get this message." He placed the telephone on the receiver then looked at Brandon. "I can't get a hold of Randall right now. Hopefully, he'll check his messages and call us."

Brandon felt discouraged, as if Randall had only pretended to befriend him. He got up and started to walk out of the office.

"Wait a minute, son. Let's give Randall some time to call back."

"He ain't gonna call. He don't know me like that."

"Well, how about letting me pray for you before you go?"

"Nah, I ain't into all that. I came here to talk to Randall, but since he ain't here, I'm gonna go take a walk."

"If Randall calls back, what do I tell him?"

"You tell him that I knew he didn't really care." Brandon left the church in tears.

When Randall and Amaryllis got into the car, Randall realized that he'd left his cellular phone on the dining room table. "I forgot my cell phone. I'll be right back, Precious."

"No, I'll go up and get it. I left Aunt Bessie's gift upstairs too," Amaryllis offered.

Randall's phone was ringing when Amaryllis walked in the front door. She walked over to it and looked at the name of the caller. She saw the church's name and telephone number. She knew that it was Cordell calling to get Randall to come to church instead of hanging out with her. When she thought that enough time had passed for Cordell to leave his message, she listened to it and erased it. She grabbed her aunt's gift and left the condo. Before she walked out of the building, she looked at Randall's phone again. She turned the power off so that Cordell wouldn't get through to Randall if he called again. She got in the car and gave the telephone to Randall.

"Here you go, Black. Now we can go." Randall placed the phone in its holder on his belt, started the car and drove away.

The Price family was loud and wild. Whenever they got together, it always turned into a party. Amaryllis and her mother, Veronica, were more like sisters than mother and daughter. They talked like two teenage girls with no home training. There was absolutely no respect whatsoever. Curse words flowed freely in this household, and Randall was in the midst of it all.

When Amaryllis introduced Randall to Aunt Bessie for the first time, Bessie turned to her sister and said, "Veronica, you were right. He *is* fine."

Veronica held a glass of Alizé Red in one hand and a cigarette in the other. She admired Randall from his bald head to his shining Stacy Adams. "I told you my baby know how to pick 'em."

Randall walked into the living room and sat down on the sofa. The cigarette smoke was so thick that he could hardly see in front of him. Amaryllis asked if he wanted anything to eat.

"No thanks, Precious," he declined. Randall thought that if he actually ate something, he would have to stay there longer. "But I would like something to drink."

Amaryllis went to the kitchen to fulfill Randall's request as two of her uncles unfolded a card table. Another uncle walked in with a Keno board game. They set the table up and asked Randall if he wanted to gamble.

"No thanks, I'm not a gambler," Randall replied.

Amaryllis heard Randall's answer as she was bringing his drink from the kitchen. "Well, I am. I want three boards."

Randall took the drink from Amaryllis and gave her a look that told her that he wasn't pleased by what she was getting ready to do.

"Why are you looking at me like that?" She asked Randall.

"Because we didn't come over here to gamble. And you promised me that you were going to stop gambling."

"Actually, a game of Keno isn't gambling; it's too much like Bingo."

"Amaryllis, I'm not going to sit here and watch you drink, smoke, and gamble. If this is what you wanna do, then I'm going to church and will come back and pick you up after men's night is over."

"If you think you are so holy that you can't spend a little time with my family, then you go ahead and leave. And you don't have to worry about coming back for me, ever."

She turned away from Randall, sat down at the card table and took about fifty dollars from her purse. She never gave Randall another thought. He sat there steaming for the next two hours as he watched her lose all of her money. By this time, he had drank three glasses of juice. When it was time to go, Randall had fallen asleep on the sofa and Amaryllis had to wake him. "Come on, Black, it's late. Let's go home."

Randall stood up and lost his balance, falling back onto the sofa. One of Amaryllis's uncle's saw this and made fun of Randall. "Man, if you can't hold your liquor, you shouldn't be drinkin.'"

Randall looked at Amaryllis with a puzzled look on his face. "What is he talking about?"

"Momma spiked the punch with gin," Amaryllis said nonchalantly.

Randall's eyes grew wide. "What?!"

"Calm down, Black. I only gave you one glass."

"Amaryllis, I went and got two more glasses. Why didn't you tell me that it had gin in it? You know I don't drink."

"I wanted you to loosen up. You are always uptight when you get around my family."

"Because y'all do stupid crap like this." Randall slowly stood up and staggered to the door. He yanked it open and walked out without saying good-bye to anyone. Needless to say, Amaryllis had to drive home. Randall let his seat back and fell asleep.

When they got home, he stripped out of his clothes immediately and got into bed with his back to Amaryllis—something that he'd never done before. Amaryllis saw the red light blinking on the caller identification box, which was on her nightstand. She walked over to it and saw the church's name and erased it, but not before she made sure that Cordell hadn't left a message.

Chapter 5

The radio alarm clock woke Randall at 4:45 AM, Tuesday. Something in the pit of his stomach didn't feel right. He looked on the left side of the bed for Amaryllis and saw that she wasn't there. He sat up on the bed, and for a few seconds, the bedroom turned pitch black. When everything came back into view, his temples started throbbing. He attempted to get out of bed and stand, but his legs felt like Jell-O when the soles of his feet made contact with the floor. With squinted eyes, he glanced at the alarm clock again and saw two of them.

"Amaryllis?"

At the sound of his own voice, Randall felt an axe slice him right between his eyes. His nostrils were inhaling something his stomach didn't like. When his abdomen began having a tumultuous affair and started to boil, he placed his hand over his mouth and staggered to the bathroom. He made it just in time to empty his stomach completely. Amaryllis came from the kitchen and looked at him. "What's wrong, Black?"

Randall moved over to the sink to splash cold water on his face. "I don't know, but I feel terrible. What stinks?"

"Nothing stinks. I'm cooking breakfast."

"You need to check that bacon. It smells bad, and it's giving me a headache."

"Black, what you have is a hangover."

Randall had begun to apply toothpaste to his toothbrush. He started brushing his teeth. "What do you mean a hangover? A hangover from what?"

"From the gin and juice you drank last night."

Randall got dizzy again. He let go of the toothbrush and leaned over to rest his arms on the sink to balance himself. "Amaryllis, I can't believe you did that to me. How am I supposed to drive a train today?"

"Don't get so dramatic, Black. It's only a slight hangover; nothing that two Tylenol and a cup of strong black coffee can't cure. Come on in the kitchen and put something in your belly. You didn't eat dinner last night, and drinking alcohol on an empty stomach doesn't set well."

Randall looked at her as if she'd lost her mind. "And you knew this and still gave me alcohol? What's wrong with you, girl?"

Amaryllis became defensive. "I suggest you lower your voice while talking to me. I'm not your child."

"You behaved like a child last night when you gave me that stuff. You know I don't drink. And what's even more childish is that you let me drink on an empty stomach."

"Black, you're making way too much of this. Hangovers are not uncommon. You learn to get used to them. You don't see me trippin' do you?"

Amaryllis's nonchalant attitude was beginning to tick Randall off. It took all that was within him not to curse at her. "You know what, Amaryllis? I'm going to take a shower and get out of here before I say or do something I'll regret."

While Randall was showering, Amaryllis fixed a plate with bacon, scrambled eggs, and orange slices. She placed it on the dining room table complete with two Tylenol capsules and a cup of strong black coffee. Randall stepped out of the shower, looked in the mirror and didn't recognize his own face. His eyes were red and puffy and his vision was still a bit blurred.

In the bedroom, Amaryllis had laid out his work uniform. She was sitting on the bed polishing his work boots. Randall got dressed in complete silence. He walked out of the bedroom toward the front door.

"What about breakfast, Black?"

Randall walked over to the dining room table, picked up the plate, took it to the kitchen and threw the entire plate into the garbage can. He walked past Amaryllis, grabbed his sunglasses off the cocktail table, and walked out the front door. Randall was so caught up in his anger that he forgot his daily routine—getting on his knees and praying before leaving the condo.

He got to work and signed his name in the logbook at the clerk's desk.

"Randall, what happened to you? You look like crap." The receptionist said.

"Good morning, Carmella. Let's just say that I got up on the wrong side of the bed this morning."

She got up and came around the desk to Randall. She unbuttoned his shirt, then buttoned it correctly and fixed his collar. "There you go. At least you look half decent. I don't have any drops for your eyes, so I suggest you put your shades on because the yardmaster is on the platform today."

Randall followed her advice and reached in his shirt pocket for his sunglasses.

"Thanks, Carmella, I appreciate it. Lunch is on me tomorrow."

"I'm going to hold you to that, Randall. Have a good day."

Randall reached the platform and was glad he didn't see the yardmaster. Every Tuesday is discipline day, and yardmasters were always on the prowl looking for anything out of place, from wearing proper uniforms and work shoes to getting the trains into service on time. According to his watch, Randall had exactly one minute before his train was scheduled to leave Ninety-fifth Street.

He boarded the train hoping to see Brandon sitting where he had been sitting yesterday, but he wasn't there. Randall wondered if Brandon had decided to accept his invitation to men's night last night. He made a mental note to call Cordell at the church the moment he got north to the Howard Street station.

It took Randall one hour and ten minutes to get to the north side of town. After walking through the eight train cars and confirming that every passenger had disembarked, Randall locked the motorman's cab and proceeded to leave. As he was exiting the train, the headline of an abandoned copy of *The Chicago Sun-Times* newspaper on one of the seats caught Randall's attention.

'South Side Black Teenage Male Found Dead With Gunshot Wound To The Head, Police Assume Suicide.'

Engrossed in the article, Randall was walking on the platform but stopped abruptly as if he had run out of concrete. Suddenly, his feet were glued to the ground. *No, it can't be. Please God, don't let it be him.* Randall ran to the office to call Cordell.

"Good morning, Holy Deliv . . ."

"Wanda, get Cordell on the phone, quick," Randall said, cutting Wanda off before she could finish her greeting.

Although Wanda and the entire church knew that Cordell and Randall were best friends, Randall never made the mistake of calling Pastor Bryson by his first name in the presence of other church members. "Randall, is that you?"

Lethargic and bewildered, Randall had lost all five of his senses. He couldn't see, hear, taste, touch, or smell. "Where's Pastor Bryson?"

"He's in a meeting right now, Randall, are you all right?"

Randall was anything but all right. "Get him now, Wanda, *right now.*"

"Randall, I just can't walk in and interrupt his meeting. You know the pastor doesn't play that."

"Tell him it's me calling and I gotta talk to him."

"Look, Randall, I don't know what this is about, but you know how he gets when he's interrupted."

Randall closed his eyes and exhaled. He was still nauseous from last night, and now, he was nervous. Of course he could hang up on Wanda and call Cordell's cell phone, but he realized that wouldn't do him any good. Whenever Cordell was in session, his cell phone sat on his secretary's desk. "Wanda, please. He'd want to talk to me. This is urgent, and it can't wait. Get him on the phone."

"All right, Randall. I'll get him. But if Pastor yells at me, I'm yelling at you."

Randall's palms were sweating as he gripped the

telephone. He prayed to God for this not to be his Brandon. The article only mentioned the young man's first name and the neighborhood he lived in.

"Randall, I'm glad you called," Cordell said when he picked up the phone. He didn't sound the least bit upset about the interruption.

Randall shot straight to the point. "Did that young man I called about show up last night?"

"Yes he did, but did you read the newspaper this morning?"

Randall closed his eyes and silently prayed again. "Tell me it's not him, Cordell. Tell me it's not the same Brandon."

"I'm sorry, Randall. As soon as I heard about it, my heart went out to you."

"Are you sure it's the same Brandon?"

"Yes, the picture in *The Chicago Defender* confirmed it."

Randall felt faint and had to lean against the desk. "Aw, man, Cordell, if only I had gotten to him. I knew he was going through a rough time. My God, I can only imagine what his mother is going through."

From that statement, Cordell knew he didn't have all the information.

"There's more to Brandon's story than you know, Randall."

"What don't I know?"

Randall listened as Cordell told him what type of day Brandon had on yesterday.

"Cordell, I'm sick. I feel responsible, man."

"Brandon was looking for you last night. I could tell that something was bothering him, but he wouldn't open up to me. He said he only wanted to talk to you."

"Why didn't you call me, Cordell?"

"I did call. First, I called your house and didn't get an answer, then I called your cell phone and got your voicemail. I left a message for you to call me here. I tried to get Brandon to hang around and give you time to call back, but he wouldn't stay."

"What did Brandon say? He must've said something."

"Randall, I don't think you wanna know."

"Cordell, if Brandon wanted me to know something, tell me what it is."

Cordell wanted to spare his friend, but Randall was persistent.

"What did he say, Cordell?"

Cordell exhaled. "Randall, before I tell you this I want you to know that it's not your fault what happened to Brandon. He'd already lost one of his jobs and family before he got here last night."

Randall lost patience and raised his voice. "What did Brandon say?!"

"He told me to tell you that he knew you didn't really care."

Randall was speechless. God had put Brandon in his life for a reason and he had failed to do what he was supposed to do. He let God down, he let Brandon down, and he let himself down. And for what? A night of watching a bunch of drunks throw money around. And if that wasn't bad enough, he, too, was full of the devil's juice.

"Don't get quiet on me, Randall. What are you thinking?"

"I don't know what to think. I just don't know what to think. I don't understand how I missed your call last night. I had my cell phone with me."

"Well, check to see if your battery is low."

Randall took his phone from its holder on his belt loop and looked at it. "It ain't even on, Cordell. Why is it off? I never turn my phone off unless it's charging or when I'm in church."

"You probably hit the power button by mistake. It happens, Randall."

"Nah, Cordell, not me. Something ain't right. You said you left a message?"

"Yes, around a quarter 'til eight."

"Hold on a minute." Randall dialed his mailbox and heard a message from Amaryllis. She had called twenty minutes ago to apologize for last night.

"The only message I have is from Amaryllis, this morning."

Every time Randall mentioned her name, Cordell got agitated. "Didn't you just leave her? What could she want already?"

Randall didn't answer. Something about her message stuck in his mind. *I'm sorry about last night.* Was Amaryllis admitting to powering off his cell phone? "I know she didn't do what I think she did."

"What are you talking about?"

"We left for her mother's house between 7:30 and 7:45. I remember the time because *The Parkers* had just come on television and she was rushing me, saying that she wanted to get there before eight o'clock. But when we got down to the garage, I realized that I'd left my cell phone upstairs. Amaryllis insisted that she get it for me. That had to be about the time you called because it normally takes about fifteen minutes to get to her mother's house and we got there at eight on the dot."

"So, what are you saying, Randall?"

"I'm wondering if Amaryllis turned my phone off when she went back to get it."

"Even if she did, you'd still get my message on your voicemail."

Randall closed his eyes again. "Cordell, I messed up, man. Amaryllis has the access code to my voice mail-box."

Cordell couldn't stand Amaryllis, but the pastor in him just couldn't believe anyone would do something so devious. "Come on, Randall, you don't think she's capable of something like *that* do you?"

"I don't wanna think it, but I'm telling you that other than being at church or when it's charging, I never, ever turn my phone off. Something just doesn't add up."

"Listen, Randall, before you accuse her of doing anything, you have to make sure that there is no way possible that you could've hit the power button yourself by accident."

"Are you sure you left a message on the right cell phone?"

"Absolutely. I heard your voicemail greeting."

Was Amaryllis capable? She was certainly capable of getting me to drink. "I gotta tell you something, Cordell."

"So, tell me."

"I got a hangover."

Cordell laughed in Randall's ear. "Yeah right, from what? Kool-Aid?"

"From drinking three tall glasses of gin and juice last night."

Cordell was stunned. "How did that happen? Have you forgotten that you don't drink alcohol?"

"That's what I don't understand."

"You're losing me, Randall."

"While we were at her mother's house, I asked Amaryllis for something to drink and she brought me what I thought was fruit punch. I couldn't tell any alcohol was in it. By the time the evening was over, I had drank three glasses of the stuff. I passed out and she had to wake me up to leave. She said she gave it to me so that I would loosen up around her family."

"That's dangerous, Randall, very dangerous."

"Yeah, I realize that. So, Pastor Bryson, what do you think happened to your message now?"

Randall ended the call with his best friend, boarded the train, and headed back to the south side of Chicago. He thought about calling Amaryllis at work. But he really wanted to wait until tonight to question her just so he could look in her eyes when he asked about his cell phone. One thing his mother taught him as a young boy was if someone couldn't look him in the eye, it usually meant they were secret-keepers. But it was early in the day and there was no way he could make it through hours without knowing if she was guilty or not. He was sure that he hadn't accidentally turned off his phone. Amaryllis was guilty; there was absolutely no other reasonable explanation.

Of course, she would deny it. Randall was already expecting that. But what if Amaryllis actually admitted to doing something so devious? What would he do then? No, he couldn't wait until tonight. He had to know now. He called her work number.

"Parker & Parker Law Offices. How may I direct your call?" the receptionist answered.

"Good morning. Will you put me through to Amaryllis Price's extension please?"

"Yes, sir. Just a moment."

One moment turned into two long minutes—too long to listen to elevator music. Randall could hear his train approaching the platform at Howard Street. It was time for him to take it south to Ninety-fifth Street.

Come on Amaryllis, I don't have all d. . . .

"Amaryllis speaking."

"You got a minute?" Not a 'good morning' or 'how are you doing?'

"Black?"

"Yeah, it's me. You got a minute?"

The tone of Randall's voice told Amaryllis he was hot and bothered about something. But since she'd already called and apologized for getting him drunk, she couldn't imagine why he was being so short with her. "I got a few. What's up?"

He decided to use reverse psychology on Amaryllis to see if she'd trip herself up.

"Actually, I'm returning your call."

"Oh, well I just wanted to apologize for last night."

"What exactly are you apologizing for?"

"You know, for giving you gin. It was wrong, I shouldn't have done it, and I'm sorry."

"So, is that it?"

"Is what it?"

"Is that all you're apologizing for?"

"What else is there?"

"I don't know, *you* tell *me*." Randall was losing patience. He knew without a shadow of doubt that Amaryllis was guilty.

"Are you talking about the gambling?"

"What do you think, Amaryllis?"

She noticed Randall didn't use her pet name. "What happened to 'Precious'?"

"I'm still hung over, which means I ain't in my right mind. So the only name I know is 'Amaryllis'." *I wanna call you something else right now.*

"Come on, Black, don't be like that. I said I was sorry. What else do you want from me?"

"I want you to answer my question. Are you only apologizing for giving me gin?"

"Okay, the gambling too, Black. Is that what you wanted to hear?"

Nah, that ain't it, but keep talking. "I just wanna make sure that you got everything off your chest."

"That just about covers it as far as I'm concerned, but I got a question for *you.*"

"I'm listening."

"Why was your phone off when I called you earlier?"

Oh, no. She will not turn this on me. "What makes you think it was off?"

"It didn't ring. I got your voicemail immediately."

"I was on an important call and didn't wanna click over. You know it's funny that you mentioned that, because I talked to Cordell today and he said he called my cell phone last night and left a message because I didn't pick up. He claims he called right around the time you were upstairs getting my phone and your Aunt Bessie's gift."

"Yeah, and?"

"I'm trying to put a puzzle together, Amaryllis. For the life of me, I can't figure out how my phone got turned off when I know for a fact I didn't do it."

"Are you accusing me of something, Randall?"

Are you guilty of something, Amaryllis? "What happened to 'Black'?"

She presented a pregnant pause and Randall caught the delay. "Are you there, Precious?"

"Yeah, I'm here. I just don't know what you're getting at."

"I'm trying to figure out how my phone got turned off and I'm not gonna rest until I do. I missed a very important call last night and that bothers me."

"Well, now that I think about it, I probably touched the power button by mistake because I was trying to carry my purse, keys, your phone, and Aunt Bessie's gift. Maybe I pressed the power button and didn't realize it."

Bingo. "Well, that may explain the phone being off. But even though it was off, I still should've gotten Cordell's message."

"I don't have an explanation for that, Black. Maybe your mailbox is malfunctioning."

"Nah, that can't be it, because your message came through with no problem, didn't it?"

"Well, I don't know what to tell you. Why don't you call your phone company and report it. There could be a discrepancy."

Most definitely, and her name is Amaryllis. "Yeah, okay. I gotta get this train back to the south side. I'll see you at home."

"Okay, Black. Don't forget to get your phone checked out."

"I'm gonna take care of it right now." He hung up from Amaryllis then dialed his mailbox and changed the access code to his voicemail. *No more discrepancies.*

Amaryllis's co-worker, friend, and gambling partner, Bridgette Grayson, sat at a desk directly across from her and had heard every word she said to Randall. "I gotta give it to you, Amaryllis, I didn't think you were gonna be able to pull that off. It sounded like you were being backed into a corner, but as usual, you came through with flying colors."

Amaryllis chuckled. "You know me, Bridgette, I'm always on top of my game. If you ever need a way out of a sticky situation, call me."

"I got your number, girl. Tell me something. How are you gonna go to the river boat this weekend when you just apologized to Randall for gambling?"

"Bridgette, what's my name?"

"Your name is Amaryllis."

"And what Amaryllis wants?"

"Amaryllis gets," Bridgette responded.

"And don't you forget it. We'll just go on Sunday morning instead of Saturday night. You see, Bridgette, if there's one thing I learned from Randall about this church thing, is if there's a will, there's a way. And I'm willing to go to the boat while he's at church."

"What if he doesn't go to church?"

"Black, not go to church? Now that's funny, Bridgette." Amaryllis laughed at Bridgette so hard she almost wet her powder-blue lace thong.

"But wasn't Randall with you last night instead of being at church?"

Amaryllis stopped laughing because Bridgette had a point.

Chapter 6

As he guided the southbound train to Ninety-Fifth Street, Randall couldn't concentrate on what he was doing. Disappointed with himself for letting Brandon down, he couldn't pull himself together. His head began to throb as he was driving and thinking that this was all Amaryllis's fault.

"YOU LET THIS HAPPEN," the Lord spoke to him.

"But, Lord, she turned my phone off. If she hadn't done that, I would've gotten Cordell's call."

"CALL OR NO CALL, YOU HAD AN ASSIGNMENT."

Randall's next stop was at Thirty-first Street, which had a rail supervisor stationed on the platform. Without realizing it, at fifty-five miles an hour, Randall drove the train past the station without stopping. The wind from the speeding train caused the passengers on the platform to stumble backward.

"I know, Lord, I'm sorry. I just wanted to please Amaryllis by going with her to her mother's house."

When Randall didn't stop the train at the Thirty-first Street platform, the rail supervisor immediately contacted the Control Center at the Chicago Transit Authority's headquarters on his radio.

"Rail supervisor 931 to the Control Center, come in."

The dispatcher answered the call immediately. "Control Center to rail supervisor 931. What's your message?"

"Run number 904 just blew by me without stopping."

"Ten-four, rail supervisor 931. You are instructed to take the next train and follow run 904. I will dispatch a surface supervisor car to intercept the train farther down the line. I shall also attempt to contact the train operator."

The rail supervisor did as he was told, and the Control Center dispatcher tried to reach Randall on his radio. "Control Center to operator 904. Come in."

Randall didn't respond, so the Control Center dispatcher tried again. "Control Center to operator 904. Come in."

Again, there was no response. The Control Center dispatcher attempted a third time to reach Randall. "Control Center to operator 904, respond to your radio."

Nothing from Randall, so the control center contacted the rail supervisor. "Control Center to rail supervisor 931, come in."

The rail supervisor was already on the next train following Randall. "Rail supervisor 931 to the Control Center. What's your message?"

"I just got a report that run number 904 has also failed to stop at Forty-third Street, and all attempts to contact the operator have been to no avail. Are you on the following train?"

"Ten-four, I'm on the follower."

Randall's mind was in another world, oblivious to the calls on his radio and the emergency alarm the passengers had set off as he sped past the Forty-third Street station. A passenger who missed her stop was banging on the motorman's cab door, yelling for Randall to stop the train.

"AM I NOT THE LORD, THY GOD?"

"Yes, Lord, You are. But what was I to do when Amaryllis practically threatened me to stay with her?"

"YOU HAD AN ASSIGNEMT, RANDALL. PUT NO MAN BEFORE ME."

Randall saw debris lying on the tracks, but before he had a chance to stop the train, he'd already hit it and part of the train lifted off the rail. The front wheels derailed and passengers hit steel poles and windows. Other passengers, who were standing, were thrown to the floor. Randall applied the brakes and the train skidded along the rail for about twenty seconds before coming to a complete stop.

Randall wasn't hurt, but he could hear passengers screaming and crying. He called the Control Center to report the derailment.

After the ambulances had come and the injured passengers had been taken to various hospitals, the general manager of the Red Line, William Nichols, approached Randall and asked if he was hurt.

"No sir, I'm fine," Randall replied.

"Apparently there was large debris lying across the tracks. You didn't see it?"

"Not until it was too late for me to stop the train."

"How fast were you going?"

Randall didn't know. "I have no idea, Mr. Nichols. I was thinking about something and lost focus."

"This derailment happened not even ten feet from

the end of the Forty-third Street platform. As you leave any platform, according to the guidelines in your instruction manual, the rate of speed should be no more than five miles an hour. If you were following the proper procedure, that debris would've been spotted before you left the platform."

"Yes, sir, you're right. I don't know how something like this could've happened."

"I have several reports from passengers stating that you drove straight through the Thirty-first Street station and had gone through Forty-third Street also when the derailment happened. You want to tell me what you were thinking about that had you driving this train so carelessly?"

Randall was at a loss for words. He had been driving trains for seven years, and this had never happened to him before. "Mr. Nichols, I don't know what to tell you. I was thinking about my personal problems instead of concentrating on my job. I'm sorry."

"Well, Mr. Loomis, I want you to think about this; not only has service been interrupted for passengers heading south due to the fact that we've got to get something out here to lift this train, but we have dozens of passengers headed to hospitals."

Randall hung his head in shame. "I'm sorry," was all he could say.

"I'm instructing you to board the next train, accompanied by rail supervisor 931, and head straight to the Ninety-fifth Street Terminal where you will be interviewed by a transportation manager for a breathalyzer and urinalysis testing. This is a direct order. Are these instructions clear, Mr. Loomis?"

"Yes."

"Do you completely comprehend these instructions?"

"Yes I do, sir."

"Okay then, you and rail supervisor 931 may proceed to the terminal."

At the Ninety-fifth Street terminal, Randall told the transportation manager the same story he had told Mr. Nichols. He was subjected to breathalyzer and urinalysis testing, removed from active duty, and given instructions. He was informed that once the breathalyzer and urinalysis tests results were received and an investigation was completed, he would be notified when to return for a final disposition of the incident.

Randall didn't know what to do next. Was this the day from hell or what? When he stepped outside of the Ninety-fifth Street terminal, he called Amaryllis. "Guess what I just did."

She was still annoyed at Randall for trying to trip her up, and didn't want to be bothered. "Black, I'm busy."

"I may be out of a job."

"What?"

"I derailed a train at Forty-third Street. I ran over something lying on the tracks."

"Oh, honey, are you okay?"

"I'm fine physically, but emotionally, I'm messed up."

"I'm sorry I can't be with you right now, but why would you lose your job? It was an accident."

"I had to take drug and alcohol tests, Amaryllis. I know they're going to come back positive because of last night."

"Oh, Black, I'm so sorry."

"Yeah, me too." He disconnected the call. What was he going to do now? Instead of going home he found himself at Holy D, in Cordell's office.

Cordell was in complete awe of Randall's story. "Sounds to me like you've had a heck of a day, Randall."

"Yeah, it just keeps getting better and better."

"So, what happens now?"

"I sit at home and wait for the C.T.A. to call and tell me that I'm out of a job."

"Don't jump to conclusions. Power and death lies in the tongue. Just wait and see what happens."

Randall leaned forward and put his face in his hands. "Cordell, I don't understand how something like this could happen to me. I'm always careful. What am I going to do, man?"

"Don't sit here in my presence and act like you don't know what you gotta do, Randall. You are allowing this woman to affect your life in such a way that will eventually cost you more than you can afford."

"You can't blame this derailment on Amaryllis. She wasn't there when it happened."

"You're right, Randall, she wasn't there. But wasn't your mind on her at the time of the derailment? Yes, it was. First of all, Amaryllis turns off your phone, according to you. Second, she purposely gives you alcohol when she knows you don't drink. Now let's think about that for a minute, Randall. Would you have come here last night to counsel Brandon if you could have?"

"What kind of question is that? Of course I would have."

"Okay, so tell me again why you weren't reachable."

"Because Amaryllis turned my phone off."

"Hold that thought. If your breathalyzer and urine tests comes back positive, what happens?"

"I could lose my job."

"Now tell me why your tests could be positive."

"Because Amaryllis gave me gin last night."

"So, a young man's life could have been spared and your job would not be in jeopardy but for Amaryllis's actions. Do you understand what's happening, Randall?"

"Yeah, I understand. I understand that I should've checked my phone when she gave it to me. And I shouldn't have gone to work today with a hangover."

Cordell was fit to be tied. "Don't make excuses for her, Randall. Why should you have to check behind Amaryllis? And why should you be in jeopardy of losing your job because she did something so selfish and foolish?"

"She apologized for that."

"So what!" The words were out of Cordell's mouth before he could catch them, not that he really wanted to. "Randall, think about it. How many times in the last two years has Amaryllis apologized for doing something that cost you either money or time with God? What about the time you put your tithes money on the dresser and she took it without asking you what it was for and gambled with it? She lost all of your money at the blackjack table, and you couldn't pay your tithes. She apologized for that. What about the time she invited her family over to your place? Remember how they used your Bible for an ashtray and a coaster? She apologized for that. Do you remember that time when you came home from church and the police were at your place because a neighbor called and said that Amaryllis had the music too loud? You had to pay your landlord a fine that night. Amaryllis apologized for that."

"So, what are you saying? If something bad happens to me, it's Amaryllis's fault?"

For the past two years, he'd been singing this same song to his best friend. "Randall, what is wrong with you? Are you that booty-whipped that you can't see what's happening?"

Randall looked angrily at Cordell.

"Yeah, I said 'booty-whipped' and I meant it. You exercised poor judgment when you approached Amaryllis two years ago, and you've been suffering for it ever since. Don't you know by now that she's not the woman for you?"

"Look, Cordell, I'm not gonna sit here and let you bad mouth my woman. I love Amaryllis. I feel like I can really help her find God if I just continue to pray for her. Aren't we ambassadors for Christ? Let me ask you something, Cordell. What if Hosea had turned his back on the prostitute of a wife God had for him? Besides, I see that Amaryllis is changing for the better."

Cordell threw his hands in the air in frustration. He completely ignored Randall's comparison to Hosea. Cordell had discerned Amaryllis's foulness the moment Randall introduced them. "How, Randall? How is she changing for the better? Giving you gin last night, was she doing better then?"

"I told you she apologized for that."

"Until when? The next time? Randall, man, open your eyes."

Randall stood up to leave, and Cordell stood up too. "Where are you going?"

"Home to wait for my job to call."

"Let's have a word of prayer before you go."

"I don't feel like praying."

Cordell stood in shock. Had he heard Randall correctly? "What did you just say?"

"I gotta go, Amaryllis should be on her way home from work. I wanna be there when she gets there."

"What's happening to you, man? I don't understand you anymore. Do you realize that you said that you don't feel like praying? Tell me something, when was the last time you really spent time with God?"

He thought about Cordell's question. "I don't know, it's been a while."

Randall walked out of his best friend's office and went home. Cordell sat down in his chair, put his face in his hands and sighed. He had to do something to loose Randall from the enemy's grip. But what could he do? Randall refused to face reality and it was impossible to help someone who didn't want to be helped.

Cordell got down on his knees and talked to God on Randall's behalf. He prayed that God would open Randall's eyes before Amaryllis did anything else to cost him more than his job. He also prayed for strength and patience for himself to deal with his best friend.

Amaryllis was waiting for Randall when he got home. He walked in the door and saw balloons and party favors all around. On the dining room table sat a small vanilla sheet cake that read, "Things Will Work Out."

"What's all this?" Randall asked.

Amaryllis stood next to him and began slicing the cake. He saw that she wore a crimson red, sheer teddy. Her hair was pinned up into a French roll and Randall couldn't take his eyes away from her perfectly lined and glossed lips.

"Just a little something to make you feel better. I'm so sorry about your job, but I'm glad that you're okay. I don't think I could live with myself if anything would've happened to you because of something that I'd done."

"Something did happen, Amaryllis. I wasn't hurt, but a lot of other people were. Can you imagine the lawsuits that are already in the making?"

Amaryllis stopped slicing the cake and placed her arms around Randall's neck and hugged him tight. He wrapped his arms around her waist and pulled her closer to him.

"You smell so good. And you look nice in this red thing," he complimented.

She kissed his ear, lingering on his lobe. She moved to his cheek and onto his lips. The cake sat on the dining room table forgotten as Randall lifted Amaryllis and carried her to the bedroom. An hour later, they finally got around to the cake. They were eating when the telephone rang. Amaryllis answered it then looked at Randall. "It's the C.T.A., Black."

Randall hesitated before he nervously got up and took the telephone from her.

"Hello? Yes . . . okay . . . tomorrow morning at 10:30. Okay, Mr. Nichols, I'll see you then. Good-bye." Randall lost his appetite and went to bed.

The telephone woke Randall up at 8:30 the next morning.

"Randall Loomis?" the caller asked.

"Speaking," Randall replied.

"Randall, this is Sebastian Shelton, your local transit union representative. I was informed this morning that you are scheduled to meet with Mr. William Nichols, the general manager of the Red Line at 10:30 this morning. Are you aware that such a meeting is to take place?"

"Yeah, I'm aware of it."

"Do you plan to attend this meeting, and if so, would you like union representation?"

"Yes."

"All right then, I will meet you at the coffee house across the street from the station at 9:30 so that we can discuss what happened yesterday. I was also informed that you took breathalyzer and urine tests. Is there any chance of them coming back positive?"

Randall closed his eyes. "Yes."

"Okay, Randall, I'll see you at the coffee shop at 9:30."

Randall got out of bed, went into the bathroom and started the water in the shower. He leaned on the sink and looked at his reflection in the mirror. Seven perfect years with the C.T.A., and now this. As he stared at himself, he saw tears forming in his eyes. What if he lost his job because of this? How was he going to support himself? Better yet, Amaryllis was living there rent-free. What would she do if he couldn't support them anymore? How would he go on living without her? At the thought of losing Amaryllis, he broke down and cried hard. Why was God doing this to him?

After his shower, Randall noticed that Amaryllis had laid out an outfit for him to wear.

He went into the kitchen for a glass of orange juice and saw that Amaryllis had made breakfast for him. His plate was on the kitchen table covered with saran wrap. Next to his plate was a sealed envelope. Randall opened it and read the letter.

Black, whatever happens today just know that I love you. We can make it through anything as long as we're together. I love you and I'll always be by your side.

Yours truly,
Precious

Randall warmed his plate in the microwave, sat down to eat without saying grace, and read the letter again. What was he so worried about Amaryllis for? He knew she loved him. He should be ashamed of himself for thinking that she wouldn't stick by his side through this mess. Just as he was finishing his plate, the telephone rang for the second time that morning.

"Hey, man, what's up?" Cordell greeted cheerfully.

"Nothing that's good, Cordell."

"Talk to me about it."

"I've got a meeting with the general manager of the Red Line this morning. And from what I've heard in the past, he doesn't go easy on alcohol-related incidents, so I'm not real optimistic right now."

"Well, I'm calling to offer you moral support and to let you know that I'm here for you, no matter what. And remember that with God, all things are possible. Maybe He'll work a miracle and the tests will come back with a negative result."

"I doubt it, man. Ain't nothing going right for me lately."

"Randall, that's the wrong attitude to have. Think positive thoughts. Let's get on one accord, and talk to God together right now."

"Cordell, I don't have time for that, I've got to meet my union representative at 9:30."

Cordell became upset by Randall's attitude toward prayer. "You know what, Randall? You're gonna mess around and lose everything that God has blessed you with because of your attitude. All this talk about not wanting to pray and not having enough time to pray can cost you big. So, my suggestion to you is to stop what you're doing and repent to the Lord. You need to get back in touch with God and acknowledge Him as your personal Savior. You've lost focus on what life is all about and you need to realize it before it's too late. Do you think it's a good thing to ignore God?"

Randall was in no mood for Cordell this morning. He was frustrated, upset, and anxious. The last thing he needed was someone his own age telling him what to do.

"Who in the heck do you think you are, telling me

about God? I know and love Him just as much as you
do. I'm sick and tired of you telling me what I should
and shouldn't be doing. Are you my keeper? I don't
think so. Just because you got a license to preach doesn't
mean that you're holier than anyone else. Learn to
stay out of my business, Cordell."

Cordell was thrown at Randall's outburst. They had
had their differences in the past and things had sometimes gotten heated between, them but this was the
first time that Randall had told Cordell to leave him to
his own troubles. They were extremely close, and had
always pulled each other through trials. "Randall,
where is this coming from? We've always been able to
talk to one another about anything. I'm your friend
and your pastor and I'm only trying to help you do the
right thing."

"No, what you're trying to do is run my life. Ever
since I met Amaryllis, you've been telling me how to
live. So what, she gambles, and so what she drinks
and cusses sometimes. I love her, and she loves me. It
took me a little while, but I figured out what your motive is, Cordell. You want Amaryllis for yourself. Ain't
that the real deal?"

Cordell almost laughed in Randall's ear. He wanted
to tell him that he wouldn't deal with Amaryllis if she
was the last woman on earth. "Randall, you're out of
line and way off base. And I don't appreciate the way
you're talking to me. You need to realize who really
loves you and has your back. It certainly isn't Amaryllis because she's the reason you're in this situation.
I'm telling you, man, she's a snake and I know one
when I see one. But you know what? This is your little
red wagon; you can pull it anyway you want to."

Randall cursed, slammed down the phone and went
to get dressed.

He didn't like what Amaryllis picked out for him to wear, but knew if he changed outfits, she'd be very upset. Amaryllis was very specific about what she wanted done and how it was supposed to be done. Once Randall was dressed and ready to leave, the telephone rang again.

"Have you calmed down so we can pray?" Cordell asked.

"I'm running late." Randall responded coldly.

"Randall, you need to pray about this."

"Cordell, you're the pastor, *you* pray. I gotta go." Again, Randall hung up on Cordell and left the condo.

Sebastian Shelton met with Randall and informed him how the meeting with the general manager may transpire. He advised Randall that if the tests showed no alcohol in his urine, he would only be suspended for three days for failure to operate the train cautiously. However, if the tests were positive, and knowing Mr. Nichols' zero tolerance for alcohol-related incidents, Randall may have something to worry about.

At the meeting, Mr. Nichols informed Randall and his union representative that he had tested positive for alcohol. He was intoxicated at the time of the accident. Neither Randall or his union representative disputed this fact. Therefore, Randall was informed that pursuant to his union contract, first-time substance abuse offenders with more than five years of service may be suspended to the (EAP) employees assistance program in lieu of discharge if they prefer. He was further informed that the suspension would be without pay for six months and he must satisfactorily complete the program or he would be discharged. After he successfully completed the program, he could return to work, but would be subjected to random breathalyzers and urine tests for twenty-four months. If he tested positive at anytime during this period, he would be immediately discharged.

Randall accepted the suspension and conditions. Little did he know, his life was about to change drastically. If there was ever a time when he needed to put on the whole armour of God, it was right then.

Chapter 7

After one month of not receiving any income, Randall thought he would have to apply for another job just to make ends meet. Amaryllis was high maintenance. When Randall had a steady paycheck every two weeks, paying for her hair and nails wasn't an issue. Money was unlimited and it flowed freely from his hands to hers. Not once in two years had he ever paid attention to the charges on her credit card bills. He just looked at the balance and wrote a check for the amount due. But now rent was due, and Randall sat at the dining room table with a calculator and all of their bills spread out, trying to figure out what would get paid and what wouldn't.

Randall earned a nice living with the Chicago Transit Authority, which had enabled him to sacrifice half of his net income to a credit union for his savings account. The other half was more than enough to support himself and Amaryllis. But looking at the bills before him told Randall that his primary checking account would soon be overdrawn if he kept withdrawing without depositing. He had never had to dip into his savings for anything, but that was about to change.

Living on Michigan Avenue, downtown in the Loop, cost Randall $1,500 a month. His underground parking space was included in the rent, but when Amaryllis moved in, that added another $200 to lease a parking space for her car. Back then, it wasn't a problem for Randall. He would've paid a thousand dollars extra if he had to. When it came to his precious Amaryllis, money was no object.

He looked at the light bill. For the two of them to be gone for most of the day, he couldn't figure out why the bill was $220. Then he remembered that Amaryllis slept at night with the hallway light on. She had to see her way to the bathroom in the middle of the night. But in the morning time, it was hard to tell that the hallway light was still on because the sun shined so brightly through the floor to ceiling windows. So, they sometimes forgot to turn it off.

Randall had a solution to this problem. Today he would buy Amaryllis a flashlight to use at night. He put the light bill in the 'pay' pile. He picked up the gas bill and looked at the amount due. His eyes grew wide when he saw $161. But there was nothing he could do about the gas bill but pay it. Amaryllis was an excellent cook and made Randall breakfast every morning and a home-cooked meal every night. Throughout the week, he found her in the kitchen baking something sweet. She kept him well-fed, and he loved it. The gas bill was placed in the 'pay' pile. Next was the telephone bill and Randall almost fell out of his chair. "Three hundred thirty-eight dollars? For what?" He looked at the detailed listing of the calls. More than $220 worth of calls were made to a psychic hotline last month. Randall wanted to curse, but he bit his tongue. He was sure the telephone company made a mistake. He placed the telephone bill in the 'do not pay' pile.

He lined all three of Amaryllis's Visa bills next to one another. The first had a balance of $917. The second balance was $656 and the third balance was $1,292.

Randall let out a loud sigh and shook his head from side to side. *What is Amaryllis doing?*

For the first time in two years he looked at her charges. Shoe stores and clothing stores dominated the bills. And what did she buy at For Real Men Only, a lingerie boutique for men? According to the date of this charge, she had made the purchase a month prior, and Randall hadn't received a gift. He would definitely question her about this.

Randall didn't hold Amaryllis responsible for any bill in the house. She could use her own money for whatever she wanted. He wondered why she couldn't pay cash for her things. What was she doing with all of her money? Grocery and gas for her car cost only a fraction of what she made. But Randall did what he had to do to keep his woman happy. He placed all of her Visa bills in the 'pay' pile. Next was his own Visa bill. Two thousand sixty-seven dollars, in bold black numbers, stared him in the face. "Oh, my God."

That was all Randall could say as he looked at two thousand dollars worth of cash advances from the river boat casino. The remaining sixty-seven dollars was charged on the Home Shopping Channel. All of these bills had meant nothing to Randall in the past, but without any income, they stood out like a midget on a basketball team. He put his Visa bill in the 'do not pay' pile. Their car notes were already paid and their insurance wasn't due for another four months, so Randall had some time to work with those. But there was still a matter of Amaryllis's allowance of $250 a week, plus her beauty money. He was going to have to cut back big time on a lot of things. But what?

They had to have light, gas, and a telephone. Would he be less of a man if he told Amaryllis that she had to start helping out with the bills? If they split them fifty-fifty, things should be okay. But Randall would still have to dip into his savings just to support his own half. Could he risk losing Amaryllis if he told her she had to pay for her own hair and nails? Would he dare put his foot down and tell her that he was no longer supporting her gambling habit?

Randall sat at the dining room table weighing his options. *No, I can't risk losing Precious. I'll figure out a way to keep her happy.*

He was still at the dining room table trying to figure out a way to keep their heads above water when Amaryllis walked in from work. She came into the dining room and looked at all of the bills on the table. "Hey, Black, whatcha doing?"

Randall leaned back in the chair. He tried to cross his legs, but they were numb from sitting in one position for over an hour. "Trying to figure out a way to pay all of these bills."

Amaryllis sat down in a chair across from Randall and looked at the two different piles on the table. "Why do you have some bills on one side of the table and some on the other?"

"I separated them based on how important they are. The ones that must be paid no matter what, I put in one pile, and the ones that can wait until next month, I put in another."

She picked up the telephone bill from the 'not pay' pile and held it up. "Why can't you pay this one?"

"Because the telephone company billed us for calls we didn't make. They're trying to charge us for $200 worth of psychic calls. I'm not going to send them a check until I clear this mess up. I'll give them a call in the morning and straighten it out."

"Those calls are legitimate, Black. I made them," Amaryllis confessed.

Randall sat up and looked at her. "You called the psychic hotline?"

"Yeah, what's the big deal?"

"The big deal, Amaryllis, is I have to pay the bill."

"You've always paid the bill. Why are you making a big deal of it now?"

He couldn't believe she was questioning him on this. "Are you telling me that you've called these numbers before?"

"I've been calling them for over a year. What is the problem?"

"The problem is that I can't afford to pay it this time. I never looked at the bills before, and you know that. I just wrote a check and put them in the mail. And why do you need to talk to a psychic anyway?"

"I don't *need* to talk to a psychic. I do it for fun."

"Well, the fun is over, so stop calling those numbers because money is tight, and it will be for the foreseeable future. And as far as your credit cards go, you need to take it easy and start paying cash for the things you want."

Amaryllis stood up and put her hand on the hip. "Excuse me?"

"I mean it, Amaryllis. We gotta start budgeting."

"Black, you make good money. Why are you limiting me like this?"

"In case you've forgotten my situation, I'll remind you. I don't have any money coming in. My checking account is almost empty, and I got to start dipping into my savings to keep us current in everything."

"I don't understand. You should've been prepared for something like this. I don't appreciate being told that I can't use the telephone or my own credit cards."

"You can use your own credit cards whenever you want if you start paying your own bills. And why did you use my Visa and withdraw over two grand to gamble? I don't understand why you're always broke when you have a full-time job and no bills to pay. For the past two years, you've been having a good time spending my hard-earned money, but it stops right now. You have to start paying for your own things. You can afford to get your hair and nails done yourself. And what did you buy at For Real Men Only for ninety-eight dollars?"

The look on Amaryllis's face was as if her heart had skipped two beats. Randall could tell that she was surprised that he had actually looked at her charges.

"Bridgette and I were window shopping downtown on our lunch break and she saw some underwear that she wanted to get for her man, but she didn't have any cash on her, so I made the purchase for her."

"You told me Bridgette didn't have a man."

"She met this guy about two months ago."

"And already she's buying him boxers that cost an arm and leg?"

"Black, I don't get in her business like that. She asked me to buy them for her, and I did. She paid me back the money."

"Amaryllis, I don't like the fact that you're buying underwear for another man. If Bridgette can't afford to buy her man some drawers, that's her problem. And after I pay your three Visa cards off this time, I suggest you cut them up, because I can't carry you anymore."

Amaryllis was too outdone. What did this mean? "So

what are you saying, Randall? That you can't take care of me? How did you let this happen?"

"May I remind you that I didn't let this happen? *You* did when you got me drunk."

"Don't blame that on me, Randall. You knew you had alcohol in your system before you went to work. If you had any sense, you would've stayed at home that day."

Randall couldn't believe her gall. "What?"

"You heard me. If you had not gone to work, we wouldn't be going through this."

"Correction, if you had not given me gin, we wouldn't he going through this."

"Well, you know what, Randall? You're gonna have to figure out a way to pay these bills, because my money is tight too."

"How is your money tight, Amaryllis? You don't pay for a thing."

"You don't know what I do."

"You're right. Forgive me for making that statement. Tell me what you do with your money."

"What happened to 'Precious'?"

"Don't mock me, I'm serious. Where is all of your money going?"

"I don't have to answer to you. I've told you once before that you're not my father."

"Again, you're right. I'm not your father. And guess what? You're not my wife either. So, as of right now, your bills are your responsibility and my bills are my responsibility. We will split every household bill in half, including the rent. You let your mouth write a check that your butt can't cash. I was only asking you to take it easy on the telephone and credit cards, but since you want to be difficult, I can go there too. Your car note is yours, your $200 a month parking spot is yours, your car insurance is yours, and your allowance had been suspended."

Randall watched as Amaryllis grabbed her purse and keys and walked out the door. He wrote a check for the balance of his Visa bill, put it in the envelope and sealed it. He'd drop it in the mail on the way to his employee's assistance program in the morning. On the calculator, he totaled the light, gas, telephone, and rent bills. Two thousand two hundred nineteen dollars was the total cost. Divided in half it came to one thousand one hundred nine dollars and fifty cents. Randall added another two hundred dollars for Amaryllis's parking spot to her half.

He put all three of her Visa bills on one side of the table. On the telephone, light, and gas bills, he wrote down half of the amount and highlighted it next to the balance. He highlighted the due dates and put these bills in another pile. On a blank sheet of paper, he wrote Amaryllis a note.

Amaryllis, your total for half of the bills for this month comes to $1,109.50. Remember to add an extra $200 if you want to keep your underground parking spot. Please note that I've highlighted the due dates. I would appreciate your payment a week before each bill is due.

Randall placed his note, and the telephone, light, and gas bills next to her Visa bills. He got up from the table to take a shower when the telephone rang. He answered the phone after looking at the caller ID.

"Hey man, what's up?" Cordell greeted in his usual chipper tone even though Randall had been avoiding his phone calls since his suspension three weeks ago.

"Nothing much, Cordell. What's up with you?"

"I'm calling to see how you're doing. You haven't been to church in almost a month."

"Yeah, well I had to take some time off to get myself together. There's a lot going on that I really don't want to get into." Not only had Randall taken time away from church, he had also taken time away from God altogether.

Cordell knew Randall was skating on thin ice. He wasn't in his right mind and Cordell was afraid for him. He was seeing his best friend moving farther and farther away from God. "Randall, I understand that there's a lot going on, but staying away from church is not the way to solve your problems, man. If anything, church is where you ought to be."

"I'll get back there eventually, but right now, I gotta work through some things."

"You can't work through nothing without the help of the Lord. And you know this is true. Have you talked to God about your situation?"

"Cordell, God is omniscient, right? He knows what I'm going through."

"Yeah, that's true, but He still wants to know that we need Him. If we don't seek and search for God, we won't find Him. He wants to be chased and sought after."

"Well, you know what? I ain't got time to chase after nothing right now. For the next five months I will be unemployed, and already, these bills are kicking me in the butt. And I just told Amaryllis her free ride is over."

Cordell smelled a faint aroma of victory. He knew Amaryllis loved money more than she loved herself. If Randall stopped her allowance, she wouldn't linger around much longer. This could easily be the beginning of the end of their relationship. He smiled, but couldn't let Randall know it. "Wow, I can only imagine how she took that. Where is she?"

"When I told her that she would get no more gambling money, she walked out."

"Hopefully, she'll understand and realize that it's times like these that should bring a couple together rather than separate them." This was the best Cordell could come up with to comfort Randall. He didn't dare say what he was really thinking.

"Time will tell."

"Hey, man, let's go out and get a bite to eat. I'll come by and pick you up."

"Cordell, are you deaf? Weren't you listening to me? I don't have any money to go anywhere."

"Did I ask you for any money? This is my treat. There's no sense in sitting around having a pity party about your situation, because it won't help. Be downstairs in twenty minutes."

"I don't feel like going anywhere, Cordell."

"Be downstairs in twenty minutes." Cordell didn't care what mood Randall was in. Amaryllis had walked out and he felt like celebrating.

"I don't want to go."

"Be downstairs in twenty minutes.

"I'm not going."

"Be downstairs in twenty minutes." He hung up on Randall.

When Cordell drove up to Randall's building, he was standing outside waiting. Randall walked to the car and knelt down to the passenger window. "Didn't I say that I wasn't going?"

"Then why are you down here waiting?"

"To tell you that I'm not going."

A woman drove up behind Cordell and blew her horn.

He was blocking her way into the parking garage. "I'm not moving until you get in."

The woman blew here horn again.

"Cordell, just go. I'll call you later." He walked back into the building and turned to see Cordell still sitting in his car. The woman behind him was pressing her horn. Cordell put his gear in park and turned the ignition off. He reclined his seat and closed his eyes. Another car pulled up behind the woman, and blew its horn. The woman got out of her car and walked to Cordell's window. "Excuse me, I'm trying to get into the garage. Can you please move?"

"I'm not moving until my friend, Randall Loomis, who lives in apartment 808, gets in this car." Cordell pointed toward the door. "That's him standing in the building. That's Randall Loomis who lives in apartment 808."

Randall saw Cordell pointing at him and the woman looking his way. He walked out to Cordell's car. "Man, what are you doing?"

"Get in the car, Randall," Cordell said.

Another car pulled up.

"Cordell, you are causing a scene. Would you please leave?" Randall pleaded.

The woman looked at Randall. "Are you Randall Loomis from apartment 808?"

"Yeah," he replied.

"Well, could you please get in the car so we can get into the garage?"

"No, I'm not going anywhere."

Cordell yelled from the car. "Get in the car, Randall!"

The woman looked at Cordell. "I'm calling the police." She walked back to her car and started dialing on her cellular phone. After placing the call, the man who was parked behind her got out of his car and approached her. They talked for a minute then he walked over to Randall. "Are you Randall Loomis from apartment 808?"

Randall looked at Cordell. "Why did you tell that woman my name and apartment number?"

Cordell didn't answer and the man asked Randall again.

"Yeah, I'm Randall Loomis."

"Could you do us all a favor and get in the car?"

"I'm not going anywhere."

"That lady called the police."

"Let her do what she gotta do," Randall said.

Cordell yelled at Randall again. "Get in the car, Randall!"

"Shut up, Cordell!" he yelled back.

The man that was in the car behind the man that was in the car behind the lady walked up to Randall and asked, "Are you Randall Loomis from apartment 808?"

"Yeah, that's me, but I'm not going anywhere with this man."

"You know, man, out here in the street is no place to have a lover's quarrel. We are trying to get in the garage. Why don't you and your boyfriend take this some place else?"

Randall became angry. "What are you talking about? This ain't no lover's quarrel."

Cordell got out of the car, walked to Randall, and lifted the back of his hand and kissed it. "Come on, baby, don't be like that. We don't want everybody to know our business. Let's go some place where we can be alone."

Randall was humiliated. "Cordell, you are crazy. Why did you do that?"

Another man walked over to them and asked why they couldn't get in the garage. The first man looked at him. "We're trying to get Randall Loomis from apartment 808 and his boyfriend to move out of the way."

Randall looked and saw nine cars lined up in the street waiting to enter the garage. Cordell opened the passenger door for Randall. "Come on, sweetheart, before the police comes. You know what happens to men like us in jails."

Randall was so embarrassed he didn't know what to do. Not only did everyone know his name and apartment number, they also thought he and Cordell were lovers. He hung his head and got in the car. Cordell did a feminine walk to the driver's side and the people on the street applauded. The first man looked at Randall saying, "I hope you two can work this out, Randall."

Cordell started the car and drove away. He knew Randall was mad, but he didn't care.

"So, what do you want to eat?"

Randall didn't say a word. He wanted to say something, but the only thing on his tongue were curse words.

"You're not talking to me, honey?"

"Cordell, I can't believe you did that. How am I supposed to face my neighbors? And you call yourself a pastor."

"How else was I going to get you in the car?"

"Why couldn't you accept the fact that I didn't want to go?"

"Because you don't need to be alone right now. That's why."

Cordell took Randall to Catch 35 Seafood Restaurant on Michigan Avenue. The waiter seated them, gave them their menus, and said that he'd give them a few minutes to look them over. Randall set his menu face down on the table without glancing at it.

"I think I'll have the shrimp platter, Randall. What do you want?"

Randall refused to break bread with him. "I ain't hungry."

"You're gonna make me eat by myself?"

"Serves you right for acting like a fool."

The waiter returned with a pad and pencil. "What can I get for you?"

Cordell spoke first. "I'll have the shrimp platter and a glass of raspberry lemonade."

The waiter turned to Randall. "And for you, sir?"

"I don't want anything."

Cordell looked at Randall. "Honey bunch, you've gotta eat to keep up your strength. You don't want to faint at the altar, do you?"

The waiter looked at them both like they were crazy. Randall became furious. He wanted to reach across the table and hit Cordell in his jaw. "Cordell, don't start that gay crap in here."

Cordell picked up his napkin and pretended to cry and wipe tears from the corners of his eyes. Not only did the waiter have a front row seat for the drama, others seated close to them, saw Cordell's performance. Randall leaned on the table and whispered to Cordell. "Why are you doing this to me?"

Cordell was aware of the audience and kept up the act. "Because I want what's best for you. I'll feel much better if you eat something."

Randall was so hot and mad, Cordell could see steam evaporate from his ears. Randall picked up the menu and searched for the most expensive meal. He told the waiter to bring him the steak, seafood, and lobster platter. It came with a hefty seventy-nine dollar price tag. When the waiter walked away, and everyone turned his or her attention elsewhere, Randall looked at Cordell. "Just for this little charade you're doing, it's going to cost you big."

Cordell wasn't fazed by Randall's threat. "There's no price tag on my friendship. What do you want for dessert?"

"I want you to mind your business and let me do what I wanna do."

"That's not on the menu. Order something else."

Randall spoke through clenched teeth to keep from shouting out. "Why can't you leave me alone?"

"Because you're my brother and I won't let you go out like this."

"What are you going to do, hold my hand like I'm a child?"

"If that's what it takes."

Chapter 8

Randall lay in bed Sunday morning as his alarm clock sang beautifully. As he listened, he thanked God for the birds. After they had flown away, he rolled over to see that Amaryllis's side of the bed had not been slept on again. It had been four days since she walked out on him. When she didn't come home the first night, he called her at work the next day and got a message saying that her voicemail was full. He pressed zero for the operator, and she told him that Amaryllis was in a meeting and couldn't be disturbed.

Randall decided that he would try calling her mother's house. When he asked if Amaryllis was there, he only got cursed out and threatened.

"I don't appreciate you putting my daughter out on the street. You betta watch your back because all I have to do is buy my brothers a six pack of beer and a carton of cigarettes, and they will gladly take care of you 'Price' style." Veronica told him.

For fifteen more minutes, Randall was on the phone

trying to explain to Veronica that he didn't put Amaryllis out, but that she'd freely walked out.

"I know my daughter, and she ain't gonna walk away from money."

"What money?"

"Your money."

"Is that all you taught your daughter? To get with a man who's got money?"

"It never hurts to have security and stability."

"What about loving someone?"

"What's love got to do with it? You can always learn to love somebody, but you've got to make sure they can take care of you first."

That was the most ridiculous logic Randall had ever heard. No wonder Amaryllis was jacked up. "Well, I can see where Amaryllis gets her attitude."

"I taught my daughter well."

"You taught her wrong."

"What's wrong is how you did her. But that's okay, 'cause once my brothers find out about this, all hell is gonna break loose. You best watch your back."

Randall heard the click in his ear and placed the phone on its receiver. He really didn't feel like going to church today, but he had promised Cordell he'd go. So, he got out of bed, showered, and dressed. When he got down to the garage, he looked at his Jaguar but didn't recognize it. The first thing he saw was a huge hole in the hood of his car. Acid had burned through the shiny black paint and melted through to the engine. The windshield was shattered, the radio was missing, and the passenger's side air bag was deflated and lying on the seat. The convertible top had also been slashed to shreds. Randall walked around his car and saw all four tires flattened. The trunk was wide open and his ten

CD changer and his four JL audio speakers, that cost him four hundred dollars each, were gone.

His body shook from head to toe as he looked at his baby. All the time and money he had put into this car had been wasted. Randall had prayed, fasted, and laid holy hands on this car for nine months while he saved up for the down payment. His Jaguar was his pride and joy. He'd nicknamed her 'Joy.' His license plates read, I GOT JOY.

Randall opened the passenger's door, moved the air bag out of the way, and sat in the car. He hung his head and cried.

For about twenty minutes, he thought about his situation. The sadness turned to anger when he thought about the conversation he had with Veronica just this morning. There was no way he was gonna let them get away with this. He wiped away tears and on his cellular phone, he called Cordell at home.

"Praise the Lord, Pastor Bryson speaking."

"Come to my garage."

"Randall?" Cordell almost didn't recognize the voice.

"Yeah, man. Come to my garage," he said calmly but sternly.

"I'm on my way to church, and why aren't you in Sunday School? You promised me that you'd be in church today, Randall."

"I'm telling you right now that if you're not here, in my garage, in ten minutes, I'm going to kill somebody." Randall shut the power off. He'd give Cordell exactly ten minutes before he went to Veronica's house. On the way there, he would stop at Maxwell's Gun Shop on State Street.

Cordell drove up in record time, seven minutes to be exact. He jumped out of his car and ran over to

Randall's. No words could explain the look on his face.
With his mouth and eyes wide open, Cordell couldn't
move. Randall didn't say a word. He sat in his car looking at his friend. Cordell walked over to where he sat.
"Who did this?"

"Amaryllis's uncles."

"Her uncles? Why?"

"This morning, I called over to her mother's house
looking for her and Veronica cussed me out and told
me that I'd better watch my back because her brothers
were looking for me. Evidently, Amaryllis told her that
I put her out."

Cordell sighed. "Jesus, Mary, and Joseph. This girl
is something else."

"This is my Joy and she knew it. She knew how
much I loved my Joy."

Cordell saw tears streaming down Randall's face
and knew he was about to explode. "Get out of the car
man, we gotta call the cops."

"Nah, Cordell, the cops ain't gonna do nothing about
this. I ain't got no proof that they did this. I'm gonna
take care of this myself."

"What are you gonna do?"

"First, I'm gonna pay Maxwell a visit. Then I'm going
to go over to her mother's house and start capping."

"No, that's not the way to handle this. Come on, let's
go upstairs and call the cops. You've got to report this,
Randall."

Randall didn't move. He sat in his car looking at
Cordell. "I told you what I'm getting ready to do."

Cordell looked at his friend and knew that he was
serious. He had to come up with a plan to keep Randall put until the police came. He checked the time on
his watch. It was almost ten o'clock. Morning worship
began in a half hour. He silently prayed and asked God

for direction. He couldn't risk leaving Randall and allowing him to do something crazy. But what about the church?

"Okay, Randall, if you wanna go by Maxwell's, I'll take you."

"You will?"

"Yeah, come on." Cordell would repent later for the lie he just told Randall.

Randall got out of his car and into Cordell's. Once Randall shut his door, Cordell pushed a button on his key remote that locked the doors from the inside. When Randall heard the beep, he knew he was locked in because his own car alarm had the same feature. He looked at Cordell and yelled, "Open this door, man!"

Cordell ignored Randall's outburst and called Holy D on his cellular phone.

"Wanda, this is Pastor. Is Elder Mackey there yet?"

"Yes he is, but where are *you*? We've got to get you into your robe and wired up."

"Uh, something came up this morning, Wanda. I need you to get Elder Mackey on the phone."

While he was waiting for Elder Mackey, Cordell saw how Randall was eyeing him. If looks could kill, he'd be dead as a door knob.

"Pastor, are you okay?" Elder Mackey asked.

"Elder, I need you to preach for me this morning."

"You've got car trouble? I could come get you."

Cordell tried his best not to sound anxious. "No, it's not that. There's a matter that I gotta tend to and it can't wait. Are you prepared to preach?"

"You've taught us to always be ready."

"Okay. Just announce to the people that I had an urgent matter to deal with this morning and I apologize for not being there."

"Okay, Pastor, consider it done. Do you need some-one to come and assist you?"

The way Randall was eyeing him, maybe Cordell should've told Elder Mackey to send two armour bear-ers to keep Randall off of him. "No, I'm okay. Call me on my cell after the benediction."

Once Randall gave his statement telling the police about his conversation with Veronica and who he thought the possible suspects were, the police went to the garage security guard and asked if he had seen the crime. He said that his shift had started at eight o'clock this morning, and he hadn't seen or heard anything unusual. The police asked him to play back last night's surveillance tape.

Randall watched as three men, who hadn't bothered to cover their faces, terrorized his car. They weren't Amaryllis's uncles. In fact, Randall didn't recognize any of the men. The police took the tape and told Ran-dall that they would try and match the faces with mug shots they had on file. They also dusted his car for finger-prints. After the police had gone, Randall and Cordell were left standing in the garage alone.

"Randall, the police said that since they've already dusted for fingerprints and taken pictures, you can have the car towed away."

"For what? It can't be fixed; look at it."

"You don't know that, and you just can't leave it sit-ting here like this. You need to call your insurance company."

"It's Sunday. They're closed."

"You can still call AAA Motor Club and get it towed somewhere. You don't want your neighbors to see this."

He took Cordell's advice and had the car towed to a

body shop. As the tow truck was hauling Joy away, Cordell looked at her and noticed the license plates were covered with spray paint. "You see the plates, Randall?"

"Yeah, but what's the purpose of covering up my plates?"

"What color is the paint?"

"It looks black."

"What does Amaryllis call you?"

Randall placed his hands on the sides of his head and let out a lion's roar. "I know she didn't do this. Tell me she didn't do this, Cordell."

Cordell noticed a white substance falling from Randall's gas tank. "Is that sugar in your tank?"

Randall balled up his lips and started pacing back and forth. "Cordell, man, I feel like blowing something up."

Cordell walked over to Randall, grabbed his arm and led him to his car. "Let's go for a ride."

Thirty minutes had passed while they were riding. Randall was so wrapped up in his anger that he hadn't realized they were no longer moving. Cordell parked his car in front of a small Cape Code house in Riverdale, Illinois. When Cordell turned the engine off, Randall looked to his left and saw his mother standing on the porch of the house he grew up in, with her arms spread wide open. He couldn't move. He looked at his mother's smile and remembered how her hugs use to make every ache and pain disappear.

"Why did you bring me here, Cordell?"

Cordell got out of the car and walked around to open the door for Randall. He grabbed his friend by the elbow to help him stand.

"I called Ma'Dear while you were talking to the cops.

I asked her to skip church today because you needed her. She told me to get you here as fast as I could."

Randall was in a trance. It had been a long time since he had seen his mother. He stopped his weekly visits because when he called her and said that he'd met Amaryllis and she'd moved in with him, Ma'Dear told Randall that he was not living according to God's Word. He told her that he was a grown man, and he could live his life any way he wanted. From then on, every telephone conversation between Randall and his mother was brief and to the point. And he hadn't taken the opportunity to visit because Amaryllis knew how his mother felt about their relationship. She always convinced Randall that Ma'Dear was trying to control him and break them up.

But right now, all of that was forgotten as he looked at the one woman who never betrayed him. They slowly moved toward each other. When they met, she wrapped her arms around him and squeezed him tight. "Welcome home, baby."

Randall put his face in the crook of his mother's neck and cried like an infant. He held nothing back. He moaned and cried. Then he cried and moaned. They held each other until Randall caught a case of the sniffles. Cordell helped her guide him into the house and they sat him down on the sofa. Ma'Dear sat next to Randall and guided his head to her lap. She started to hum like she did when she was in the kitchen cooking dinner. She made Randall's problems vanish. She started to caress his bald head. Within five minutes, Randall had sniffled and cried himself to sleep just like he used to do when he was a child. Cordell kissed her on the cheek. "Go ahead, Ma'Dear, and handle your business."

He watched as she reached for her Bible on the cocktail table, opened it and began to read, pray, and prophesy over her son. Cordell then walked over to the other sofa, kicked off his shoes, loosened his tie, and laid down. Cordell listened to his godmother sing, hum, and prophesy for as long as he could before he, too, was in dreamland.

Chapter 9

On their way back to Randall's condo, both he and Cordell were full. Ma'Dear's beef stew and hot water cornbread sat comfortably in their bellies. They were heading northward on Michigan Avenue toward Randall's high rise. Cordell's cellular phone rang.

"Pastor, this is Elder Mackey."

"How did it go this morning, Elder?"

"Awesome! The Holy Spirit tore the house down. Two backsliders came back home and three souls came forth as candidates for baptism. We didn't have church we had 'chuch.'"

Cordell chuckled. "I'm glad to hear that, although I hate I missed it."

"I'm telling you, Pastor, folks were leaping over pews and rolling on the floor. And one of the candidates testified that he was driving to work last week when a van ran a red light and smashed into the driver's side of his car. He said the impact was so forceful, his car door had to be cut and sawed open to free him. But when the firemen removed the door, he was able to step out and walk away without a scratch. You should have seen the saints rejoicing."

"Now that's what I like to hear, Elder. Watching folks praise God like they've lost their minds just does something to me."

"You know how we do it here at Holy D."

"Yeah, I know. I'm pleased that everything went well."

"How's your situation, Pastor?"

"All is well, Elder. All is well."

"Don't forget about deliverance service tonight at seven o'clock."

"I'll be there."

Cordell drove Randall to his door. Randall had been listening to Cordell's conversation with Elder Mackey and felt bad that Cordell missed church because of him. "Cordell man, I'm sorry that you couldn't be in church today. Amaryllis is my problem and I shouldn't involve you in it. I need to deal with this myself."

"As a pastor, my ministry is not limited to the church. That's why our communities are so messed up; because the saints are confined within the church walls. The majority of the people who come to church are already saved, so we need to minister outside on the street corners to reach those who don't come to church. So, don't worry about me missing church. And besides, we're brothers, I'll do whatever it takes to keep you strong."

"Thanks, man. I appreciate you and Ma'Dear. Listening to her brought me to my senses. Now I know that I gotta go ahead and get Amaryllis out of my house, permanently."

"You're doing the right thing, Randall. I gotta go home and prepare for this evening's service. You want me to come by here and pick you up?"

"Nah, I've inconvenienced you enough for one day. I'll catch a cab."

"Randall, it's no big deal. I want to make sure that you're there. It's a very important service."

"I promise you that I will be there, and thanks again, Cordell. I mean it."

"I know you do."

Randall walked into his unit and knew that Amaryllis was there. The living room was spotless. The carpet had been vacuumed and the tables were newly dusted. The dining room table was cleared of the bills, and in their place sat a crystal vase that held a dozen red roses. Randall saw only one table setting and next to the plate was a money order made out to him for $1,309.50. He walked into the kitchen to see Amaryllis standing at the stove with her back to him.

It seemed as though her hair had grown since he'd last seen her. He noticed that her highlights were brightened. She wore a white camisole that was cut high at the hips. He stood there looking at her and wondered how he was going to tell her that she had to go.

"What are you doing here, Amaryllis?"

She turned around and Randall had to lean against the wall to keep from fainting. At the sight of her beauty, he had actually lost his balance. Either she had been out in the sun for too long or she had gotten a professional tan from somewhere, because her high yellow skin was darkened to a rich caramel color, and Randall loved it. She had gotten her eyebrows arched to a perfect thin line. Today, she wore eye shadow that matched the golden highlights in her hair. Randall could tell that her eyelashes were longer and thicker.

Her face was smooth as silk. Her lips were lined just right with a gloss that shined so bright, Randall thought he could see his reflection in them from across the kitchen where he stood. *Amaryllis, such a beautiful name for such a beautiful face.*

He looked down and saw the camisole she wore was not only backless, but it was also strapless and sheer.

Amaryllis saw the way Randall was looking at her and knew that she had him just where she wanted him. "What did you say, Black?"

He was mesmerized. He forgot the question he asked her. "Um, um."

She approached Randall and kissed him on the lips softly and very gently. Randall inhaled the scent coming from her body that caused him to close his eyes and open them again. Amaryllis's fumes were so intoxicating, he became dizzy. She relished in the effect she had on him and grabbed his hands to wrap them around her body.

"I cooked neck bones and black-eyed peas. I made dinner rolls and baked a lemon pound cake."

Randall loved everything she cooked for him, but his belly was still full from eating at Ma'Dear's house. "I'm not hungry, Amaryllis, and we need to talk."

Amaryllis moved her body closer to Randall's and her smell almost knocked him off of his feet. He wanted her, and he wanted her badly. But he promised himself that he was going to set her straight and send her packing no matter what. "Somebody vandalized my car last night."

"Oh my goodness, who would do such a thing?"

"I was hoping that *you'd* tell me."

"Why would I know who damaged your car, Black?"

"Because your mother threatened me and said that

I'd better watch my back for putting you out. Why did you tell her that I put you out, Amaryllis, when you know it's not true?"

"Black, I didn't tell Momma that. She asked why I was home and I told her that we had an argument and I needed to stay there for a couple of days."

"Well, where would she get the idea that I put you out?"

"I honestly don't know. You know how Momma is. She's always making something out of nothing."

"And you don't know who tore up my car?"

"No, I don't, and I'm insulted that you would ask me something like that, Black."

"It's mighty funny how things happened when you left."

"I'm telling you that I had nothing to do with it."

Randall didn't know if he should believe her. The surveillance tapes confirmed that her uncles weren't involved. He had no proof that Amaryllis was behind it. And besides, would she be there preparing dinner if she was guilty?

"What's up with that money order on the table?" He nodded toward the dining room.

"That's my half of the money for the bills."

"I thought you said your money was tight."

"I borrowed it from Bridgette."

"The same girl who couldn't afford to buy her man drawers gave you $1,300.00?"

"Yeah, we went to the river boat last night, and she got lucky."

"How are you gonna pay her back if your money is tight?"

"I'll give her a little each pay period until I'm paid up."

"So, what are you gonna do next month and the month after that?"

"Black, don't worry about it. I'll figure something out."

Randall had already forgotten that she wasn't supposed to be there after today. Once again, Amaryllis wormed her way back in.

"Are you sure that you don't wanna eat anything?"

"Nah, not right now. I'm going to lie down and take a nap because I'm going to church for evening service. Why don't you come with me?"

Amaryllis would rather do anything else than go to church. She knew Randall still had his doubts about her involvement with his car so if she could do anything to further convince him that she was innocent, it would be worth it, even if it meant sitting in a boring church. "Okay, Black, I'll go with you this time."

Randall couldn't believe what he heard. He just knew that she was going to come up with another excuse why she couldn't go with him. "Seriously, Precious, you'll go?"

"Sure, if it'll make you feel better," she faked a smile.

Randall grabbed her and pulled her close to him and squeezed her tight. "Thank you, baby. I am so happy. I'm gonna have my Precious in church with me tonight."

Amaryllis looked into his eyes. "You know I love you, right, Black?"

"Yeah, baby, and I love you too."

"You go ahead and get some rest, and I'll put the food away."

Randall got undressed and into bed, but before he could drift off, Amaryllis had come into the room and called his name. When he opened his eyes and saw that her body was rid of the camisole, they did everything but sleep. Randall had taken two steps forward and three steps backward. He was once again back in Amaryllis's grip. All of the praying and prophesying his mother had done earlier in the day had no effect whatsoever.

As they were leaving for church, Randall gave her $200 in cash.

"What's this for?" Amaryllis asked.

"Since Joy isn't in my parking space downstairs, you can park your car there and that'll save you money on *your* parking space."

They walked out the door and Amaryllis completely forgot to get the Bible that Randall bought for her. It was still on the top shelf in her closet, where it had been for almost two years.

Randall walked into Holy 'D' proudly with his trophy on his arm. Amaryllis wore a dazzling Roberto Cavalli navy blue minidress that fit her every curve. She carried a silk navy Chanel clutch and four-inch navy silk sling back House Of Dereon stilettos decorated her feet. Her earlobes carried the weight of three-carat Lorraine Schwartz diamond studs. Amaryllis was as sharp as a tack and she knew it. She sashayed into the sanctuary with her arm looped through Randall's and her nose in the air.

JoAnn Banks, the president of the sanctuary choir, saw them come in and approached them with a smile and hugged Randall. "Hey, Brother Loomis, long time no see. Where have you been hiding yourself?"

"How are you this evening, Sister Banks?" Randall replied.

"God is still in the blessing business. I have no complaints. I've missed you these last few weeks."

What did she say that for? Amaryllis was in the church for only two minutes and already she had an attitude. *Who is this woman hugging on my man, and what is she doing missing him?*

Amaryllis didn't appreciate being ignored and Randall knew better. She stood there hanging on to him. She listened to them chit chat for another minute before she decided to make her presence known. "Ahem."

Randall was in mid-sentence with Sister Banks, but immediately stopped his conversation and looked at Amaryllis. She had on dark Versace shades. He couldn't see her eyes, but he knew what the 'ahem' meant.

"Oh, excuse me. Sister Banks, I want you to meet my lady friend, Amaryllis. Amaryllis, Sister Banks is the president of the Holy Deliverance Sanctuary Choir."

Amaryllis extended her hand, but Sister Banks stepped to her and hugged her.

"Welcome, my sister. Amy? Amaro? Uh, how do you pronounce your name again?"

Amaryllis was ticked off. Not only did this woman totally ignore her, then grab and hug her like she was her best friend, but she had the gall to mispronounce her name. She looked at Sister Banks like she was stupid and said her name correctly but Amaryllis broke down every syllable with a very nasty attitude. "It's A-ma-ry-llis, but if it's too complicated for you to say, just call me 'Precious.'"

Randall couldn't believe how she was speaking. But Sister Banks was a forty-eight-year-old missionary and she knew how to handle young women who were too pretty for their own good and stuck on themselves. "I beg your pardon, young lady?"

Amaryllis removed her arm from Randall's and put her hand on her hip. "Are you dumb and deaf?"

Sister Banks stared at Amaryllis in shock. It was good, for Amaryllis's sake, that they were within church walls. She held in a few choice words that would quickly

put her in her place. Randall had enough of the rude-
ness. He looked apologetically at Sister Banks.

"Excuse us, Sister Banks," Randall said. He grabbed
Amaryllis forcefully by her elbow and led her out into
the vestibule. "What is your problem, Amaryllis?"

Amaryllis snatched her arm from Randall's grip and
straightened her dress. "I don't have a problem. You
need to ask that broad what her problem is. I saw the
way she was hugging on you talkin' about how much
she missed you, then acted all phony and hugged on
me like she knew me. She heard you say my name.
She was trying to be funny."

"Amaryllis, Sister Banks is almost fifty years old.
There is no way she's interested in me. She has two
sons my age *and* a husband. She is highly respectable
and was genuine in her greeting. If you looked around,
you'd see that everybody is hugging everybody. And you
know that your name is not common. It took me a
whole month to pronounce it right."

"Look, Black, I don't care what you say. I know
women, and she was coming on to you and disrespecting me."

"You're wrong, Amaryllis, she's old enough to be my
mother. Your problem is that you weren't raised to recognize good manners."

Amaryllis was hot and ready to fight. She removed
her shades so Randall could see her eyes. "What the
. . . what are you saying, Black, that Veronica raised
me wrong?"

"Watch your mouth. This is church, and you just
proved what I'm talking about. Veronica is your mother
but you call her by her first name, which is wrong. You
talk to each other like two teenagers, and it takes
nothing for you to cuss each other out. And what about
gettin' high together, Amaryllis? You think smoking

dope with your mother is exercising respect and good manners?"

Cordell and his armour bearers were coming upstairs from his office. He heard Randall's last question to Amaryllis. He noticed her body language and knew things were getting our of control. Her neck was rotating with an attitude and he walked over to them just as Amaryllis was blasting off.

"You know what, Black? You can kiss my . . ."

Cordell got to them just in time to cut Amaryllis's words off. "Good evening, Randall." He hugged Randall tight and whispered in his ear. "What are you still doing with her?"

He didn't have time to get an answer now but he would definitely talk to Randall later.

Cordell let go of him and looked at Amaryllis and forced a smile. "Good evening, Amaryllis. It's good to see you. Welcome to Holy D."

Amaryllis knew Cordell couldn't stand her and the feeling was mutual. He could be phony if he wanted to, but that wasn't her style. She was glad she had this moment to put Cordell on blast. "Since when is it good to see me? For the past two years, you've done everything in your power to avoid contact with me and break me and Randall up. So, why is it so good to see me now? You wouldn't be lying in the church would you, Cordell?"

Randall stepped to her. "Amaryllis, please."

Cordell didn't need Randall to go to bat for him. "It's okay, Randall. She has a right to say how she feels."

Cordell focused on Amaryllis's eyes. He wanted to send a message that she didn't intimidate him. "Amaryllis, in spite of how we feel about one another, we are in the house of the Lord, and we will conduct ourselves accordingly." He turned and walked into the sanctuary.

Randall grabbed her by the elbow again. "While you're in the church, you are to address him as Pastor Bryson, okay? Praise and worship is about to start. Can we please go in and sit down?"

"Humph, he's lucky I didn't call him what I *wanted* to call him. And let go of my arm." She snatched her arm away and walked into the sanctuary.

When Pastor Bryson announced that his text would be coming from the book of Isaiah, everyone opened their Bibles. Amaryllis mistook a hymnal, that was in a slot on the back of the pew in front of her, for a Bible. Randall was embarrassed and he quickly took the hymnal away from her and placed it back in its slot.

"This is not a Bible, Precious. It's a hymnal."

"They look alike. What's the difference?" She inquired.

Randall looked over his shoulder at the people around them, hoping and praying that no one heard her. "A hymnal is a book of songs and a Bible is the Word of God, better known as 'Good News' or the Gospel."

"Whatever *that* means."

"I'll explain it to you later. Where is your Bible I bought for you?"

"I forgot it."

Randall placed his Word on her lap and turned to the book of Isaiah.

Pastor Bryson told his congregation how they could be delivered from the things that were hindering them from spiritual growth. "We must first be deprogrammed, then be reprogrammed. We must knock down the boundaries that are limiting us from going farther in life. We need to change our way of living and start walking according to God's Word. We have to do what God tells us to do and not what *we* wanna do. Our maturity grows through our obedience to God. He's already given us the authority to live a righteous life. We can change our minds to change our attitudes to change our positions. God wants us to confess our sins and repent so that we may be justified and righteous. First, we've got to face our intimidators. Intimidators are people or things that make us timid by threats. Stand up to them and say, 'No. No matter what you say or do to me, I am no longer going to be bound. I will be free to live the life that God wants me to live.'"

Randall knew that God was speaking directly to him through Cordell. Many times, he'd come close to telling Amaryllis to move out, but could never go through with it. If only she wasn't so fine. Amaryllis had a jacked up attitude and he knew it. But where her way of living lacked, her beauty more than atoned for.

He looked around the church at the saints. Some were on their feet applauding. He looked at his Precious and saw her picking at the acrylic on her fingernails. She was totally uninterested in the sermon.

Pastor Bryson invited anyone who had something in their lives that was hindering them from spiritual growth, to come and stand around the altar. A few people made their way to the front of the church, but Randall didn't move.

Cordell looked at his friend still sitting. "Those of you who are battling with yourselves with making the right decision about an issue, come to the altar."

Six more people walked to the altar and got on their knees. Cordell looked at Randall who was still seated. The blood in Randall's veins was running a marathon. He saw Cordell look at him, focus his eyes on the rest of the congregation, and look at him again. Through Cordell's glances at him, Randall knew he was sending him a spiritual backbone. "If you're in a relationship that you know you shouldn't be in, make your way down to this altar."

God was pulling Randall's spirit one way, and Amaryllis was pulling his soul in the opposite direction. He contemplated what to do. He desired to do the right thing, needed to do the right thing, but what about Amaryllis? Was she worth holding on to? Better yet, did she appreciate *his* worth?

Randall could sit no longer. Slowly, he got up to go to the altar and Amaryllis grabbed his hand. "Where are you going?"

"I gotta do this, Amaryllis."

She looked at Cordell and stood up and yelled from the back of the church. "Why can't you mind your own business, Cordell?"

Everyone stopped what they were doing and looked at her, but she didn't care. For two years, Amaryllis had been wanting to give Cordell a piece of her mind, and now she had finally gotten her chance. She glanced around and saw that all eyes were on her.

"What are y'all looking at? Yeah, I said it. Anybody wanna do something?"

Randall wanted to die. Amaryllis humiliated him in front of his entire church family. He grabbed her by the arm and practically dragged her outside the church.

"How dare you embarrass me in my church? Something is wrong with you, girl! Something is really wrong with you." Randall's anger had reached level ten. His nostrils flared each time he inhaled.

"Why do you always blame me for everything, Randall? How are you gonna let that punk tell you that you shouldn't be in a relationship? I'm sick and tired of the way you let him run your life. Are y'all messing around? Huh, Randall? You and Cordell on the down

low?" Amaryllis raised her eyebrows and folded her
arms across her chest waiting for an answer. "Tell me
something. I mean, what's *really* going on?"

Randall wouldn't even entertain Amaryllis's sick
and twisted questions. "Amaryllis, Cordell is my pastor. It's his job to watch over the church and preach the
Word of God."

"Well, it's *my* job to speak up for my man when he
can't speak for himself."

"I *can* speak for myself, and Cordell is right; the way
I'm living is wrong."

"What?"

"You heard me. This relationship ain't right. I love
God, and you don't. I want to get married, and you don't.
You gamble, drink, smoke dope, and cuss, but I don't.
We don't have anything in common. I really think that we
should separate and evaluate what we mean to each
other."

Amaryllis stepped to him. "Is that how you really
feel?"

"Yeah it is. For the past two years I've been trying to
make us click, but it just ain't working out."

"So, you're gonna let your friend, who don't even
have a woman, break up your relationship?"

"Amaryllis, I don't think what we have can be called
a relationship. It's more like an arrangement. And it
ain't got nothin' to do with Cordell. It's about doing
what is right."

"Well, guess what else we don't have in common,
Black?"

"What's that, Amaryllis?"

"A way home."

She walked to her car, got in, and drove off. Randall
stood on the church steps. Too humiliated to go back

into the service, he walked to the bus stop. It took him almost an hour to get from the church to his condo.

When he walked into the bedroom, Amaryllis was under the covers with her back to him. He got undressed and into bed with his back to her. Randall could smell her perfume, and it took all that was within him not to reach over and touch her. After a few minutes, she rolled him onto his back and straddled him. "I'm sorry, Black."

He looked at her and didn't say anything.

"I'm really sorry."

Randall pulled her to him and held her tight. She lay with her head on his chest. They kept that position until the radio alarm sounded at six o'clock AM, Monday.

Chapter 10

Bridgette was already at her desk when Amaryllis got to work. The two of them rotated days to bring coffee and donuts. She didn't see a white paper bag in Amaryllis's hand and frowned. "Did you forget something?"

Amaryllis sat down and let out a loud sigh, but didn't acknowledge Bridgette. As talkative as Amaryllis was, Bridgette knew something had to be wrong. "Hello?"

Amaryllis looked across the office at her. "Huh?"

"Where's the grub?"

"It's not my morning to bring in the donuts, is it?"

"Yes it is, and I'm starving."

"Bridgette, girl, I'm sorry. I completely forgot. As soon as I change my shoes, I'll run down to the bakery."

"What's wrong with you, you didn't get any action last night?"

"Please, I've got Randall's nose so wide open, it's pathetic. I can get what I want, when I want it and how I want it just for being beautiful."

Bridgette snapped her fingers three times in the shape of the letter Z. "Alright now, go on with your bad self. Is it really like that?"

"That's the way it is."

"It must be nice."

"Oh, it's very nice, but there's one problem that needs to be eliminated, and I gotta do it as soon as possible."

"What might that be?"

"It's not a what, it's a whom."

"Okay, whom might that be?"

"Cordell Bryson." Amaryllis spat his name out in disgust.

"His church buddy?"

"The very one. He's got to go."

"Is he still trippin'?"

"More now than he has been. Wait 'til you hear what this fool did in church last night."

"Whoa, stop the presses. You went to church, Amaryllis?"

"As a favor to Randall. He grilled me about his car, but I told him that I had nothing to do with it."

"Did he believe you?"

"I'm sure he did. It only cost me one night with Darryl for his posse to honor my request. Nothing can lead to me."

"Speaking of Darryl, what are you going to do with him now that you don't need him anymore?"

"Well, I'm not quite done with Darryl just yet. I'll keep him around a little bit longer. Pastor Cordell Bryson could use a makeover just like Joy."

"Dang, Amaryllis, is he *that* bad?"

"It's either him or me, Bridgette. One of us has got to go. I see signs of Black gettin' weak, and I can't have that."

Bridgette brought her chair closer to Amaryllis's desk. "Tell me what happened at church last night."

"After he got through preachin,' Cordell told everyone who had problems to come to the altar. I guess he was going to pray for them or something. Anyway, he called the people about three or four times. He kept looking at Randall, but Randall wouldn't move. So, Pastor boldly tells those who are in relationships they know they shouldn't be in, to come to the altar and be delivered. That's when Black stood up. I grabbed his hand to stop him and stood up and hollered at Cordell to mind his own business."

Bridgette's eyes grew wide and she covered her mouth with both hands. "Oh, my God. Amaryllis, you didn't."

"Yes, I did too. I didn't care that I was in church. Forget a church. Cordell needs to mind his own business and someone should've told him that long before I did."

"You did this to the pastor in front of everybody?" Bridgette was too outdone.

"I sure did and there was no shame in my game."

"Ooh wee, I wish I could've been there to see that. What did Randall do?"

"He pulled me outside and told me that I was out of line and should respect Cordell. I told him that he needed to open his eyes and see that Cordell is trying to run his life. Then he tells me that we need to take time out from each other because things ain't working out."

"Uh–oh. I'm afraid to ask what your response to that was, but I gotta know. What did you say to that?"

"Nothing, I got in my car and left him there."

"You just left him standing outside the church? How did he get home?"

"I guess the best way he knew how. That wasn't my concern." Amaryllis replaced her walking shoes with black leather pumps.

"Well, don't leave me hanging, Amaryllis. What happened when Randall got home? Did y'all have a fight?"

"No, we didn't fight. I had it all planned out. I was already in the bed when he got home, but I was naked and smelling good. I could tell that he was mad and he tried to hold on to that anger, but as usual, I was irresistible. And this morning, Black brought me breakfast in bed."

Bridgette was impressed. "Girl, girl, girl. How do you do it?"

"What's my name?"

"Amaryllis."

"And what Amaryllis wants?"

Bridgette chuckled, "Amaryllis gets."

They both laughed. Then Bridgette asked her, "So, you're gonna have Darryl's crew pay Cordell a visit?"

Amaryllis took ten dollars from her wallet and stood up. "You know what, Bridge? I think I'm gonna handle Cordell personally."

"How do you plan to do that?"

"I haven't figured it out yet. What kind of donut do you want?"

As soon as the elevator doors closed, Amaryllis's extension rang and Bridgette answered it from her desk. "Amaryllis Price's desk, how may I help you?"

"Good morning, Bridgette, this is Randall. Has Amaryllis gotten there yet?"

"Hi, Randall, yes she was just here, but she went down to the bakery. Should I have her call you at home?"

"No, I'm leaving in a few minutes. Tell her to call me on my cell."

"Okay, I'll tell her."

"Hey, Bridgette, I want to thank you for helping Amaryllis with her bills. I'm sure she already thanked you, but I want you to know that I appreciate it too."

"What are you talking about?"

"The $1,300 you gave her. She said you got lucky Saturday night at the river boat. You must've won a lot of money to be able to give her that much."

Bridgette was caught totally off guard. She had no idea what he was talking about.

"We didn't go to the river boat Saturday night. Are you sure she said that it was *me* who gave her money?"

"Yeah, but maybe she meant another friend and said your name by mistake. By the way, how about the four of us getting together next weekend?"

"The four of who?"

"Amaryllis and I with you and your new man."

"Are you trying to be funny, Randall? You know I don't have a man."

"Wow, that was fast. What happened, he didn't like the expensive boxers you bought for him?"

"What boxers? Randall, are you high? I don't have a clue what you're talkin' about."

"I'm talking about the underwear that Amaryllis bought at For Real Men Only."

"Oh yeah, but she didn't buy them for me. I should be asking you if *you* liked them, and were you able to get out of the handcuffs?"

Randall was confused. "What handcuffs?"

"The chocolate edible ones Amaryllis bought with the boxers."

Randall was quiet, and Bridgette thought he'd hung up on her. "Hello, Randall are you there?"

"I gotta go, Bridgette. Tell Amaryllis to call me."

Ten minutes later, Amaryllis returned to the office

with the goodies. Bridgette looked at her with a frown. "Randall just called. He wants you to call him on his cell, but before you do that, let me tell you what just happened."

Amaryllis placed the white paper bag of donuts on Bridgette's desk. She sat at her own desk and logged on to her computer. "What?"

"He thanked me for giving you $1,300 to pay your bills."

Amaryllis looked at Bridgette and froze.

"Did you forget to tell me something, Amaryllis?"

"I meant to call you on Saturday to tell you that Darryl had given me money and to have you cover for me if Black asked you about it, but I forgot. What did you tell him?"

"I told him that I didn't give you any money."

Amaryllis's heart sank down to her abdomen. "Bridgette, you didn't."

"I had no idea what he was talking about. You should've told me, Amaryllis."

She set her elbows on her desk and placed her face in her hands. "Oh, my God. What am I gonna do?"

"You need to figure out a way to explain those boxers and handcuffs you bought last month, because he mentioned those too."

Amaryllis felt like she was on a roller coaster going downward at one hundred miles an hour. "What about the boxers and handcuffs?"

"He asked if my man liked them. I told him that I didn't have a man and that you bought the boxers and handcuffs for him. I was with you when you bought them. Why didn't you tell me they were for Darryl and not Randall?"

"It completely slipped my mind. Bridgette, you're killing me. What else did Black say?"

"Nothin'. He got quiet for a moment then told me to have you call him. You know Randall and I go there with each other. He's always in my business, and I'm always in his. You really should have told me what you were up to, Amaryllis."

Amaryllis knew she had to pull herself together. Randall had always been putty in her hands. Why should this time be any different? "Before I call him back, I gotta find a way out of this."

"Well, if anybody can do it, it's you, Amaryllis. And next time, clue me in when you use me."

On her lunch break, Amaryllis went back to For Real Men Only and bought another pair of boxers and chocolate handcuffs. She told the cashier that she'd made the exact purchase last month and needed a copy of that receipt.

Back at her desk, Amaryllis shredded today's receipt and placed the old receipt in the bag with the new boxers and handcuffs. On her computer she printed a personal letter.

Black,
   On this day I could only think of you. So I decided to do some shopping. I hope you enjoy wearing your gifts just as much as I enjoyed buying them for you.
                          Love,
                          Precious

Amaryllis called a travel agent and made reservations at a spa in Lave Geneva, Wisconsin for the upcoming weekend. Bridgette watched Amaryllis in action with total admiration. "Is there anything that you can't get out of?"

"Nope. Now all I have to do is wait for Black to ask me about this, and I'll say that I was planning a surprise trip this weekend and was going to give him the gifts when we got to Lake Geneva. I'll say that I didn't want him to find out about it, so when he saw the charge on my bill, I had to say that I bought them for you. I purposely left the receipt with last month's date on it in the bag, to make sure he sees it."

"Amaryllis, your life ain't nothing but a soap opera. You need to teach a class or write a book on getting out of sticky situations."

"That's not a bad idea, Bridgette. I could call it *Precious Ways To Outsmart Your Man.*"

They laughed. Then Bridgette thought about something. "Where are you going to tell Randall you got the thirteen hundred dollars from?"

"Oh, that's easy. Randall knows that I took two thousand dollars from his credit card. I'll say that it came from that."

"I hope your plan works."

"It will because I've got reinforcements."

"And what might that be?"

"On the way back from For Real Men Only, I stopped at a lingerie store and bought something that will knock him off his feet the moment he walks in the front door. And this outfit has five-inch spiked heels to match it."

"You are too much, Amaryllis."

"That ain't nothing, Bridgette. Guess what else I'm going to do?"

"I'm afraid to ask."

"Randall's program dismisses at three o'clock, and you know how much he likes to eat. So, when he gets home, I'll be dressed in my new outfit and lying across

the dining room table with lasagna covering me from
my neck to my thighs."

"Ooh girl, that's good *and* nasty."

"Absolutely, and I guarantee that once Black gets a
taste of me, he won't even remember to ask about the
boxers, handcuffs, or money." Amaryllis did half of her
own work, gave Bridgette the other half plus one hundred dollars, and left work for the day.

The evening went exactly the way Amaryllis had
planned it. Randall walked in, saw her spread across
the dining room table and all other thoughts were forgotten. Later in the evening, Cordell called to ask if
Randall was coming to men's night.

"No, I'm too tired to make it tonight," Randall said
into the phone receiver.

"What were you doing with Amaryllis yesterday? I
thought you were gonna kick her to the curb. What's
up?"

"Nothing."

"Where is she?"

"Lying next to me watching television and eating ice
cream."

Cordell couldn't believe that after all she put Randall through, he'd taken her back. "*What?*"

Amaryllis reached over Randall to unplug the telephone cord from the jack in the wall. Randall quickly
ended his call with Cordell. "I gotta go man. I'll talk to
you later."

Chapter 11

All week long, Amaryllis had been insisting that this weekend's rendezvous to the spa in Wisconsin was going to be her treat. On Friday morning, though as they were getting ready to go about their day, she confessed to Randall that she had blown all of her money on the black jack table Tuesday night. Unless he paid for the hotel, she would have to cancel the reservations.

"Precious, if you've planned to treat me this weekend, why would you risk your money gambling?"

"I had hoped to be a winner, and for a while I *was* winning, then all of a sudden, I lost everything."

"Amaryllis, you know that my savings is all that I have, and I need it to pay the bills."

"Okay, Black, I'll just cancel the reservations."

Randall watched as she sat at her vanity table looking disappointed.

"I'll tell you what, Precious, I'll pay for the weekend and you can pay me back."

Amaryllis smiled, ran to Randall, and put her arms around his neck. "I love the way you love me, Black."

"Yes, Amaryllis, I love you very much."

On his way home Friday afternoon from his employee assistance program, Randall stopped at the credit union and withdrew one thousand dollars from his savings account. He'd been depressed about his job and money issues. He thought that this weekend with his beauty may be just what the doctor ordered. His insurance company wasn't cooperating regarding his car. The car had been totaled beyond repair, but the insurance company was dragging its feet as to whether Randall should get a brand new Jaguar.

They checked into the spa resort on Friday evening and didn't emerge from their suite until they checked out on Sunday afternoon. It was then that Randall found out that the suite Amaryllis booked cost him $3,000 a night.

The room service alone totaled $200. It cost Randall fifty dollars in gas for Amaryllis's car one way. Before they left for the spa, her gas tank was on empty.

They were late checking into the spa because Amaryllis had taken too much time getting her hair and nails done, which cost Randall one hundred dollars.

Just as quickly as he had withdrawn one thousand dollars, he had spent it. What was supposed to have been a free luxury weekend for Randall turned out to be a free luxury weekend for Amaryllis. But Randall didn't care. As long as his precious was happy, he was too.

They got home at approximately 5:45 PM. Sunday, and there were three voicemail messages. The first was

from Ma'Dear, calling to check on Randall. The second
was from Bridgette, calling to find out how the roman-
tic weekend turned out. The third message was from
Cordell. He was calling to let Randall know that Apostle Donald Lawrence Alford, pastor of the Progressive
Life-Giving Word Cathedral, in Hillside, Illinois would
be the guest speaker for the evening service.

Randall and Amaryllis were fashionably late. Praise
and worship was over and Apostle Alford was
standing at the podium taking his text. Randall had
on a tailor-made charcoal gray pinstriped double-
breasted Armani suit, and Amaryllis wore a matching
tailor-made charcoal gray pinstriped double-breasted
Armani coat dress. Almost every eye in the church was
on them as they were ushered to their seats. Everyone
remembered Amaryllis and the scene she had caused
when she was there last. Cordell was sitting in the
pulpit trying to stay focused on what Apostle Alford
was saying, but couldn't help but notice the prime candidates for the paparazzi and their dramatic entrance.

The usher stopped at the sixth pew from the back of
the church and held out his hand for them to enter the
row. Amaryllis came to church to be seen. She wanted
everyone to know that Randall was her man and she
was his woman. So she was going to be seen. She got to
the sixth pew and looked at the usher.

"This is too far back. Do you have any seats up
front?" Amaryllis asked.

The usher wasn't used to this question. At Holy D,
whatever pew the usher brought you to was where you
sat. He looked at Amaryllis as if he didn't understand
her question. She saw the way he was looking at her,
and she said to Randall, loud enough for the usher and
all the people around them to hear, "Obviously he can't

hear. Black, go up front and see if there are any seats available."

The usher whispered. "Miss, the only available seats up front are reserved for the mothers of the church."

Amaryllis always got what she wanted, and she wasn't going to let an usher stand in her way of sitting where she could be seen. "Well, Pastor Bryson's mother is dead and Randall's mother isn't here, so we'll take their seats. Come on, Black."

She grabbed Randall by the hand, brushed past the usher, and walked to the second pew from the front of the church. There was room for them, but they had to step over nine mothers before they were able to sit. And it wasn't Amaryllis who said 'excuse me' as they stepped over knee after knee, making their way to the middle of the pew. It was Randall. He said the phrase nine times. He knew that they didn't belong on the mother's pew, but Amaryllis moved so quickly, he had no choice but to follow her. And even if he had spoken up, she would've caused a bigger scene.

Cordell was furious. How dare they disrespect the usher and the mothers?

Randall realized that he'd left his Bible at home and Amaryllis's Bible was still on the closet shelf. She wasn't interested in reading the Bible anyway. Randall had to look on with the mother seated next to him. Cordell saw that Randall didn't have his Word, and he got even angrier. When he couldn't detain himself any longer, he walked out of the pulpit over to Randall. "Excuse me Brother Loomis, may I speak with you?"

Amaryllis gave Cordell a nasty glare, but he ignored her. Randall whispered something in her ear and excused himself. He followed Cordell to the choir's room.

"Cordell, before you say anything, let me tell you

that I didn't know that Amaryllis was going to do that."

"That's beside the point, Randall. Before she got to the mother's pew, you should've stopped her. Actually, you should've stopped her from disrespecting the usher. She didn't even have good manners to say 'excuse me' as she was stepping over the mothers. *You* had to say it for her."

"Cordell, what can I say? When I told her that I was going to church, she insisted on coming with me. So, it was either bring her with me or stay at home."

Cordell wanted so badly to tell Randall that he should've kept his hind parts at home, but he knew God would not be pleased with such a suggestion. "Randall, I have no problem with Amaryllis coming to church with you. God knows that girl needs all the church she can get. My concern is how disrespectful she is when she's here. Now this is the last time that I'm going to tolerate her behavior in my church. That pew she's sitting on is for the holy women of God, and Amaryllis is far from holy, but I'm not going to say anything to her today because I know she'll act a fool and disrupt service. But she needs to know that she can't come in this church and demand things. Now when church is over, bring Amaryllis down to my office, and I'll have a talk with her about church etiquette."

Randall knew Amaryllis wouldn't take kindly to anything Cordell said to her. "No. Please let me do it. I'll talk to her when we get home. She'll take it better coming from me."

"I'm not kidding around with you, Randall. You need to nip this in the bud, now."

"I said 'I'll talk to her.' "

"Make sure that you do. And where's your Bible?"

"I left it at home."

"I've never seen you come into the sanctuary without your Bible."

"I didn't leave it on purpose, Cordell."

"I want you to sing with the choir tonight."

"What? I haven't been to choir rehearsal in almost two months."

"That's okay, they haven't learned any new songs."

"I just can't walk into the choir stand and sit down. You know Sister Banks don't play that."

"I'll deal with Sister Banks. You need to sing tonight, Randall."

"What about Amaryllis?"

"What about her? She's not a child who can't sit by herself."

"She's gonna get mad if I don't sit with her."

"Is that supposed to mean something to me?"

Cordell walked to the robe rack and looked for Randall's name on the tag inside the robes. He found it and brought the robe to Randall. "Put this on."

Randall got robed up, and Cordell escorted him to the choir stand. Then he went to the pulpit, sat down, and looked at Amaryllis. She wasn't looking at him. Her eyes were fixed on Randall. Cordell saw that Randall had his head hanging down.

At the height of Apostle Alford's sermon, everyone in the entire church was on their feet except Amaryllis. She sat as if nothing was going on. The music was high, and so was the Holy Spirit. An elderly mother next to her got happy and started to dance. With her eyes closed, she accidentally stepped on Amaryllis's brand new Jimmy Choo stilettos. Amaryllis stood up and stomped down on the mother's shoe. The mother went from praising God to hollering out in pain. The mother sat down, began rubbing her foot and looked at Amaryllis who now had her eyes closed imitating those around her in praise. She was waving her hands in the air and pretended to be holy dancing as though she hadn't stepped on the mother's foot.

When the church calmed down and everyone sat down, the mother looked at Amaryllis again. Amaryllis knew she was looking at her, but she kept her eyes focused on the pulpit. At offering time, the baskets were passed along the pews. Amaryllis placed a twenty dollar bill in the basket and took eighteen dollars out of it. After the benediction, Randall walked over to her. "I'm sorry, Precious, but Pastor Bryson wanted me to sing."

"Look, Black, I didn't come here to sit by myself. If I wanted to be by myself, I could've stayed at home."

"It won't happen again, I promise."

"Are you sure about that?"

"Yeah, I'm gonna resign from the choir." It didn't even dawn on Randall that the enemy had defeated him yet again.

On his way home from his employee assistance program the following Monday afternoon, Randall stopped at Holy D to tell Cordell about his decision to resign from the choir.

Cordell was livid. "You're gonna do what?"

"Calm down, Cordell, it's just for a little while."

"This has Amaryllis's name all over it, doesn't it?"

"Not in the way you think. It wasn't her idea at all. I'm doing this so that she'll start coming with me more often. The goal is to get her here every week, but she'll only come if I sit with her. So, I figured that if I sat with her for a few weeks, she'll get used to coming, and then I can sing again."

"That's crazy, stupid, and dumb. Why are you allowing her to do this to you?"

"She isn't doing anything. You're the one that's always talking about doing what we gotta do to get people off the streets and into the church. This is how I can get Amaryllis here."

"I did say that, didn't I?" If Cordell was double-joined, he'd kick his own behind for allowing those particular words of advice to flow from his lips to Randall's ears.

"Yeah, you did."

"But there's a difference. Other people who come from the streets show an interest unlike Amaryllis who yawns and picks at her fingernails throughout the service."

"Well, I don't know what to tell you. I want her to come to church and this is what it takes to get her here regularly."

Cordell leaned back in his chair and shook his head. Then he looked across the desk at his best friend of twenty-eight years. "You listen to me and listen real good. Against my better judgment; I'm excusing you from the choir for only one month, and if Amaryllis doesn't know how to sit by herself and act like she's got some sense by then, it's just too bad. Do you hear me, Randall? You've got four Sundays to do what you feel you need to do."

Randall stood up to leave. "I heard you, man. That's all the time I need."

Cordell got up, came around the desk, and hugged him. "I love you, man."

"I love you too, man. Thanks for having my back and understanding."

"I'll always have your back no matter what, but understanding you is a different story."

When they released the embrace, Randall saw disappointment in Cordell's eyes.

"What are you worried about?" Randall asked.

"Nothing, let's pray before you go."

"I ain't got time. I gotta go downtown and pick up Precious."

"You can't pray with me for two minutes?"

"Nah, man, I'm already late."

"Are you coming back for men's night?"

"Yeah, I'll be here."

Randall opened the door to leave. He turned to look at Cordell's eyes. Worry was still present. "Stop worrying man. It ain't that bad."

After his best friend left his office, Cordell sat down in his chair and looked at the closed door. "It is that bad, Randall."

Before she and Randall started their days, Amaryllis seasoned a pot roast and cut white potatoes into chunks and placed them in a crock pot with carrots to simmer all day. When they walked in the front door, they could smell what promised to be an excellent feast. The only thing Amaryllis had to do was put the crescent rolls in the oven for twelve minutes before dinner would be served.

At 6:15, they were eating at the dining room table. Amaryllis had on a very short dark purple lace nightgown with spaghetti straps. He looked at her lips as she chewed. She noticed that he had stopped eating and his eyes were fixed on her. "What are you looking at?"

"You."

"Why?"

"Because you're beautiful and gorgeous." Randall was sincere. In that moment, he had fallen more in love with Amaryllis.

"And you're handsome and gorgeous."

"Can you imagine what our baby will look like?"

Amaryllis's pot roast went down the wrong way as she was trying to swallow. She had to swallow three or four times and drink water to get it down smoothly. Randall reached for a napkin and gave it to her. "Are you okay, Precious?"

"Yeah, I'm fine. You threw me with that baby thing."

"I know we've never discussed it, but don't you wanna have kids?"

"I don't have time." Truth be told, she hadn't had the desire. Although Randall afforded Amaryllis all the benefits of a wife, she wasn't in love with him. Her only purpose for being with Randall was to be a kept woman. If children came onto the scene, she'd have to share the benefits. Amaryllis could never let that happen.

"Don't you want us to be a family?"

"Black, God told Eve to be fruitful and multiply, He didn't say anything to me."

"If you would read your Bible that I bought for you, you'd know that God was talking to all mankind."

"Why are you trying to fix something that ain't broke?"

"What does this relationship mean to you, Amaryllis? Where do you see us in another two years?" Randall began to wonder exactly what Amaryllis's intentions were with him if children weren't in their future.

"I don't know, Black, I can't predict the future."

"No one can, but we can at least plan it and set goals."

"I don't have any goals. My life is fine just the way it is."

"Well, I *do* have goals, and I don't want to be in this same situation in two years. I want to get married and have children. I want to move out of this building and buy a four-bedroom house. I would like to start my own business and buy property. And I want to be able to retire from my job in the next three to five years."

"Black, all of that sounds good, but it ain't likely to happen. Especially the married with children part— not with me anyway."

Disappointed, Randall threw his napkin on his plate, got up from the table, and went to start the water in the shower. It became clear to him that he'd wasted the last two years of his life waiting for something to happen that was never in God's plan. And if Ma'Dear told Randall once, she'd told him a thousand times that he should never allow a woman to live in his house permanently if she didn't even visit God's house occasionally.

"Where are you going?" Amaryllis asked him.

"I'm going to church. It's men's night."

"I wanted you to watch the eight o'clock movie with me."

"I told Cordell that I was coming to church tonight."

"You're gonna put him before me?"

"I'm going to church because I wanna go. It has nothing to do with Cordell. And you just told me that we have no future together so why should I sit around watching the Lifetime Channel with you?"

"Black, just because I don't wanna get married and have kids doesn't mean we can't be together."

Randall stood next to Amaryllis and looked down at her. "Don't you see, Amaryllis? That's exactly what it means. I really thought we were building a future, but it turns out that the last two years of my life have been wasted on false hope."

Now Amaryllis threw her napkin into her food. "I don't get it. You've been content for this long. If you would live your life the way you want to instead of letting your boy dictate your every move, we'd be very happy together."

"I'm sick and tired of you blaming Cordell for everything. The way I wanna live my life has nothing to do
with him. It's about doing what's right. I wished that
I'd listened to him when he told me not to move you in
here." Randall walked into the bathroom and slammed
the door. After his shower, he went into the bedroom to
get dressed. Amaryllis was lying across the bed watching television. When Randall opened the closet door to
select his attire for the evening, she sat up on the bed.

"How are you getting to church?"

"Since you're not going anywhere, I thought I could
drive your car."

"You can't take my car."

"Why not?"

"Because I said so."

"I pay the note on that car, Amaryllis."

"You didn't pay it this month, and if you take it, I'll
call the police and report it stolen. And if you think I'm
playin', just try me."

Randall was so mad, his ears were burning. "You
ain't stoppin' nothin', Amaryllis."

He picked up the telephone and called Cordell at
home. "Hey, man, can you swing by here to pick me up
on your way to church?"

Cordell told Randall he'd be there within twenty
minutes. Randall advised Cordell to call when he got
near so he could meet him downstairs.

He got dressed, grabbed his Bible from the dresser,
went into the living room, and sat down on the sofa to
wait for Cordell to call. When he left the bedroom,
Amaryllis took the telephone off the receiver.

Cordell sat downstairs calling Randall's house phone.
He kept getting a busy signal. He called his cellular phone and got his voicemail. He parked his car

across the street from Randall's building and went in just as someone else was entering. He rode the elevator to the eighth floor and knocked on the door. Randall got up from the sofa and opened it.

"You didn't have to come all the way up here. I told you to call me when you got downstairs."

"I got a busy signal on the house phone. Where's your cell? My call went straight to your voicemail."

"Oh, my bad, it's on the charger."

Just then Amaryllis placed the house phone back on its receiver, came out of the bedroom, and went into the kitchen. Cordell abruptly stopped talking and watched Amaryllis walk into the kitchen.

Randall turned around to see what had captured Cordell's attention and saw her standing at the stove, naked, with her back to them. "Amaryllis?"

She turned around to face them. "What is it, honey? Oh, my goodness, I didn't know Cordell was here." She covered her bottom half with her hands, but left her double-D-size girls fully exposed.

Cordell shook his head in disgust. He turned and walked toward the elevator. "Come on, Randall, let's go."

Randall grabbed his cellular phone from the charger, walked out, and slammed the door. Amaryllis stood in the kitchen laughing.

Chapter 12

Randall was more than halfway through his employee assistance program. With two months to go, he was still without a car. His insurance company had been giving him the run around for the past three months. Ever since that night Amaryllis clowned about her car, that *he'd* been paying for since she came into his life, he promised himself he'd never ask to use her car for anything.

One of the advantages of working for the Chicago Transit Authority was that his company identification badge could get him around the city free of charge on buses and trains. Public transportation got him wherever he wanted to go, and Cordell was his way to church.

Since that night Amaryllis bared her essentials, Cordell vowed to never step foot in Randall's condo again as long as she was living there. If Randall wanted a ride to church, he would have to be downstairs waiting at a time they agreed on.

Today was the third Sunday in October and Holy D's

fortieth anniversary. The kitchen staff prepared a feast for the church. After morning service, the congregation had dinner downstairs in the fellowship hall. After dinner, the afternoon service began at four o'clock. It wasn't until after seven that Cordell took Randall home.

Amaryllis was sitting at the dining room table waiting for him. Randall stepped on rose petals that led from the front door all the way to his seat at the table. He looked at her and knew by the expression on her face that she was highly upset. The table was set beautifully with purple flowers in a tall thin vase. Two white candles had been burned and wax melted all the way down and hardened around the candlesticks. Amaryllis sat in front of a plate that had very little food on it, but the plate she set for Randall was filled with meatloaf, mashed potatoes, biscuits, and gravy. "Where have you been, Black?"

"First of all, good evening to you too, and I was at church."

"All day?"

"Yeah, it was the church's anniversary today."

"Why didn't you call and tell me you weren't coming home after morning service to eat?"

"Precious, I tried to wake you up to go to church, and you acted like you didn't want to be bothered, so I left you alone. Before I walked out the front door I told you that I was going to eat at church and stay for the afternoon service."

"How do you expect me to hear you talking to me when I'm asleep, Black?"

"You *did* hear me. When I told you I was eating at church your exact words were 'Yeah whatever,' then you turned over and pulled the sheets over your head."

"I don't remember that."

"Well, that's not *my* fault."

Randall saw her neck rolling. "It *is* your fault. I've been sitting here for hours waiting on you. You think I don't have anything better to do than wait on you hand and foot? I slaved over that hot stove all afternoon, and you don't even appreciate it enough to come home and eat. And why is it that every time I called your cell phone, I got your voicemail?"

"I turn my phone off because I don't want to be disturbed when I'm worshiping God, Amaryllis. You know that, don't act like you don't."

Randall might as well have told her that she wasn't important. He could tell she was becoming irate. Amaryllis stood from the table, put her hand on her hip, and rolled her neck like she was working a miniature hula hoop.

"Oh, so now I'm a disturbance, huh? Is that what I am to you, Black? A disturbance?"

Randall wished that he'd packed an overnight bag and stayed at Cordell's.

"Precious, calm down. That's not what I'm sayin'. The saints go to church to get delivered from things, receive blessings, and hear the Word of God. No one wants to hear pagers and phones ringing because it distracts them."

Amaryllis's neck continued to dance. "So, not only am I a disturbance, but I'm also a distraction?"

"You're putting words in my mouth. You know that's not what I'm sayin'."

"Well, I don't like not having access to you twenty-four seven, Black, you know that."

To Randall, this conversation was getting more ridiculous by the second. He was a grown man, and Amaryllis was not his wife. "Look, the only time my phone is off is when I'm at church. Any other time, you can reach me. You're just gonna have to understand that. I'm sorry that you went through all this trouble, but I *did* tell you that I was eating at church today. So just wrap my plate up for me, and I'll have it for dinner tomorrow night."

Amaryllis picked up Randall's plate, smashed it in his face, and dropped the plate on the floor. "*You* wrap it up." She went into the bedroom and slammed the door.

Randall stood in the middle of his dining room in shock at what she'd just done. He cleaned the table and floor as best he could. He could only hope the gravy stain would come out of his suit jacket and shirt. He took a shower and washed the food from his head. When he tried to enter the bedroom from the attached bath, the door was locked from the bedroom side. Randall then exited the bathroom and tried to open the bedroom door from the hallway and found that it too, was locked from the inside.

"Amaryllis, open this door."

She didn't answer him.

"Open the door, Amaryllis."

Randall leaned his forehead against the door for a minute then went to the linen closet for sheets and a blanket. He spread the sheet over the living room sofa, laid down and pulled the blanket up to his neck. He went over the events of the evening in his mind for two hours before he drifted off to sleep.

Amaryllis was gone when he woke up Monday morning. He went into the kitchen for his breakfast and saw the plate she left for him. She'd gone into the trash can and dug out the meat and potatoes Randall cleaned from his clothes and floor then put them on a plate and covered it with saran wrap. Next to the plate was a note.

*Since you treated me like garbage yesterday, see
how you like eating garbage. Have a good breakfast.*

Precious

Randall threw the entire plate into the garbage can
and left to go to his program. He called Amaryllis at
work on his lunch break and Bridgette informed him
that she had called in sick. He called her mother's
house, and Veronica said she hadn't heard from Amaryllis. Randall switched his cellular phone to vibrate and
went back to his program.

Amaryllis was in a seven-bedroom estate in Long
Grove, one of the wealthiest towns in north suburban
Illinois. She climbed off of Darryl and started to get
dressed.

"Wait a minute, baby. Where are you going?" he asked.

"It's twelve o'clock. I should at least go to work for
half a day," Amaryllis replied.

"You're just gonna love me then leave me?"

"What's in it for me if I stay?"

"Open the top left drawer of the dresser."

Amaryllis did as she was told and saw many crisp
one hundred dollar bills. She looked at Darryl and
smiled. "Is this for me?"

"Ten of those got your name on them, but it depends
on what you're willing to do."

She took ten bills out of the drawer and put them in
her purse and got back into bed.

"Dang, girl, you love money, huh?"

"My momma taught me that closed legs don't get
fed."

It wasn't until after three that Amaryllis called the
law firm. "Bridge, it's me. You busy?"

"Just doing your work *and* mine. Where are you?"

"I'm at Darryl's house. You wanna go to the boat tonight?"

"I don't have any boat money."

"Let's just say that I earned a bonus today, and I'm gonna split it with you for handling my work load."

"You better make it worth my while, Amaryllis. I typed six briefs for you today."

"How does $500 sound?"

Bridgette was elated. "It sounds like 'ka-ching, ka-ching'."

"Uh huh, that's what I thought you'd say. What time are you leaving the office?"

"It's 3:30 now, and I'm working on my last brief, so I'm hoping to get outta here no later than 5:30, then I gotta go home and get in a pair of jeans."

"Cool, I'll meet you at the blackjack table at seven o'clock. Did I get any calls today?"

"Yeah, Randall called this morning. Then I got busy so I let your other calls go into your voicemail."

"What did you tell him?"

"I told him you called in sick. Was that the wrong thing to say?"

"No, you told him the truth, because I'm sick of him."

"Amaryllis, you two have been fighting a lot lately. What's going on?"

"Girl, he's been getting on my nerves doing stupid stuff. Like yesterday, I cooked dinner for him, and he didn't come home to eat."

"Where was he?"

"At church with Cordell, where else?" Amaryllis answered as though Bridgette should have already known the answer.

"What time did he finally come home?"

"Some time after seven. He claims he told me he was going to stay at church all day before he left, but I don't remember that."

"What did you do?"

"I threw his food in his face and locked him out of the bedroom."

"Amaryllis, you can't fault the man for wanting to be at church. Sometimes I wonder why Randall puts up with you."

"Because I'm fine."

They both laughed and Bridgette saw that she was misspelling words. "I gotta go, 'cause you're making me mess up. I got typos all over the place. I'll see you at seven."

It was after midnight when Amaryllis came into the bedroom to undress. Randall was asleep, but she woke him when she got into bed. When she finally stopped moving, he sat up. "Amaryllis, you smell like Boss."

"What?"

"You smell like Boss cologne."

"Do I?"

"Yeah, and it's strong like you sprayed yourself."

"I was next to a man at the blackjack table tonight, and I thought he smelled a lot like you."

"What was he doing, rubbing against you?"

"No, he was just sitting next to me, but if it bothers you, I'll take a shower."

"It bothers me."

Bridgette was surprised to see Amaryllis sitting at her desk so early. "You must've slept here last night, 'cause that's the only way you'll beat me here. What are you doing here so early?"

"I didn't wanna see Black this morning. When I got in the bed last night, he could smell Darryl all over me. And that scared the heck out of me 'cause I had showered before I left Darryl's house. I made up an excuse about a man with strong cologne being next to me at the blackjack table. Then I took another shower."

"Amaryllis, you're slipping. You ought to know that you can't lay with one man then lay with another. The second will always pick up the scent of the first. Did Randall believe you?"

"I don't know, he didn't say anything else about it."

"How could he when you were gone before the rooster crowed?"

"I just didn't want to deal with him this morning."

Bridgette sat at her desk. She didn't see the white paper bag. "Where's my coffee and donut?"

Amaryllis exhaled. "It can't be my morning again."

"It *is* your morning, and I'm hungry."

Amaryllis took ten dollars out of her purse and headed for the elevator. "If Black calls, tell him I'll be in meetings all day."

Chapter 13

For the remainder of the week, Randall said no more than two words to Amaryllis. He'd wake up without saying 'good morning,' and go to his class. From there, he'd go straight to church. He purposely wouldn't get home until well after ten o'clock P.M.

On the fifth night of non-communication, Amaryllis sat up and waited for him to get home. Cordell brought Randall home from Bible Study at 9:45. He walked in the front door to see a trail of lighted candles leading to the bedroom. He blew out each candle as he walked through the condo. Randall opened the bedroom door and heard jazz music coming from the stereo and Amaryllis was sitting on the middle of the bed in her birthday suit.

He didn't acknowledge her existence. He undressed, unplugged the stereo, got into bed, and turned his back to her. She looked at him, wondering how he could ignore her for an entire week. She'd always been able to weaken him with her beauty. Where was he getting his strength?

"Black, why are you ignoring me?"

Randall pulled the sheets up to his neck and didn't say a word. She got out of bed and walked around to his side and stood nude in front of him. "Look at me."

He opened his eyes and looked at her. She smiled at him, but he didn't smile at her.

"Black, I'm trying to seduce you. Why are you behaving like this?"

"I got a headache, Amaryllis."

"A headache? You've never had a headache before."

"Well, I have one now, and as long as you're here, I'll keep one." Randall then got out of bed, and took his pillow and the sheets with him into the living room, and slept on the couch.

On Saturday evening, Randall had just come in the front door from taking the garbage down to the dumpster when he heard Amaryllis talking on the telephone in the bedroom. He walked lightly and stood outside listening.

"I don't know if I can do it, Darryl," she half whispered.

Randall wondered who Darryl was.

"He's been having an attitude all week. He wouldn't even touch me last night, but that's okay, I ain't trippin'."

Her voice got lower so Randall actually put his ear on the door.

"Well, I was gonna go to the boat, but my money is funny and rent is due next week."

Randall was still listening.

"You'll pay me how much? How many men will be there? All I have to do is dance? If you throw in another grand, Darryl, I'll do it."

Randall's face frowned. *Is she getting ready to go and strip?*

"What's the address? Oh, it's at *your* house? Okay, that's cool, I'll see you at seven."

She hung up the telephone and Randall quickly grabbed his cellular phone and keys and left. He got down to the lobby and called Cordell. "Hey, man, I need to use your car to go see Ma'Dear. She said she can't get her cable to act right."

"Okay, I'll come and get you then we can go together." Cordell said.

That was not an option. Cordell couldn't go. "Well, after I fix her cable, we were gonna go by my Uncle June Bug's house. I don't know how long we'll be. I know you dedicate Saturday nights to study your sermons for Sunday service, and I don't wanna keep you from that."

"Okay, man, I filled the tank up last night. The car is yours."

As he followed Amaryllis, Randall had to pay three forty-cent tolls as they headed north on Interstate 294. He was relieved when she exited on Grand Avenue, because he was almost out of change. He followed her into a gated community of mini-mansions and estate homes. He tailed her to a security guard and watched them talk for a moment. Then she was allowed to proceed through the iron black gates. He drove up to the guard and let his window down. "I'm here for Darryl's party. You just let the stripper in. I'm her bodyguard."

The gates opened and Randall drove through. He followed Amaryllis until he saw her pull into a wide circular driveway filled with Cadillacs, Lexuses, Mercedes, and Porsches. Every light in the mansion was on, and he heard loud music all the way to the corner, where he sat and waited.

Amaryllis got out of her car, wearing a long red wig and a khaki colored trench coat. Randall squinted his eyes and saw fishnet stockings on her legs and silver stilettos on her feet as she retrieved a duffel bag from the trunk and went inside. Randall exited Cordell's car and walked toward the noise. He went to the side of the mansion and looked through a first floor window.

He recognized professional basketball and football players. He watched as they laughed, drank from bottles of alcohol, and passed marijuana from one to another. All of a sudden everyone assembled in the living room, where Randall saw his Precious descend down a spiral staircase wearing his favorite blue outfit. He couldn't believe his eyes as Amaryllis danced, shook, and wiggled all she had in a room full of men. The dancing and wiggling wasn't what got to Randall as much as their fondling and groping her. The look on her face was pure enjoyment. It was sickening to Randall.

He watched as one man in the middle of the floor on top of a chair that resembled a king's throne, grabbed Amaryllis by the hand and knelt her down before him. He unzipped his pants and lowered her head to his waist. She jerked her head away and he slapped her in the face. Again, the guy guided Amaryllis's head, but this time, he didn't hit her.

The men were laughing and chanting something Randall didn't understand as they all took turns sitting on the throne in front of Amaryllis. Randall had seen enough. He got nauseated, ran down the street, and regurgitated beside Cordell's car.

He was a mess driving to Cordell's house. Twice he lost control of the steering wheel and almost crashed into cars driving south alongside him on Interstate 294. Randall had flu symptoms. He was sweating, yet was chilled to the bone. He was crying uncontrollably and couldn't stop his body from trembling. Through his tears, he barely saw where he was going. Why hadn't he listened to Cordell when he said that Amaryllis was no good for him? He felt like such a fool.

He got to Cordell's house and rang the doorbell profusely. Cordell opened the door to a distraught Randall who fell into his arms. "Whoa, what happened, Randall?"

He couldn't say anything. The only thing he could do was cry.

"Did something happen to Ma'Dear?" Cordell literally had to carry Randall into his living room and sit him down on the sofa. "Talk to me, man, are you hurt?"

Randall took a deep breath and told Cordell what he had just seen.

"Oh, my God. How did you know?" Cordell asked.

"I heard her talking on the telephone to this guy name Darryl, then I followed her to his house and watched her through the window. Man, it was crazy; they were using her like she was a rag doll, and when I couldn't stand to see any more, I threw up. I should've listened to you, Cordell. You told me two years ago not to trust Amaryllis, and I was hard-headed. I feel so stupid."

"Randall, don't beat yourself up over this. I just hope you finally realize what you gotta do. You're worth more than this, man."

Randall was sitting on the living room sofa when Amaryllis came in the front door.

"Hey, Black. Why are you sittin' in here looking funny?"

He stood up and walked to her. "You've got one week to get everything you came here with and get out of my house. If you are not gone by next Saturday, I'm throwing all of your stuff out the window."

Amaryllis couldn't understand Randall's attitude. "What's the matter with you?"

"Where were you tonight, Amaryllis?"

"I went to the boat with Bridgette."

Randall raised his hand to send her flying across the living room, but caught himself. "You are lying and you have the nerve to stand here and look me in the eye while doing it. I'm not stupid, Amaryllis."

"Black, I was at the boat. I won enough money to pay my half of the bills. See, look at this." Amaryllis took about three thousand dollars in cash from her purse and showed it to Randall.

He took the money from her hand and forcefully shoved the bills in her mouth. "Since you like to put nasty things in your mouth, chew on this."

Amaryllis fell to the floor, coughing and gagging. Randall looked down at her. "Be out of here in one week."

So that he wouldn't have to see or talk to Amaryllis, Randall moved in with Cordell for seven days. He didn't want to be in the same house with her. On Saturday evening, he told Cordell that he was going home.

"You want me to come with you, man?" Cordell asked.

"Nah, man, I'm cool. She should be long gone by now."

Cordell walked him to the door. "You did the right thing, man. I'm proud of you. Call if you need me."

When Randall stepped off the elevator and walked to his unit, he saw that the door was ajar. He walked in and didn't see any furniture. The entire condo-

minium was empty. He walked into the kitchen and
saw the cabinets open and bare. He opened the refrigerator to see that it only contained a box of baking
soda.

In the bedroom, Amaryllis had stripped the windows of their shades. His underwear were thrown into
the corner where the chest of drawers used to sit. Next
to his underwear on the floor were his watches, chains,
and rings. Only Randall's clothes were hanging in the
closet. He saw his suits, jeans, shirts, and on the closet
floor were all of his shoes. After all Randall had done
for Amaryllis, she took almost everything he had.

He accepted her lifestyle, moved her into his home,
paid all of her bills, and gave her everything she asked
for. She came into his home with one suitcase and left
with all of his dishes and furniture. With tears in his
eyes, he walked into the bathroom for Kleenex but
there were none.

Gone were the toothpaste, toilet tissue, paper cup
dispenser, soap, soap sponge, and everything else that
wasn't a solid fixture. On top of the sink sat his toothbrush, bottles of cologne and deodorant. Randall was
outdone. Everything that he'd worked for was gone.
His black leather living room set sat in layaway for a
year and two months before he could bring it home,
and now it was gone. The pictures of his family and
friends had been stripped from their expensive frames
and were left lying face down on the living room floor.

Randall walked back into the kitchen to call Cordell
when he noticed the phone too was gone. In the corner
he spotted the tall garbage can. On top of the garbage
that was overflowing, Randall saw the Bible he'd bought
for Amaryllis.

The fourteen-karat gold lettering that spelled her
name had been carved out of the front cover. He took the

Bible and walked into the living room and sat on the floor against the wall. He opened it and read his dedication.

> *To my precious Amaryllis, such a beautiful name for such a beautiful face. It is my deepest prayer that you will come to love and honor this book just as I do. I give this gift to you as a guide through your everyday trials. The powerful words on these pages are an inspiration to me, and I share them with you. I look forward to studying this book with you as we, together, reach for everything that God has in store for us. May God bless your life in such a way that you won't be able to stand it.*
>
> > *Yours truly,*
> > *Black*

Randall closed the Bible and hung his head and cried. "Why, Amaryllis? I loved you so much."

He sat on the floor remembering everything that he'd done for her including sacrificing his relationship with God, his mother, and his best friend. He reached for his cell phone on his belt loop and called Cordell. Crying, he could hardly pronounce his words. "She took everything."

"Randall?"

"Everything is gone, Cordell. She took everything."

Cordell heard Randall, but could barely understand what he was saying. "Calm down. What do you mean 'everything is gone'?"

Randall cried louder and didn't answer Cordell.

"Randall, what do you mean everything is gone. What happened?"

"She took everything out of here. The only things

she left were my pictures and her Bible. She even took
the toilet paper and the ice. Man, I'm telling you,
Amaryllis took everything."

"Okay, Randall, I'm on my way over there."

"Nah, man, you ain't gotta come. I don't wanna be
here. I'm going to take a walk."

"No. Don't go anywhere. Wait for me, and we'll walk
together. I'll be there in ten minutes."

Cordell rang Randall's bell without getting an answer. He called upstairs from his cellular phone and
heard the operator, "The number you are trying to
reach has been temporarily disconnected." His call to
Randall's cellular phone went directly into his voicemail. He was frustrated. He saw a man exiting the
building and quickly walked in when he opened the
door.

"Hey, man, you just can't walk in here," the man said
sternly as Cordell brushed past him into the lobby.

Cordell completely ignored the man and ran past
the elevator and up the stairs to the eighth floor. When
he got to Randall's unit, he was tired and breathless.
The door was wide open. He walked in and looked all
around and saw nothing. "Randall?"

He saw Amaryllis's Bible on the floor and picked it
up. He looked at the space where 'Amaryllis Denise
Price' had been engraved. He had been with Randall
when be bought the Bible for her and remembered
that the gold lettering wasn't cheap. The clerk at the
jewelry store told Randall that he was the first to have
someone's name engraved on a Bible in fourteen-karat
gold. And at fifteen dollars a letter, she was too happy
to service him and receive the commission.

Cordell opened the Bible and read what his friend
had written to the woman he had loved more than he
loved himself. He closed it and again looked at the

space where her name was. "That's just like you, Amaryllis. May God have mercy on your soul."

He walked through the condo and was shocked at what Amaryllis had done. Randall wasn't a cheap man. He spent a fortune for his things and was known as the lay-away king. He didn't mind putting furniture on hold and getting it out when he could. His bedroom suite alone cost more than $3,000, and it sat in lay-away for what seemed like forever. It had been delivered only a week before Amaryllis moved in.

Cordell stood in the empty bedroom and looked around. Even the custom-made window shades Randall designed to match his king-sized comforter were gone.

Cordell tried Randall's cellular phone again. "Hey, man, I told you to wait for me. I know you're hurting and upset, so you don't need to be by yourself right now. I don't know where you could be, so I'm going to head back home, and that's where I'll be if you need me. I love you man, and you don't have to go through this alone. I'm here for you so call me."

Many hours later, the telephone rang as Cordell was in the middle of studying his sermon for the next day.

"Cordell, I need you man."

"Randall, where are you?"

"I don't know, I'm just out here walking."

"Get to a corner, look at the street signs, and tell me where you are."

Randall walked to the corner and looked up. "I'm at 183rd and Halsted Street."

"What? That's about thirty miles from where you live. Did you walk all the way there?"

"Yeah and my feet hurt. I'm tired and hungry."

"Stay put until I get there and keep your phone on. Do you hear me, Randall?"

"Yeah, I hear you, man. Hurry up."

Cordell quickly got dressed and went to get his friend. It took him twenty minutes to get to where Randall was. When he pulled up to the corner at 183rd Street, he saw Randall sitting on the curb with his knees propped up and his head hanging down. Cordell got out of his car and walked over to him.

"How in the world could you have possibly walked all this way from downtown?"

When Randall raised his head to look at Cordell, his eyes were bloodshot red. "I was just walking, man."

Cordell noticed that his speech was slurred. "Have you been drinkin', Randall? I know you're not drunk."

"I just had a little sip of somethin', that's all."

"A sip of what?"

Randall reached behind his back and grabbed three empty forty-ounce bottles of Corona and gave them to Cordell.

"Just a sip, huh?"

Randall laid back on the grass and started crying. "Cordell, what's happening to me? How did I end up like this? This is not what I'm supposed to be doing with my life."

Cordell helped Randall to stand. "Come on, man, let's go."

It was difficult, but Cordell managed to get Randall into his car. He reclined the seat for Randall. "Go ahead and lay back, but don't throw up in my car. I ain't playing. If you think you're getting sick, just tell me and I'll pull over, okay?"

Randall closed his eyes and didn't answer. Then Cordell reached over and shook him and yelled, "Okay, Randall?"

The axe that sliced Randall between his eyes the morning after he drank at Amaryllis's mother's house, sliced him again when Cordell yelled. He put his hands on his forehead and winced his eyes. "Yeah, man, okay. Please don't holla."

"You've got a problem, Randall. Do you wanna know what it is?"

"Only if you can tell me without hollering."

"It's two o'clock in the morning, it's gonna take about twenty minutes to get home, and I'm sleepy."

"So, how is that my problem?"

"I gotta do something that'll keep me awake until we get to my house, and I know that I can't depend on you for conversation. So, guess what I gotta do?"

Randall knew what was getting ready to happen and he slowly sat up and looked at his friend with begging in his eyes. "No, Cordell. Please don't do it, man. Please don't do it. I promise to stay up and talk to you all the way home. Please don't do it, Cordell. I'm begging you, man."

"You promise to keep me awake?"

"Yeah, man, whatever you want. Just don't do it, please."

Cordell started the car and drove away from the curb. He knew Randall was tired, sleepy and worn out. He got on the Bishop Ford Expressway and pushed the button for the cruise control. He tuned in to the jazz station, and with the volume down low, Grover Washington's saxophone was soothing and mellow. Cordell lowered the windows just enough to let the perfect amount of fresh air into the car. The mood was set to relax anyone who had a bad day and was full of alcohol. He waited five minutes then looked over at Randall. He was laid back with his mouth wide open, sawing logs.

Cordell set the bait and Randall took it. He laughed at what he was getting ready to do. He thought back to

how Randall was begging for mercy. *Oh no, Cordell.
Please don't do it, man. I'm begging you.*

Cordell muted the volume on the radio then switched
to a hard rock station on the AM dial. He looked at Randall again and saw that he was almost comatose. He
raised the windows and quickly turned the volume on
the radio up to the maximum level. Randall sat straight
up. At the sound of the loud drums and guitars, he covered both ears and yelled, "Cordell, turn that down!
My head hurts!"

Randall wanted to die. His head began to throb. He
reached for the volume knob, but he wasn't fast enough.
Cordell quickly grabbed the knob and held on to it.
Randall covered his ears again and looked at his friend.
Cordell was looking straight ahead. Randall called his
name, but not loud enough. He called his name louder,
but Cordell still didn't acknowledge him. Randall yelled
out Cordell's name as loudly as he could and immediately, the axe sliced him between his eyes. He hollered
out in pain then laid back in his seat, moaning and
crying. When he let go of his ears to caress his aching
head, the loud music rushed to his eardrums and the
axe sliced him again.

Between the heavy metal music and the axe, Randall was delirious. No matter how he tried to shut the
noise out, the axe didn't stop slicing and the drums
didn't stop banging. Randall cried as he tossed and
turned in his seat. Cordell laughed all the way home
as he held on to the volume knob.

Getting Randall into the house was a chore for
Cordell. He picked him up and put him over his shoulder, then carried him downstairs to the basement
where he kept his office. He sat Randall in a corner
and leaned him against the wall. Randall tried to lie

down on the floor, but Cordell wasn't sleepy anymore. And if he wasn't getting any sleep tonight, neither was Randall.

"Oh, no you don't. You ain't getting off that easy. Wake up," Cordell ordered his friend.

Randall tried to open his eyes but couldn't. "I can't, man. Just leave me alone. My head hurts."

Cordell walked over to Randall, knelt down, and yelled, "I said 'WAKE UP'!"

Randall winced in pain, and looked at Cordell through one eye. "Man, what did you do that for? Why are you doing me like this?"

"Why am I doing *you* like this? I should be asking you that same question, Randall. I'm the one who has to be in the pulpit in a few hours, and you *will* be in the choir stand."

Randall tried to lie down again. "I can't go to church. I'm too tired. Please let me go to sleep."

Cordell got angry. In the twenty-eight years that he and Randall had known each other, he'd never been as angry with him than he was right then. For the past two years his relationship with Randall had been an emotional roller coaster. Not only had Amaryllis turned Randall's life upside down, being his best friend and pastor caused Cordell to take unwanted flips, turns, and loops. He was forced to watch Randall go from bad to worse, and there was nothing he could do about it but stay on the battlefield on Randall's behalf. Cordell had often fasted and warred in the spirit; yet Randall continued to rebel. Witnessing his best friend deteriorate before his very eyes was taking a toll on Cordell. Randall was acting out like a child without his favorite toy. If Randall wanted to behave like a two-year-old, Cordell would treat him as such.

"I said 'wake up.' You got work to do."

Randall moaned. "What work are you talking about?"

Cordell man-handled Randall. He pulled him up and guided him to a chair next to his desk. "Since you've forgotten how to pray, we're gonna do it right now. Together, me and you, just like old times."

Randall's head was spinning a mile a minute, and he was half out of his mind. Pray was the last thing he wanted to do. "Come on, man, I ain't prayin' right now."

"You what? Randall, don't get crazy, 'cause I'm not having it. You are in my house, and as for me and my house, we're gonna serve the Lord."

Randall's entire head was throbbing. He got up from the chair. "Well, how about if I leave your house then, huh? How about that?"

Cordell pushed Randall down in the chair. "You ain't going nowhere because this is the first and last time you're gonna call me out of my house in the middle of the night to come and get your drunk behind from a street corner way across town. Amaryllis has you sprung like a two dollar ho, Randall. You've got some issues, and we're gonna deal with them right here and now."

Randall stood again. Cordell pushed him back into the chair. "You think I'm playin' with you, Randall?"

"Man, what is wrong with you?"

"I told you that me and my house will serve the Lord."

Randall knew that he had to get out of Cordell's house. And the only way to do it was by going head to head with his pastor. He jumped up and pushed Cordell. "You can't make me stay here."

Cordell pushed him harder. "Randall, the only way you're leaving this house is over my dead body. I suggest you sit your drunk behind down and chill."

Randall stepped into Cordell's personal space. "You think you can take me, Cordell? Huh, do you?"

Cordell pushed Randall. Then Randall pushed Cordell. Randall tried to land a few blows, but he was no match for the sober pastor. Cordell blocked his blows until Randall was too tired to raise his arms. He collapsed to the floor and Cordell sat down next to him out of breath. "Are you ready to pray, Randall?"

He was lying on his back panting. "What I wanna do is go to sleep."

"I want you to repeat after me." Cordell would not let up on his friend. *God never gave up on me,* was all he could think. So he wasn't about to give up on Randall. "My God, I'm sorry."

"Cordell, man, just leave me alone."

"You will acknowledge God in my house. Now say it!"

The alcohol made Randall's body feel as though he had been in a boxing match with a heavyweight. "Say what?"

"My God, I'm sorry."

"I'm sorry," Randall said lazily.

"Let's try it again, Randall. I want you to say, 'My God, I'm sorry.'"

His speech was still slurred, but he managed to get it right. "My God, I'm sorry."

"For turning my back on you," Cordell continued.

"For turning my back on you."

"I admit that I was wrong."

"*What?* I didn't do anything wrong. Amaryllis was the one that . . ."

"No, you were the one who made the decision that landed you in the position you're in now."

"Just leave me alone, Cordell, please." Randall refused to take responsibility for his own actions.

"I can't do that, Randall. The love I have for you as my brother won't let me leave you alone. And while we're on the subject of love, let's talk about it for a minute."

Cordell stood and got his Bible from his desk. He then sat down on the floor next to Randall. "Sit up Randall, you're in Bible Study." Cordell turned to First Corinthians, chapter thirteen. He gave the Bible to Randall and told him to read it.

"Cordell, I ain't in a mood to read."

"Read it," Cordell demanded.

Randall looked at the page and couldn't tell the words apart. They all seemed to run together. He squinted then bucked his eyes out, but he still couldn't see the words clearly.

"I can't see it."

Cordell took the Bible from Randall and put it close to his face, less than an inch from his eyes. "Read it now."

Randall read the verses. "Though I speak with the tongues of men and of angels, but have no love, I have become a sounding brass or a clanging cymbal. And though I have the gift of prophecy, and understand all mysteries and all knowledge, and though I have all faith, so that I could remove mountains, but have not love, I am nothing. And though I bestow all my goods to feed the poor, and though I give my body to be burned, but have not love, it profits me nothing. Love suffers long and is kind; love does not envy; love does not parade itself; is not puffed up; does not behave rudely, does not seek its own, is not provoked, thinks no evil; does not rejoice in iniquity, but rejoices in the truth; bears all things, believes all things, hopes all things, endures all things."

"Okay, stop right there, Randall. Do you understand what you just read?"

"Yeah."

"Explain it to me."

"What do you want me to say?"

"I want you to explain to me what you just read. Teach me somethin'."

Randall massaged his temples. He felt a migraine coming on. "Please, man, I can't do this right now. My head is pounding. Why are you doing me like this?"

"Love hurts doesn't it, Randall? You're strong, you'll be all right. Now tell me what these scriptures mean."

"They're saying that if I don't have love in my heart, I'm nothing. Even if I have the gift of speaking in tongues or casting out demons or even if I'm able to heal the sick, I am nothing without love. Even if I give all my worldly belongings to the poor and needy, it profits me nothing if I don't give it in love."

"What do you mean?" Cordell wanted Randall to really understand this passage of scripture.

"Let's say that I gave someone some money just because I was tired of them buggin' me or if I paid somebody's gas or light bill just so that my name can be in the spotlight; that's not giving in love. That's pride. And in the eyes of God, I'm just walking around making noise with my life. Love is having patience and being kind to everyone. We are to love unconditionally."

"Unconditionally?" Cordell asked.

"That means you set no boundaries on how much you're gonna love someone. You love and care for them in spite of what they do. Verse eight says that love never fails. That means that it's long suffering. You suffer through hard times with those that you love and don't turn away when you get fed up. It means that you don't hold any grudges against those that have done you wrong, but we are to forgive and love them. You can't love someone and turn your back on them at the same time."

While Randall was teaching his pastor, he was also ministering to himself. He thought about everything he was saying and started to cry. "You know what, Cordell?"

"I'm listening, man, what is it?"

Randall mentally dismissed his headache. Instead, he became remorseful. "This is exactly how *you* love *me*. When I think of how I treated you and the things I've said to you, you never turned your back on me. You didn't give up on me. I know that it was you who was praying for me, because no one else was. And if it hadn't been for your love and prayers, there's no tellin' where I'd be right now. I've said some hurtful things to you, man. Things that would've made a lot of people walk away from me. But not you, Cordell. You were always there whether I wanted you to be or not. That's the kind of love that God wants us to have. Somebody else would've left me on that curb, but not you, man. Every time I call you, you come running. And I'm sorry, man. I'm sorry for putting you through all this crap and for the things I've said. And I thank you for loving me like a true brother should."

Cordell moved over to Randall and pulled him into his arms and hugged him. "That's what I'm here for, man. I know that if it had been me who went crazy and left God, you would've done the same thing."

"Yeah, I would have. But I don't know if I would've been so tough about it."

Cordell laughed at Randall. "It's called tough love. I had to get the devil out of you. That fool set up house in you and was sittin' back chillin'. It was for your own good, 'cause it worked, didn't it?"

"Yeah, I'll give you that, but what about what you did in the car? That was unnecessary."

"Randall, my man, that was for *my* good. That's

what you get for interrupting my study time. If you could've seen your face when you jumped up. And the way you were tossing and turning trying to block out the noise was priceless. It was definitely a Kodak moment. Remember how you were beggin' me not to blast the music? That was hilarious."

"Yeah, okay, go ahead and have your fun because your day is coming."

Cordell laughed until his abdomen ached. The more Randall thought about it, he had to laugh himself. "Cordell, I hope you're laughing with me and not at me. But all jokes aside, man, I thank you for loving me right. And I'm thankful that you're my pastor. But I'm most grateful for our friendship."

"Am I my brother's keeper?" Cordell asked.

"Yes, you are."

Sunday School was less than two hours away, so it wouldn't have been wise for them to go to bed. Like two old men, they helped each other stand and prayed for the next half hour. Randall confessed to God that he was wrong for replacing Him with Amaryllis. He asked for forgiveness and repented for his actions and the choices he made, then he rededicated his life to God. They each took a shower then Cordell made breakfast for them both. Randall remembered to say grace, and it lasted for about ten minutes. He thanked God for food, shelter, love, friendship, and everything else he was grateful for. Cordell loaned Randall one of his suits. It was a blessing they were the same size in clothes.

When Cordell and Randall walked through the church doors looking like the living dead, everyone stared at them. Cordell's slow pace revealed that he hadn't slept at all the night before. Randall walked slower than Cordell, revealing signs of the loud drums beating in his head.

Wanda approached them with a horrified expression. "Pastor Bryson, what happened to you and Randall? Did you two get mugged?"

"We were in a war, but it's over. We won."

The next morning, Randall received a call from Sebastian Shelton, his union representative. He told Randall that the Chicago Transit Authority had canceled his suspension. Therefore, Randall could return to work a month early.

Chapter 14

The following Saturday, Randall and Cordell went to Evergreen Park Mall to have Cordell's new robe altered for men's day. As they sat and waited for the tailor to put the finishing touches on the robe, Randall looked at Cordell. "You know what I got a taste for?"

"No, but I'm sure you'll tell me."

"I want chocolate chip cookies."

"Man, I'm thinking you're getting ready to say steak or shrimp, but you got a taste for cookies?"

"Chocolate chip cookies."

"Yeah, well I've got a whole bag of chocolate chip cookies at the house. You can have all of them after we stop at the Fish House for fried jumbo shrimp. Now that's what I have a taste for."

"I want Mrs. Field's chocolate chip cookies," Randall said.

"You sound just like a woman, Randall. What difference does it make who made the cookies? As long as they have chocolate chips in them, you should be fine."

"Is that right? What if I said that we should stop at

a grocery store and get shrimp from the frozen food
section and put them in the microwave?"

Cordell thought long and hard. "Okay, I see what
you're saying."

"Yeah, I figured you would. Some things just can't be
substituted."

The men got chocolate chip cookies, came back for
Cordell's robe, and bought more minutes for Randall's
cellular phone. They were good to go. Something caught
Randall's attention, as they were leaving, and he stopped
walking. Cordell stopped walking also and asked Randall what was the matter. Either Randall didn't hear
him, or he was too distracted. Cordell looked in the same
direction as Randall and saw the target.

Two women were in a shoe store trying on high heeled
sandals. Coincidentally, it happened to be the same
shoe store where Randall had met Amaryllis. One of the
ladies wasn't quite Randall's type, but something about
her mesmerized him. The way she moved, the way she
walked or maybe it was her smile that captured his attention.

Randall couldn't figure it out because she didn't look
at all like Amaryllis. Her hair wasn't quite as long and
she didn't have highlights. Her skin was lighter than
Amaryllis's, and she had sort of a plain face with very
little makeup. She wore just a dab of mascara and a
light coat of cherry colored lipstick. She didn't have on
any lip liner, which Randall loved to see on a woman.
She was about five inches shorter than Amaryllis and
not as shapely. Around her neck, Randall saw a gold
crucifix. As he watched her model the sandals, he noticed that she had gorgeous feet. They were small and
petite.

The friend with her, who was also trying on sandals,
was a dead ringer for Amaryllis. From the long high-

lighted hair to the beautiful face—lip liner included. This one was fine. Her body was proportioned to Randall's taste. She was also light skinned like her friend. Randall looked down at her feet and could've hit the floor. Beautiful, well manicured toes were attached to this woman's legs. She was fine, just like Amaryllis. When he couldn't stand it any longer, Randall started to move in their direction.

Sensing what his friend was about to do, Cordell grabbed his arm. "Don't even think about it."

"What? I can't compliment a woman on her pretty feet?"

"Remember what happened the last time you walked up to a woman in this shoe store? It turned out to be your worst nightmare, and personally, I don't want to relive that dream. Do you?"

"Slow your roll, man. All I wanna do is tell her how pretty her feet are. It's all good."

Before Cordell could get another word out, Randall was on his way into the shoe store. Boldly, he walked over to the woman, the same way he had approached Amaryllis.

"Excuse me. My friend and I were walking by and I noticed you trying on sandals. I saw how gorgeous your feet are, and I wanted to let you know that the sandals you're trying on really bring out the attractiveness of your toes."

The woman wearing the gold crucifix looked at Randall and smiled. "Bless you. I couldn't make up my mind whether to get them or not, but you've just helped me make my decision."

"You should definitely get them, 'cause they look great on you."

Her crucifix sparkled. "Thank you."

He extended his hand toward her. "I'm Randall Loomis."

She shook his hand. "Gabrielle Davis. It's nice to meet you, Randall."

When she moved, her crucifix sparkled again. "What church do you attend?" Randall asked.

"I'm new in town. I work for the Board of Health. I transferred here from Dallas three weeks ago and I'm looking for a church home. Can you recommend one?"

All thirty-two of Randall's teeth became visible. "Absolutely."

They exchanged numbers and Randall invited Gabrielle to be his guest at Holy Deliverance the following Sunday. Randall was blown away after morning service when he asked Gabrielle to join him on Thursday evening for Bible Study, and she quickly responded, "Sure, I'd love to."

Randall rejoined the choir and was pleased as punch when Gabrielle joined the church on her seventh consecutive Sunday visiting. With a holy God-fearing woman in his life, Randall was on top of the world. He asked his pastor what he thought of Gabrielle.

Before Cordell answered Randall's question, he asked a few questions of his own. "Does she drink, cuss, or gamble?"

"No. She doesn't do any of that," Randall responded.

"That's good, that's very good. Are you both abstaining?"

Anyone else asking Randall this question would have caused him to blush. He knew Cordell was in his pastor role. He saw that Cordell was holding his breath—afraid of what his answer might be. "You can breathe. We're celibate."

Cordell exhaled a sigh of relief. "That's good, that's very good. You two will maintain separate residences, right?"

"Most definitely. The next woman that I live with will be my wife."

"That's good, Randall. That's very good." Cordell saw that Gabrielle was right beside Randall whenever the church doors opened up. He saw her paying tithes and getting her shout on. He saw her participating in Bible Study. But Cordell knew that everyone who attended church wasn't saved.

"Okay, Randall. One last question."

"Yes, Gabrielle is saved," Randall said proudly.

Cordell patted Randall on his back. "Well then, son. You two have my blessing."

Two months later, Randall and Gabrielle were riding eastbound on Twenty-second Street in Oakbrook, Illinois. They were coming from Just Music, Inc., where Randall had four JL audio speakers installed in his brand new late model Jaguar Coupe.

It took his insurance company a while, but they finally came the through for him. They agreed to a brand new car and the car notes were exactly the same as what Randall had been paying before. The amount of money he'd invested in Joy was deducted from the price of the new Jaguar. Randall's new license plates read *2 Joyful*.

Gabrielle tuned the radio to the gospel station and heard the song, "Take Your Burdens To The Lord."

"Oh, I love this song," she said.

"Yeah, it's nice. Do you know who sings it?"

"Uh huh, that's Ed Primer's group, The Voices of Joy. They recorded this CD a few months ago. They're right here in Chicago. I should check out one of their rehearsals."

"That sounds cool, Gabby. Find out where and when their rehearsals are and maybe I'll go with you."

Gabrielle smiled at the pet name Randall had given her. She really liked it.

She turned the volume up louder and began to sing along with the lead. Randall looked over at her and couldn't believe his ears. "Gabby, you sound just like her. I didn't know you could sing like that."

"Uh–uh. That's Ms. Damita Moore blowing. I can't touch this girl. She's definitely going places. I heard Johnny Walker, Jr. wrote this song specifically for her. Did you know he's the head musician for Ed Primers group?"

"Yeah, Johnny's a bad dude. Many of the songs the group sings comes from him. The boy is blessed."

They were riding and singing when Randall suddenly made a sharp right turn onto Tabitha Road. Thank God they were wearing their seatbelts. If they hadn't been, Gabrielle would be in Randall's lap.

"Randall, what are you doing?" Gabrielle was shaken at his abrupt turn.

"Shh, I'm listening."

"Listening to what?"

Randall was driving like it was his first time behind the wheel of a car. He slowed down and his hands were holding the steering wheel at the ten o'clock and two o' clock positions. "God is talkin' to me, Gabby."

Randall got to Toiya Lane and turned right again. He drove three blocks to Tashea Drive and turned left. Gabrielle noticed the names of the streets. "What's up with the girl's names for these streets starting with the letter T?"

Randall paid her no attention. He didn't even hear

her question because he was tuned in to what God was saying to him. He drove to an estate on a cul-de-sac at 815 Tashea Drive, put the gear in park and turned off the ignition. Gabrielle looked at the house then looked at Randall. "Whose house is this?"

Still Randall didn't answer her. He got out of the car and walked up the driveway. He could see from the outside that the house was empty and newly built. He got to the door and turned the knob and wasn't surprised to find it unlocked. He walked into the foyer and left the door open. Gabrielle got out of the car and followed him inside. When she walked into the foyer, Randall was in a daze, looking all around him.

"Randall, are you crazy? We just can't walk into someone's house."

He grabbed Gabrielle's hand and led her up a spiral and glass staircase with white marble steps to the second floor. "You can if it's yours, Gabby."

"Oh, my God, you have totally flipped."

The entire left side of the second floor was dedicated to the master suite. It ran seventy feet from the front of the house to the rear. Randall estimated that, wall to wall, it was about thirty-five feet wide. They looked to their left and saw two steps leading to an open sitting room. They walked hand in hand through an arched opening without a door that led to a huge walk-in closet. Farther toward the rear of the suite, the closet opened up to a master bath. A ceramic tiled floor with his and her marble burgundy sinks, a glass blocked double shower, a sunken burgundy Jacuzzi tub and a closed door with his and her toilets, made up this room. Randall and Gabrielle turned right, out of the master bath and into an even larger walk-in closet. A few more steps forward brought them back into the master suite. They made a U shape into one closet, through the master bath, then through another closet and ended back in the master suite. It was then that Gabrielle noticed the marble fireplace to her left.

"Randall, this is beautiful, but I don't think we should be here."

He grabbed her hand again and walked out of the master suite, down the hall to a full bath and four large empty bedrooms and a second floor laundry. "See, Gabby, I always wanted a four bedroom house but God gave me five of them."

Next to the last bedroom was another staircase made of oak wood that led down to the kitchen. When Gabrielle saw the kitchen, she screamed. It was as big as the master suite upstairs. The kitchen had lots and lots of cherry oak cabinets, and there was a stainless steel refrigerator, dishwasher, and gas stove. The kitchen had floor-to-ceiling windows and a center island with a stainless steel, flat gas range top. Off to the side, there was a breakfast area with patio doors that opened to a huge deck. Three steps down from the kitchen, the room opened to a great room with an oak wood floor and a wall-to-wall brick fireplace. Behind the spiral marble and glass staircase was another room the same size as the kitchen and master suite. Standing in this room, Randall and Gabrielle could see nothing but windows that expanded from one side of the wall to the other. They went from the base of the floor to the top of the house. They almost got whiplash looking up at the fifty-foot ceiling.

On the other side of the estate, on the first floor, was a formal dining room where Gabrielle imagined a table big enough to seat ten people. In front of the dining room, was the living room with white plush carpet.

Randall looked all around this room and thought out loud. "I can put a white baby grand piano in here next to the window with its top up."

"Can you play?"

Randall was mesmerized. "Nah, I just wanna look at it."

Gabrielle turned to her left and stopped moving. "Oh, my God. Randall, look at this."

He walked over to a wall that separated the living room from the four-car garage.

They were able to see into the garage from where they stood. The entire wall was made of glass. Randall couldn't believe his eyes. "Wow, how cool is this? We could actually see our cars from inside the house."

Through the glass wall, they saw another door. "I wonder what that door leads to, Randall," Gabrielle pointed to a door.

"Let's find out."

They walked through the dining room, down the hall that had another bedroom with patio doors leading to a terrace. This bedroom had bookshelves built into one wall and another full bath with a Jacuzzi tub.

"Gabby, I could use this room for my home-office."

To the left of this bedroom was the first floor laundry room, complete with a soaking sink. Next to the dryer was the door that led Randall and Gabrielle to the four-car garage. "Wait right here, Gabby." Randall ran into the living room to the glass wall and waved at her. She mouthed, "You are so silly," with a smile. He mouthed "I don't care."

They met up in the foyer at the spiral staircase and were getting ready to leave when Randall saw another staircase leading down to the lower level of the estate. "I didn't see these stairs when we came in," he said.

"They must lead down to the basement."

What they saw downstairs couldn't be referred to as a basement. One half of the room was more living space with wall-to-wall Berber carpet. Patio doors led to an outside terrace. At the bottom of the stairs, immediately to the left, there was a closed door. Randall opened it to see a dark room without any windows. He flipped the light switch on and saw two sofas on one step, two sofas on another step and two more sofas on a third step. Straight ahead was a movie screen.

Gabrielle sat down on one of the sofas. "I could get used to this, Randall."

He sat down next to her. "You and me both."

"How did you find this place?"

"God led me here. He told me exactly where to turn and brought us to this address."

Something dawned on Randall. "You know what, Gabby, this address is 815 Tashea Drive, right?"

"Yeah, I think the numbers eight, one, five were above the front door."

"I was baptized on August fifteenth when I was nine years old. Ma'Dear's birthday is August fifteenth. I was hired at the C.T.A. on August fifteenth seven years ago, and when I was twenty years old, I bought my first car on August fifteenth."

"Are you serious?"

"Yep, ain't God amazing?"

"Amazing and awesome."

"This house has got to cost a fortune. I don't think I can afford it."

"Randall, let me tell you somethin'. If God brought you here, you don't have to worry about money. He didn't bring you here to tease you."

Randall leaned back on the sofa and closed his eyes. "My God, you mean I can really have this?"

Two months later, Randall closed on the house at 815 Tashea Drive in Oakbrook, Il. His house note was double what he paid to live in downtown Chicago, but he didn't care. If God gave him this house, then God would surely make a way for him to pay for it.

After the closing, he took the keys from the realtor, shook his hand, and left the realtor's office. In his car, he dialed Cordell at the church. "Hey, man, I've got great news."

"You got the house?"

"Yep, I just closed the deal."

"Congratulations, Randall, I'm happy for you, man."

"Man, I feel like Jesus did when He walked out of hell after preachin' a revival with the keys and all power, in His hands. I got my keys, Pastor."

Cordell chuckled. "That's good. You're supposed to feel that way."

"Can you get away for about two hours? I want to come by and pick you up and swing by and get Ma'Dear so you two can see the house."

"Yeah, man, I've got time."

Randall hung up from Cordell and called his mother. "I got the house, Ma. I got the house."

"Oh, baby, that's so wonderful."

"I'm on my way to get you right now."

Randall's house was so massive, it took up the whole half of the circle on the cul-de-sac at the end of Tashea Drive. Both Ma'Dear and Cordell were speechless at the size of the house. Randall pulled into the driveway, got out of the car and went around to the passenger side and opened the door for his mother, but Ma'Dear made no effort to get out of the car.

"What's wrong, Ma'Dear?"

"I love you, Randall, but I ain't going to jail for you."

"What are you talkin' about?"

"You bring us all the way out here to this high-priced neighborhood, where folks are looking at us funny, and expect me to walk in this big house? Well, I ain't doing it."

Cordell was in the backseat laughing. "I ain't going to jail for you either. Now come and take us to your real house. I got a marital counseling session in an hour."

Randall left them in the car and opened the front door with his key. Ma'Dear turned around and looked at Cordell. "Is he for real?"

"I don't know, but I ain't going in unless you go in first, 'cause I don't trust him."

She looked at her son and yelled from the car, "Are you for real?"

"Ma'Dear, would I have a key if I wasn't for real?"

"You better not be playin' with me, Randall. You ain't too big for me to put you 'cross my knee for playin' with me."

"Ma'Dear, please get out of the car and come see my house."

The house was magnificent, and it spoke for itself. Cordell and Ma'Dear toured the upstairs and main level, but when they got to the lower level, Ma'Dear had run out of breath. "This house ain't got no end to it?"

Randall wanted to tell his mother and pastor just how huge his new home was when he closed the deal but wanted them to be just as surprised as he was when God brought him to the address.

Randall opened the door to the theater. "This is the last room."

The three of them walked in and sat down on one of the sofas. Ma'Dear fanned herself. "Good Lord, Randall, what do you need a television that big for?"

"It's for watching movies."

"You're gonna mess around and go blind lookin' at that thing."

"Nah, Ma'Dear. It's just like being at the theater."

She looked at the magnitude of the screen. "Lord have mercy, they actually made a movie theater in a house. What will they think of next?"

Randall looked at his best friend. "So, do you like the house, Pastor?"

"Yeah man, it's tight. But what are you gonna do in this big house by yourself?"

"Live in it."

"How much livin' can you do?"

"As much as I possibly can."

Ma'Dear spoke. "Well, don't lose yourself in this place."

"Hopefully, I won't live here by myself."

Ma'Dear stopped fanning herself and stared at him. "You ain't thinkin' about shackin' up again, are you?"

Cordell answered her before Randall could say anything. "He better not be. I'd burn this house down before I let that happen again."

Randall looked at his mother with all sincerity. "I was hoping that you'd move in with me."

"Boy, is you crazy, or is you crazy? What am I supposed to do with my own house?"

"You can sell it. Daddy's been dead for twelve years, and every man that looks your way, you roll your eyes at him. Obviously, you don't want to get married again, so I think you should move in here with me. You can help me take care of the place."

"Uh huh. I knew there was a catch to this movin' in

thing. I ain't about to be your maid, Randall. I'm too old to be sewing, washing windows, and scrubbing floors."

"Not a maid, Ma'Dear, but more like a roommate. All I want you to do is cook for me. You don't have to sew, clean, or wash anything. I just want you to cook, that's all. I'll even give you the master suite upstairs if you want it."

"Oh, no, I can't be climbing those stairs. And why are they twisted around like that? Won't you get dizzy from climbing up in a circle?"

"I'll take my time when I go up," Randall chuckled.

"Well, if I do move in here with you, I'd want that room off the dining room. The one with the shelves in the wall and the sliding doors."

"Okay, that's cool. That room has a full bath connected to it and you can wake up every morning and walk right out onto the patio and have your coffee."

"What about your office?"

"I'll use one of the bedrooms upstairs."

"Well, I gotta think about it for a couple of days."

"I really want my momma here with me. You've taken such good care of me for twenty-eight years, and now it's my turn to take care of you."

"You don't owe me anything, Randall."

He leaned over and kissed his mother's cheek. "Ma'Dear, I owe you the world."

She wrapped her arms around her son. "I am so proud of you, and your father would be too."

Cordell witnessed this beautiful moment. "I'm proud of you too, Randall. After all you've been through, I knew you'd come out on top. The devil tried to stop you from getting this blessing, but when God says enough is enough, he had to take his hands off you."

Ma'Dear looked at Randall. "Speaking of hands, go

get my Bible and blessed oil out of my purse so we can walk through this place and lay hands on everything. I ain't movin' in here until we bless every inch of this house."

"Does that mean you'll move in here with me?"

"Didn't I say I had to think about it? You know I don't like to be rushed, Randall. Now go on and get my oil."

Randall didn't replace the furniture in his condo. He used wisdom and saved his money to rebuild his checking and savings accounts. He slept on an air mattress, ate at a very small three-piece dinette set, and entertained Gabrielle in his living room as they sat on a futon and watched a nineteen-inch color television.

Randall had to fill his new house with all new furniture. The baby grand piano and living room set would have to wait a while. The day he moved in, Randall had a new bedroom set, kitchen table and chairs, two sofas, a cocktail table, and a seventy-two-inch high definition television delivered.

Ma'Dear accepted Randall's invitation to share his estate. She put her house on the market and it sold within ten days. Randall didn't want any old furniture in his new house. He was able to convince Ma'Dear to sell all of her furniture and buy herself a very elegant bedroom set. She asked Randall for permission to paint and wallpaper her bedroom. He told Ma'Dear that her bedroom and the kitchen were her two special rooms and she could do whatever she wanted with them.

As the first delivery truck was leaving, another was backing into the driveway. Ma'Dear and Randall went to the front door and looked outside.

"Randall, I thought you wanted to wait until later to get the piano and living room furniture," Ma'Dear stated.

"These are bedroom sets for the rooms upstairs."

"Why did you buy beds when there ain't nobody to sleep in them?"

"'Cause, I didn't want the house to be too empty. You can walk in those rooms and hear an echo when you talk, and I don't like the sound."

Upstairs, in the room next to his home office, Randall set up two white wicker bunk beds with a white wicker chest of drawers and writing desk to match. "This looks like a girl's room, Randall."

"Well, Ma'Dear, you never know."

Across the hall from the girls' room, Randall set up a full-size dark blue bed shaped like a racecar. In the corner was a dark blue writing desk and chair and a dark blue chest of drawers against the wall at the end of the bed. Ma'Dear looked in this room and back at Randall. "Is Gabby pregnant?"

Randall placed his hand over his heart. "Mother, you shock me. I'm a virgin."

"Humph, you can tell that lie to somebody who doesn't know any better."

"What makes you think I'm lying about being a virgin, Ma'Dear?"

"Because, I got common sense. And ain't no man gonna let a woman who isn't his wife move into *his* home and not pay *any* bills, and spend *all* of his money, and cause him to almost lose his good job, and keeps him from *his* mother, and coerces him to *drop* out of the choir, and turn on his *best friend* and pastor, and gets him so mad at *God*, that he stops praying and drives him to drink and ends up miles away from his home, *on foot*, unless she's making his toes curl."

Ma'Dear raised her right hand in the air. "Now, can I get an Amen?"

"Preach on, Evangelist, you got the floor." Randall couldn't deny it. Ma' Dear was telling the truth.

"I know I got it. I think Amaryllis put some voodoo on you, Randall."

"Ain't nobody put no voodoo on me."

"You can't be too sure about that. You need to have Cordell put you down in the baptismal pool Sunday morning just to be safe."

"I don't think so, Ma'Dear. We were talkin' about Gabby, remember?"

"Oh yeah. If she's not pregnant, why did you buy all this furniture for kids?"

"Because like I said, 'you never know.' "

Further down the hall, next to the girls' room, was a guest room with a queen-size brown oak bed with a chest of drawers to match. "And who is this room for?"

"You never know."

Chapter 15

Randall loved the way Gabrielle phoned him every morning and prayed over the telephone with him before they went about their day. He'd convinced her to join the sanctuary choir, and she was a regular at Bible class.

The time they spent together was pure and enjoyable. Randall had been celibate for six months now and didn't mind it one bit. Where Amaryllis fulfilled him in one way, Gabrielle fulfilled him in another. Amaryllis kept his belly full, but Gabrielle kept his face in the scriptures. If he was having a bad day, all he had to do was call Gabrielle and she knew just the right words to encourage him. She was so different from Amaryllis.

Gabrielle was like a breath of fresh air. He never had to beg her to go to church. If anything, she was the one encouraging him to go when he didn't feel like it. Although Randall knew her schedule, he'd still call and ask what she was doing later, just to hear her say, "I'm going to church."

Those words from Gabrielle's mouth were like music to Randall's ears. They had so much in common, it seemed they were joined at the hip. If he had trouble finishing a sentence, she'd say the words that were on the tip of his tongue. And Ma'Dear was in love with her too. When Randall had introduced them for the first time, Ma'Dear was instantly drawn to Gabrielle's spirit. She told Randall that God had taken away the trick and gave him a treat. After Amaryllis left, Randall realized what he had felt for her was not love, but only lust. Gabrielle was someone to love.

One night before bed, Randall got down on his knees and asked God if Gabrielle was the one for him. He told God that she said and did all the right things, but how could he be sure that she was his Eve? He asked God for a sign to assure him that Gabrielle was his wife.

Then one day, between runs, Randall called her at work to see how her day was going. He could hear her fellow employees in the background laughing and having a good time. He asked what all the noise was about and she said that a few of her co-workers put money on a lottery ticket and the number came in last night. Four people were to split $20,000. He asked Gabrielle why she didn't get in on it and she stated that she didn't gamble.

Randall closed his eyes and whispered, "Thank you, God."

That same night, Ma'Dear sent Gabrielle and Randall to the convenience store for Epsom Salt, rubbing alcohol, and baby oil. Gabrielle saw a new shade of lipstick she wanted to try. Randall asked why she didn't line her lips like other women. "Because my lips are fine just the way they are."

Again, Randall whispered, "Thank you, God."

Three days later, on a Friday evening, Randall held Gabrielle in his arms as they sat in front of the fireplace in the great room. He had been wanting to bring up the subject of having children for some time, but didn't want to be disappointed if she said she didn't want to have any. But if he was going to consider asking her to marry him, he needed to know where she stood on the matter.

"Gabby, do you like kids?"

She looked up at him. "Where did that come from?"

"It's somethin' that's been on my mind."

"I love kids, Randall. I've got two nephews by my brother. Before I transferred here from Dallas, they were with me more than they were with their parents. Plus, I have two godchildren."

"Well, how do you feel about having some of your own?"

Gabrielle laid her head on his chest and closed her eyes. When she didn't answer him, he lifted her chin and saw tears on the verge of falling onto her cheeks. "What's wrong, Gabby?"

"I've been tryin' to work up enough nerve to tell you, but every time I get the courage, the words won't come out."

"Tell me what?"

"Twice before, I've told men whom I dated, and they suddenly ended the relationship. I'm in love with you, Randall, and I couldn't bare it if you didn't want to be with me."

"Gabby, it can't be that bad. Just tell me."

"I'm not ready yet. It's too soon."

"I love you, Gabrielle, and nothing you tell me will change that."

She stood and walked over to the fireplace and folded her arms across her chest. She looked at Randall as the tears spilled onto her cheeks. She sighed, but still didn't say anything.

"Gabrielle, you're scaring me. Take a deep breath and tell me. I promise that it'll be all right."

She inhaled deeply then exhaled. "Three years ago, I was rushed to the hospital for severe abdominal cramps. I had developed three fibroid tumors in my uterus the size of golf balls and my fallopian tubes were loaded with many small ones."

She got choked up, put her face in her hands, and cried loudly. She couldn't finish what she wanted to say. Randall got up and came to her then pulled her into his arms. "Did you have a hysterectomy?"

She couldn't say anything but nodded her head.

"Oh, my God. Gabby, I had no idea. Baby, I'm so sorry."

"Every time I'm upstairs and I look in those bedrooms, my heart aches because I know you're preparing for something I can never give you."

"Baby, I wish that you'd told me sooner. I never would have bought the beds had I known."

Gabrielle looked up at him with a tear stained face. "This changes things, doesn't it?"

Randall knelt before her and reached in his back pocket and pulled out a three carat platinum diamond ring. "My father presented this to my mother thirty years ago. Gabrielle LaShawn Davis, you're everything I prayed for. Having you in my life assures me that God is real. I want to spend the rest of my life with you. For better or for worse, will you please be my wife?"

Gabrielle knelt down in front of Randall and looked into his eyes. The tears made her vision blurry, and she saw four Randalls. "Don't you understand that I can't fill those rooms upstairs?"

"I'll repeat what I just said. I want to spend the rest of my life with *you*. *You*, Gabby, *you*. *You* fulfill me in every way."

Gabrielle looked at this man and silently thanked God for this angel. "Yes. I'll marry you."

Randall slipped the ring on Gabrielle's finger and kissed her passionately.

After Bible class on Thursday night, Cordell, Randall, and Gabrielle decided to go to the Fish House for shrimp and fried okra.

"Gabby, why don't you show Cordell your ring?" Randall said.

She held up her left hand close to Cordell's face. "Bling, bling."

Cordell made a joke about it, but was actually impressed by the size of the diamond.

"Wow Randall, how many cracker jack boxes did you have to go through before you found it?"

"Man, you better not let Ma'Dear hear you say that."

The three of them were standing in line, laughing and talking, when Randall saw a young man at the counter ordering take-out. Randall could only see his backside, but it was something about him that seemed very familiar to him. He totally tuned Cordell and Gabrielle out and concentrated on who this young man could be.

Gabrielle noticed Randall's attention was elsewhere. "Randall, honey?"

He brought his attention back to his present company. "I'm sorry, Gabby. What did you say?"

"I asked if you wanted hot or mild sauce with your shrimp."

Randall didn't take his eyes away from the young man. "Hot sauce is fine."

Cordell noticed Randall was distracted. "What's up with you, man?"

Randall pointed to the young man. "Doesn't he look familiar, Cordell?"

Cordell could only see the back of him. "Not to me."

Randall thought for a minute. Then it dawned on him who the boy reminded him of. "He looks just like Brandon, doesn't he?"

It took a moment for the memory of Brandon to register in Cordell's brain. "Yeah, now that you mention it, he does favor him a little."

"Who's Brandon?" Gabrielle asked.

"Someone who'd still be alive if it weren't for me," Randall answered sadly.

Cordell patted Randall on the back. "Come on, man, don't do this to yourself. What happened to Brandon was not your fault."

"It was, and you know it."

Gabrielle looked at them both. "Are either one of you gonna tell me what you're talkin' about?"

"It's a long story, Gabby, I'll tell you later." Randall excused himself, walked over to the young man and tapped his shoulder. "Excuse me?"

The young man turned around and Randall looked in the face of someone who could almost be the twin brother of Brandon. "What's up, man?"

"You look very familiar to me. Are you related to anyone named Brandon?"

"I had a cousin named Brandon. How did you know him?"

"I was on my way to work one morning and we met on the El. My name is Randall Loomis."

"Randall Loomis? You're the guy whose number we found in Brandon's pocket the night he died."

"Yeah, I gave it to him in case he needed anything. What happened to his younger brother and sisters?"

"The state took them and placed them in three different foster homes. My mother and Aunt Vera were sisters, and even though we're the next of kin, the government wouldn't give them to us because my mother's a paraplegic. They said that she couldn't handle the youngest girl, Eboni, 'cause she's autistic. So, every Saturday, I drive my mother around the city to visit all three of them."

"Wow, man, that's deep. I didn't catch your name."

"Michael."

Randall shook his hand. "It's nice to meet you, Michael. You think you can put me in touch with their caseworker? I would like to visit the kids."

Michael told Randall the name of the caseworker and which family services office to go to. "By the way, if you get permission to see them, make sure to take Mike and Ikes for Eboni. That's the only way she'll give you the time of day."

Randall chuckled. "Mike and Ikes, huh?"

"Yep, they win her over every time."

"Thanks, Michael, I appreciate it. I would have attended Brandon's funeral, but I didn't know his last name or address. I checked the newspaper every day for a week, hoping to get any information regarding his funeral arrangements."

"We tried calling the number on the card you gave Brandon but a lady answered. My mother told her that we'd found your number in Brandon's pocket and we thought that you were one of his friends. My mother asked her to give you the information about Brandon's funeral and the lady told my mother that she had the wrong Randall Loomis and for us not to call that number again."

Randall felt a blow in the pit of his stomach. Through prayer he had found the strength to forgive Amaryllis for the evil things she'd done, but this new information from Michael angered him all over again. He shook Michael's hand again and walked to the table where Gabrielle and Cordell were already sitting and eating. Gabrielle could tell by the expression on Randall's face that something was wrong. "Are you okay, honey?"

"Yeah, everything's cool."

Cordell looked at his best friend. "Your shrimp is gettin' cold, man."

"I just lost my appetite."

All during the night, Randall tossed and turned, then turned and tossed. At three o'clock AM, he got out of bed and fell on his knees to ask God what was the purpose of him meeting Michael. Randall felt the Lord was trying to tell him something, but he couldn't quite grasp what it was. He stayed on his knees for an hour and still couldn't comprehend what God was saying to him.

Frustrated, he stood and paced his bedroom floor for twenty minutes. Finally, Randall went downstairs and knocked on Ma'Dear's door. He opened it a bit and looked at her sleeping soundly. Ma'Dear was an intercessor and wise beyond her years. And at 4:30 in the morning, Randall needed his mother to intercede to find out what God was saying to him. He walked into the bedroom and stood by her bed. "Ma'Dear?"

She opened her eyes and looked up at Randall, but didn't move or say anything. He saw her looking at him, but he asked the question anyway. "Ma'Dear, are you awake?"

"You think I sleep with my eyes open?" she asked sarcastically.

"Why are you lookin' at me like that?"

" 'Cause, I'm wondering why you're standing over me."

"I got somethin' on my mind and I need you to help me sort it out."

Ma'Dear looked through her patio doors and saw the moon high in the sky. "This can't wait until it gets light outside?"

"Nah, Ma, I can't sleep."

"So I'm not supposed to get any sleep either, right?"

Randall sat down at the foot of her bed. "I guess I could call Cordell, but I feel that I need my momma right now."

Ma'Dear propped her pillows against the headboard then sat up and leaned back. "What is it, Randall?"

"Somethin' weird happened last night at the Fish House."

"You went to the Fish House?"

"Gabby, Cordell, and I went after Bible class."

"Did you bring me any shrimp?"

"Ma'Dear, I'm tryin' to talk to you, and you wanna know if I brought you shrimp?"

"I'm sorry, baby, go ahead."

"Remember that young man I told you about, the one I met on the train about a year ago?"

"The one who lost his family and shot himself?"

"I don't know if Brandon committed suicide. I never found out what happened to him that night after he left Holy D looking for me. I feel so bad that I wasn't there for him when he needed me to be."

"I didn't know you were still dealing with this, Randall."

"I wasn't until I saw somebody at the Fish House tonight that looked just like Brandon."

"I can't believe you went to the Fish House and didn't bring me any shrimp."

"Ma'Dear, please."

"I'm sorry, baby, go ahead."

"I walked over and asked this young man if he was related to anyone named Brandon and he told me that he had a cousin named Brandon. His name is Michael and he said my home number was found in Brandon's pocket the night he died. Michael's mother tried to call and let me know about Brandon's funeral arrangements, but Amaryllis told her she had the wrong Randall Loomis and not to call our number again."

"Oh, my God. That girl is the devil incarnated."

"Ma'Dear, when he told me that, I got sick to my stomach and couldn't even eat my food."

"I'm so sorry, baby."

"But what I don't understand is why the police didn't contact me when my business card was found on Brandon's body. No one called me and I wasn't told to come to the police station for questioning."

"You'd think they'd come looking for you right away," Ma'Dear added.

"I asked about Brandon's brother and two sisters and Michael said the government took them and put all three of them in different foster homes. Brandon was working two jobs just so that very thing wouldn't happen. He truly loved his family, Ma'Dear, and he gave me the impression that he'd do anything to keep them together."

"Couldn't Family Services let them stay within the family?"

"Michael said that he and his mother are the next of

kin, but she's a paraplegic. She wasn't awarded custody because the youngest girl is autistic."

From the hallway light, Ma'Dear could see tears streaming down Randall's face.

"Why are you crying? You shouldn't carry the guilt, son."

"Why not? I feel responsible for Brandon's death. And the one thing he was working so hard to keep from happening, happened anyway. And I feel it's my fault. I should've been there for him, Ma'Dear. Brandon needed me and I knew he needed me because God told me that Brandon needed me. Who knows what would've happened had I gotten to Brandon that night he came to Holy 'D' looking for me. Now he's dead, his mother is dead, and his family is separated. Those kids are out there without each other to lean on. They're only kids, Ma'Dear. Can you imagine what they're going through?"

Randall's tears flowed like a river down his cheeks. He placed his face in his hands and sobbed loudly. Ma'Dear moved to where Randall was sitting and pulled him into her arms. "It's okay, dear."

Randall became angry and raised his voice. "No, it's not okay, and stop telling me that. I've got Brandon's blood on my hands. I'm the cause of his death. I am the cause of three kids being separated from one another, and I can't shake this feelin' that I need to do something. Since I saw Michael, God has put pressure on my heart about those kids, and I don't know why. I can't sleep and I can't eat. I'm praying and seeking God's face in this thing, but He's not coming through clearly. I need you to help me. Don't tell me it's okay, because it's not. I don't need you to pacify me. I need you to help me see what God is trying to say to me."

"Okay, baby, calm down and listen to me. The reason you can't eat or sleep is because God has given you an assignment. Just think about the events that have taken place in your life. He's leading you to somethin.' You've been prospering ever since you decided to live right. The next week after you told Amaryllis to leave your house, you got your job back a whole month early. That following Sunday, Pastor Bryson appointed you as the director of men's ministry at the church. Then your insurance company gave you a brand new car without the brand new price. That same day, God blew your mind by leading you to this estate. Recently, you asked the woman of your dreams to be your wife, and she accepted. But there's a bonus that comes with Gabby's acceptance."

Randall wiped his eyes with the back of his hand. "I don't understand, Ma'Dear."

"Gabby revealed to you that she can't have children, and three days later you run into Brandon's cousin. Meeting Michael wasn't a coincidence. God set you up. Do you really think you're interested in those kids just 'cause you're a good person?"

"Ma'Dear, I just wanna make sure they're okay."

"It goes deeper than that, Randall."

"I still don't understand."

"There are three kids, right?"

"Yes. A boy and two girls."

Ma'Dear grabbed Randall's hand. "Come with me." She led him upstairs to the bedroom next to his office. "Look at these white bunk beds in the spirit and tell me what you see."

Randall looked at the beds then looked at his mother. "Oh, my God. Ma'Dear, are these for Brandon's little sisters?"

"You think you bought these beds to fill the room, but God had a plan."

She led him across the hall. "Look at this race car bed in the spirit and tell me what you see."

"I see Brandon's little brother sleepin' in it."

"Now you're gettin' God's message, Randall. So what are you gonna do about it?"

"I'm gonna get those kids and bring them here to live with us. I know Brandon would want that."

"See, Randall, the devil wanted you and Gabby to think you'd never be parents, but God is gonna give you not one, not two, but three kids. Now, you let that marinate in your spirit, and I'm going back to bed."

Before Ma'Dear got to the front stairs, she turned around. "Didn't you say you lost your appetite last night?"

"Yeah."

"Then where's the shrimp you didn't eat?"

"In the refrigerator."

Instead of going down the front stairs, Ma'Dear walked past Randall and went down the back stairs to the kitchen where she retrieved the shrimp and indulged. Randall chuckled to himself as he thought, *all that interceding must have worked up an appetite.*

Chapter 16

Randall and Gabrielle were at the Department of Family and Children Services at eight o'clock AM, Friday morning. They sat before the caseworker assigned to Brandon's family. Randall told her how he met Brandon on the train and the need he felt to reach out to his family. He explained how God had given him an assignment to get the kids and make them a family again.

Thank God the caseworker was saved. When Randall testified to her how God led him to his estate in Oakbrook, and he'd already furnished the bedrooms without knowing why, it blew her mind. Randall expressed that he and Gabrielle were engaged to be married the following year and adopting the kids would literally put the icing on their wedding cake.

The only concern the caseworker had was the fact that Randall was taking on this responsibility a year before his wedding. The Department of Family and Children Services was not in favor of awarding custody of a child to single fathers. And Randall didn't just want one child, he wanted three. Randall explained to the caseworker he wasn't alone, but shared his estate with his mother, who was in his corner one hundred percent. In fact, Randall wouldn't have gotten God's revelation had it not been for Ma'Dear's knowledge and wisdom.

The caseworker told Randall that she needed to see his home and evaluate the relationships between him, his mother, and Gabrielle before his application for adoption would be considered. He invited her to his house for dinner that evening and she graciously accepted.

Randall and Gabrielle were driving back to Oakbrook when he called Cordell at the church.

"Holy Deliverance Baptist Church, Wanda speaking."

"What's up, Wanda MaeBell?"

"Didn't I tell you to never use my middle name, Randall?"

"Girl, your mother gave you that name. Don't be ashamed."

"Okay, Black."

At the sound of that name, Randall almost dropped the cellular phone in his lap. "Oh, you're tryin' to be funny, right?"

"Man, your ex-woman gave you that name. Don't be ashamed."

"Just put Pastor Bryson on the phone. I ain't got time to mess with you today."

"Oh, now you ain't got time? Did I hit a nerve?"

"Nope. But you can forget about me gettin' those discounted Fred Hammond concert tickets through my credit union for you."

"Come on, man. Don't be like that. You know God don't like ugly."

"He ain't too fond of pretty either. You should've thought of that before you said what you said."

"You started it."

"That's beside the point. You need somethin' from me, I don't need anything from you."

"You need to talk to the pastor and you can't do that unless you go through me."

"I got his cell number. You ain't stoppin' nothing."

"His cell phone is right here on my desk. So, now what are you gonna do?" Wanda had the upper hand.

"Girl, will you put him on the phone?"

"Can you say 'please'?"

"Can you say 'ouch' from gettin' hit in your eye? Now put him on the phone, it's urgent."

"How urgent?"

"Very."

"Urgent enough for you to get my Fred Hammond tickets?"

"I'll think about it."

"Okay, I'll wait."

"Wait for what?"

"For you to finish thinkin' about it."

"Wanda, I don't have time for this."

"Then I suggest you hurry up and finish thinkin'."

"You're wasting my minutes."

"I know you ain't worried about a few minutes when you're livin' in a mansion and driving a brand new Jaguar. People kill me talkin' about how they don't have any money. They're the same ones with fifty grand sittin' in the bank, but still they have no money."

"I can honestly say that I don't have any money in the bank."

"Then how can you afford the things you have, Randall?"

"I pay my tithes and offerings."

"Yeah, and that $85,000 a year job you have don't hurt you none."

"How do you know how much money I make? My own mother doesn't know how much money I make."

"Randall, please. You work for the C.T.A. and everybody knows they pay good money."

Randall laughed in Wanda's ear. "Wanda, darlin'?"

"What?"

"Somebody done told you wrong. The C.T.A. ain't all that generous, trust me. And I'm tired of talkin' to you. Put Pastor Bryson on the phone."

"You can't talk to him, Randall. Not until you promise to get me those tickets."

"Okay, Wanda, you win. I'll get the tickets for you. Now put Pastor Bryson on the phone, MaeBell."

"Now you've messed up. He's in a meeting, and I can't disturb him."

"You could if you wanted to."

"Sho' you right."

"You know, it's such a shame the Fred Hammond concert is sold out. Do you know that my credit union is holding the last four tickets for me? I guess I'll tell the clerk I don't want them. I'm sure someone else would be grateful to have them."

The next thing Randall heard was, "Pastor Bryson speaking."

"Hey, man, what are you doing tonight?" Randall asked.

"I don't know. Why?"

Randall explained how he'd been up all night wrestling with his new assignment.

"Randall, you're supposed to get married first, then have children."

"Man, look! God is giving me a second chance to help these kids, and I'm not gonna mess up this time."

"All right, if you feel led by God, then I'm behind you all the way. What can I do?"

"The caseworker is coming to dinner tonight to evaluate my household, and I need you there to back me up."

"Back you up how?"

"You know, tell her what a great guy I am and stuff like that."

"So, basically you want me to lie for you."

"Cordell, that is so not funny."

Cordell responded in his famous gay voice. "It's just a jokey joke, don't be so sensitive."

"You're settin' a bad example for your secretary. She blackmailed me in order to speak to you."

"*Sister Wanda?*"

"Yeah, 'Sister holier than thou, always got somethin' to say, need to get her some business,' Wanda."

"I'm sorry, Randall, but I just can't believe that."

"I figured you'd defend her."

"Hey, she's the only one who makes my coffee just the way I like it."

"Yeah, whatever. So, what about tonight, can you make it at seven o'clock?"

"Only if you get Ma'Dear to make her famous beef stew and hot water cornbread; tell her to put her foot in it."

Ma'Dear was watching 'The Price Is Right' when the telephone rang. She answered and heard her son's voice booming through the receiver.

"Ma'Dear, put some clothes on and make yourself presentable. The caseworker is coming to dinner tonight, and you've been requested to make beef stew and hot water cornbread."

"The hussie had the gall to say what she wanted to eat?"

"Nah, Cordell's the hussie with the gall. He's coming too."

At six 6:45 PM, everyone was present except the caseworker. Randall had been pacing the kitchen floor for the past half hour. Gabrielle came out of the great room, saw how nervous he was, and hugged him. "Randall, you're gonna drive yourself crazy. Everything is gonna work out fine. Come sit at the table and let me massage your shoulders."

No sooner than he sat down, the doorbell rang. Gabrielle felt him jump. "You want me to answer it for you?" she asked.

"Nah, I'm cool. I'll get it."

Randall opened the front door with a nervous smile. "Good evening, Mrs. Jackson. Welcome to my home."

He stood aside to allow her to enter. Mrs. Jackson couldn't take her eyes away from the marble and glass spiral staircase centered in the foyer. "My goodness, Mr. Loomis, this is breathtaking."

"Thank you and please call me Randall."

"Well, Randall, you have a lovely home."

"Thank you again. Can I take your coat?"

"Yes, thank you."

Randall hung her coat in the front closet then guided her to the rear of the house.

"Before I give you a tour, I want you to meet some people."

Randall brought Mrs. Jackson through the kitchen into the great room where Ma'Dear, Gabrielle and

Cordell were waiting. "Mrs. Jackson, this wonderful lady is my mother, Shirley Loomis."

She extended her hand to Ma'Dear. "It's nice to meet you."

Ma'Dear placed her hand in Mrs. Jackson's hand and looked at her curiously. "I know you from somewhere. Did you graduate from Lucy Flowers School in 1963?"

"Yes, I did."

"I knew I recognized you. Do you know who I am?"

Mrs. Jackson smiled. "I sure do. You're Shirley Mayfield."

Ma'Dear met her smile, tooth for tooth. "Yes, that's me. Shirley Mayfield *Loomis*. And you're Deborah Carter."

"Yes. Well, my last name is Jackson now."

Ma'Dear hugged her. "It's been almost forty years, Deborah, and you still look the same."

"You too, Shirley. It's so good to see you. How have you been?"

"I've been great. How about you?"

"Life has been wonderful." Ma'Dear was elated to see that God had sent her schoolmate. "What are the chances of my schoolmate showing up on my doorstep forty years later?"

"Ain't this somethin'?"

Randall took Mrs. Jackson lightly by her elbow. "I'm sorry to break up this reunion, but I want you to meet my best friend and pastor, Cordell Bryson."

Cordell extended his hand to her. "Good evening, Mrs. Jackson."

"Good evening, Pastor Bryson."

Randall pulled Gabrielle next to him. "And you met my lovely fiancée, Gabrielle, this morning."

"Yes, I remember. It's nice to see you again, Gabrielle."

"You too, Mrs. Jackson," Gabrielle replied.

Randall looked at his guest and smiled. "Mrs. Jackson, my mother has prepared a wonderful feast for us, but before we eat, I'm anxious to show you my home and get your opinion on whether it's suitable for the kids."

"Okay, Randall, lead the way."

Mrs. Jackson was in awe of the magnitude of Randall's estate. He told her the house sat on three lots. She was very impressed by what he'd done with the kids' bedrooms.

"You mean to tell me you prepared these rooms without knowing you'd be seeking to fill them?" Mrs. Jackson asked.

"Yes," Randall replied.

After the tour, everyone gathered in the dining room for dinner. Cordell said grace and he, Gabrielle, and Randall were completely ignored the entire time they were eating because the two school girls had a lot of catching up to do. They reminisced about who was the cutest boy in school to who was the teacher's pet. Mrs. Jackson even got Ma'Dear to reveal her secret hot water cornbread recipe.

After an hour passed and everyone was slouched in their chairs with toothpicks dangling from their lips, Randall's patience had run out and he was desperate to know what Mrs. Jackson's decision was. "Mrs. Jackson, I don't mean to sound impatient or rush you in any way, but I'm dying to know if you've made your decision."

"Randall, my decision was made before you left my office this morning. Coming to evaluate your home and family is just a formality. Listening to you speak of God the way you do, and your willingness to step out on faith to trust and obey Him, worked in your favor.

And after meeting your lovely family and seeing how you've already made room for the children, touched me deeply. So, I'm definitely gonna recommended the adoptions for Joshua, Tamika, and Eboni."

Randall let out a loud sigh. "Thank you, Mrs. Jackson, thank you so much. I'm lookin' forward to bringing them into my home, and I'm doing all I can to make them a family again. I promise to give them a good life."

"I believe in you, Randall. But I'm concerned about Eboni. She's five years old and autistic. Autism is a developmental disorder and a lifelong condition. The severity of Eboni's symptoms vary from day to day. She demonstrates repetitive behavior and has difficulty with social interaction and communication. Eboni throws tantrums often. She's very aggressive and is prone to self-injury. Eboni also has a rare form of osteoporosis in her legs. She's never learned to walk. When she stands she experiences unsteady balance. X-rays of Eboni's legs revealed the presence of fractures. So you're gonna have to make some adjustments before she's allowed to come here and live."

"I'll do whatever needs to be done. Just name it," Randall said.

"The first is that you must install an electronic wheelchair along the stairs to get her up and down. It may be an inconvenience, but the government will pay for it."

"It's no inconvenience. We'll have it done immediately on the kitchen stairs and the stairs leading down to the lower level. What else do I have to do?"

"You must hire a full-time nurse to care for Eboni. She can't walk, but she's very active. She needs care around the clock. However, this is something the government doesn't pay for. The nurse's salary has to come from your pocket or maybe your insurance company will pay for Eboni's care. And nurses are not cheap."

"Wow, I may have a problem if my insurance company doesn't want to pay for the nurse."

"Mrs. Jackson, as pastor of Holy Deliverance Baptist Church, I will authorize the church to pay the nurse's salary if Randall's insurance company doesn't pick up the tab," Cordell said.

Randall looked across the table at his best friend with tears in his eyes. There had never been a time when he needed Cordell and he hadn't come through for him. Whether it was a swift kick in the butt, a shoulder to lean on, or money to hire a nurse to care for his soon-to-be daughter, Cordell was there. "Thanks, Pastor. I appreciate it, man." Randall was choked up, but he managed to get his words out.

"It's Holy D's pleasure, Randall," Cordell assured him.

Ma'Dear looked at everyone seated around the table. "I guess this is where Romans eight and twenty-eight proves itself. Most assuredly, everything's working together. So, Randall, now we know whom the guest bedroom is for."

"Yes we do. The full-time nurse," he said.

The lives of Randall, Gabrielle, Cordell, and Ma'Dear all changed for the better when they met the children for the first time. Little Eboni had stolen Cordell's heart the moment he laid his eyes on her. Tamika took to Gabrielle immediately, constantly running her fingers through her hair and saying how pretty and soft it was.

This is my son, was all Randall could think when he saw Joshua. Ma'Dear couldn't have chosen a favorite if

she wanted to. She fell in love with all three of the
kids. Randall pleaded with Mrs. Jackson to arrange
for him to bring the kids together for a reunion while
the adoption was pending. Visiting the children in separate homes just didn't seem right. Mrs. Jackson informed Randall that although she didn't agree with
the rules of DFACS, he wasn't allowed to talk to the
children about one another or bring them together
until the adoption was finalized.

It took two whole months, but a week before Christmas, Mrs. Jackson called Randall to tell him the adoptions were final. He could get his children and take
them home.

Randall rented a mini-van, picked up Mrs. Jackson,
and drove to the first foster home to get Joshua, who
was now four years old and the youngest of the three.
The second stop was to get Tamika, the eldest at seven
years old. It was cold outside so Randall sat in the van
with Joshua while Mrs. Jackson went inside to get his
sister. The children had been separated for more than
a year and hadn't seen or talked to one another.

Tamika was bundled up, Joshua couldn't see her
face and he had no idea who was getting in the van,
but when he saw his sister's face, he yelled to the top
of his lungs. Tamika screamed Joshua's name and
hugged him. She didn't let go of him until they got to
the third house.

Outside of a small yellow frame house, Mrs. Jackson
made a phone call and five minutes later, a nurse rolled
a wheelchair onto the porch with a little girl wearing a
pink snowsuit in it. When Tamika and Joshua saw the
wheelchair, they knew it was their sister.

"Look, Josh, it's Ebby," Tamika exclaimed.

"Ebby, Ebby, Ebby," Joshua cried out.

Randall had forgotten to apply the child safety locks on the rear doors. Tamika and Joshua were out of their seatbelts and running toward their sister so fast that no one could've stopped them if they tried.

The look in Eboni's eyes when she saw her brother and sister running to her, and calling her name, was too much for Randall to bare. Tears spilled out of his eyes like a waterfall. "Thank you, Lord. Thank you, thank you."

He watched as Eboni kicked her legs and waved her hands. The smile on her face was picture perfect. Because of her relaxed tongue, she could never hold complete sentences and it took her a while to get her words out. If one listened hard enough, though, they could understand every word she said. "Miiikaaa, Joosshh."

Tamika and Joshua got to Eboni and almost knocked her out of the wheelchair.

Joshua jumped into her lap and wrapped his arms around his sister so tight, he almost took her breath away. Eboni placed her lips on Joshua's lips and tried with all her might to say his name. "Joosshh, Joosshh."

Tamika ran around the back of Eboni's wheelchair and wrapped her arms around her sister and brother. "I missed you so much, Ebby."

Although Joshua was the youngest, he was a man today as he held on to Eboni. He silently vowed to never let anything take his sisters away from him again. He held on to his sister. "I'm so happy to see you, Ebby."

Eboni's chin was wet with saliva as she tried to lift her tongue and speak. "Wwwhere y'aalll go? Wwwhere y'all go? I nnott see y'aalll. Dooon't y'aalll neevva nooo mo leeavve meee. Miiikaaa, Joosshh, me go too wwwit youuu. Ccaann me go too wwwit youuu?"

Tamika and Joshua embraced Eboni in their arms. Not even a crowbar was strong enough to separate them.

Randall was no good as he watched Brandon's family reunite.

Even Mrs. Jackson was crying. She sat in the van with Randall. "Randall, out of all of the reunions I've witnessed, I've never seen anything like this before. This is why I say that brothers and sisters should be placed together."

Randall's attention was drawn to the left side of the street. He saw a young man leaning on a light pole, watching the kids with a smile on his face. Randall squinted his eyes to get a good look at him and was startled to see that it was Brandon. His heart skipped two beats, and he nervously tapped Mrs. Jackson on the shoulder.

"Do you see that young man over there, leaning on the light pole, watching the kids?"

Mrs. Jackson looked in the direction in which Randall pointed. "No, I don't see anyone."

"Right over there, he's got on a white knit hat, a white coat, white pants, and white shoes."

Again, she looked at the light pole. "No, Randall, I can't see him."

Mrs. Jackson turned her attention back to the children but Randall never took his eyes away from Brandon as he watched his brother and sisters rejoice and smiled at the reunion. Brandon made eye contact with Randall and mouthed the words, "Thank you."

Randall returned the smile, but when he blinked his eyes, Brandon was gone.

Before the children headed to their new home in Oakbrook, Randall made a stop at Restvale Ceme-

tery to show the kids their mother and brother's head-
stones that were side by side.

The kids loved their new home. Tamika told Randall
that they never had their own bedrooms before. She
happily took the top bunk bed and Randall installed
padded rails to the bottom bed to keep Eboni from
falling out during the night.

Joshua's blue room was beyond his wildest dreams.
He expressed his gratitude to Randall and stated that
he couldn't wait to fall asleep in his racecar bed. The
nurse the church hired for Eboni was the same nurse
who'd been caring for her at the foster home. Randall
thought it best to keep her with Eboni since she'd been
with her for the past year.

The first thing Tamika asked Ma'Dear when she
saw her again was, "May we call you Nana?"

Ma'Dear looked down at this jewel and couldn't stop
her heart from going out to her. "Of course, honey."

Joshua stood next to his sister. "You're pretty, Nana."

Ma'Dear picked Joshua up and kissed his cheek.
Then she looked at her son. "They are definitely keep-
ers, Randall. Where's the baby girl?"

"Eboni had a very exciting morning. Her nurse
thought it best if she lie down and rest. She's awake in
her bed. Go and say 'hello'," Randall replied.

Ma'Dear walked across the hall to the girls' room
and knelt by Eboni's bed. "Hello sweetheart, how are
you?"

Eboni lay there looking at Ma'Dear.

"I'm your Nana, and you're such a pretty little angel."

Eboni lay motionless, staring at Ma'Dear with her
beautiful brown eyes. Ma'Dear reached under the bed
and pulled out a gift and presented it to Eboni. "I know
what it takes to get you going."

Eboni's eyes lit up when she saw the box with multi-colored jellybeans and started wiggling her fingers. "Gimmee, gimmee."

Ma'Dear opened the box and gave Eboni one Mike and Ike. She ignored the one piece and grabbed the box from Ma'Dear's hand. Randall came into the girls' bedroom and told Ma'Dear that Tamika said that she, Joshua, and Eboni had never had a Christmas tree, so he was taking her and Joshua to the forest to cut down a real one.

On Christmas Eve, Randall was overjoyed to be with his family. Cordell came by with a load of gifts for the kids, and Gabrielle had been there all day playing mommy. Randall invited Michael and his mother over to spend the first Christmas with him and his children.

At midnight, they all gathered around the Christmas tree and opened their gifts. Tamika unwrapped a black Barbie doll that was just as tall as she was. She kissed Randall and Gabrielle on their cheeks. "This is my onlyest Barbie. Thank you."

Gabrielle squeezed her tight. "You're welcome, honey. Merry Christmas. We're gonna start a collection, and before you know it, you'll have manyest Barbies."

Randall wanted to say something to her, but his words were stuck in his throat. All he could do was put his arms around Tamika and squeeze tight as he fought back tears.

Joshua leaped for joy as he unwrapped a set of roller blades and a sled. He saw Randall's roller blades and sled in the garage and told Randall that he wanted a set just like his. Now Randall couldn't wait to hit the snow with Joshua.

"Thanks," Joshua said.

"You're welcome, son."

Randall also got copies of the obituaries of both Brandon and Vera from the funeral home and made eight by ten copies of their photos and had them framed for the kids. He placed the pictures on their desks in their bedrooms.

Cordell set a large gift-wrapped box in front of Eboni and asked Tamika and Joshua to open it for her. Eboni watched as they unveiled a three-foot tall gumball machine filled with Mike and Ike's. She got excited and lifted herself toward it. Cordell took her first finger and pressed it against a big red button that released one jelly bean and she watched it spiral down in a slot. Eboni only needed to be shown one time. In less than two minutes, she had a mouth full of candy, and Mike and Ike's were all over the floor.

Ma'Dear poured eggnog for everyone and they all sat around the fireplace and thanked God for their blessings. Tamika grabbed Joshua's hand and stood next to Eboni.

"We thank God for our big new house and our new daddy and our new momma and our new Nana and our new Uncle Cordell."

There wasn't a dry eye in the family room.

Chapter 17

The day before New Year's Eve, Gabrielle drove to Midway Airport to meet her sister who was flying in from Dallas. On their way to Gabrielle's apartment, they stopped at the church. Wanda announced to Pastor Bryson that he had visitors. When Gabrielle and her sister walked into his office, he wasn't expecting to see what stood before him.

"Good afternoon, Pastor Bryson."

Cordell didn't know who was speaking. They were identical twins. He came from around his desk and stood in front of the twin on the right, whom he thought was Gabrielle. "Hi Gabby, how are you?"

The twin on the left spoke. "I'm fine, thank you."

The three of them laughed. Cordell looked at Gabrielle. "Why did you do this to me?"

"I wanted to see if you could tell us apart."

"Well, as you can see, I can't."

He extended his hand to the twin standing in front of him. "I'm Cordell Bryson and you are . . . ?"

She placed her freshly French manicured fingers in

his hand. "Evangelist Genevieve Davis, and you are as handsome as Gabrielle said you were. It's a pleasure to put a face with the image I've had of you."

At her title, Cordell's eyebrows rose, and he kissed the back of her hand. He purposely checked her left hand for a wedding ring and was elated he didn't see one. "The pleasure's all mine, Evangelist."

They stood hand in hand, smiling at each other for the longest moment before Gabrielle broke the silence. "Ahem."

Cordell was mesmerized by Genevieve's smile. "You have a lovely smile."

"So do you, Pastor," she replied.

"Please, call me Cordell."

Gabrielle stepped between them and gently took her sister's hand from Cordell's.

"I'm sorry to break up whatever's happening here, but we've got to get going. Cordell, why don't you join Randall, Genny and me for pizza tonight at Giordano's?"

Genevieve stepped closer to him. "Yes, Cordell, please join us."

He smiled at her. "Count me in."

Gabrielle grabbed her sister's elbow, and turned her toward the door. She said to Cordell, "Okay, try and be there at seven."

He kept his eyes on Genevieve. "I'll be there at 6:45."

The waiter escorted Cordell to the table at exactly six fifty-five. The first thing that he noticed was that the twins had changed clothes since they left his office. Each of them wore black turtleneck sweaters and black denim jeans. They were seated and in deep conversation when he approached them. He had no clue which twin was Gabrielle or which twin was his

future wife. He'd have to wait for one of them to acknowledge him.

"Dang, you weren't lying about the time you were
gonna be here were you, Cordell?"

The smart-alicky question could come from none
other than Gabrielle. Though she was sweet and kind,
Gabrielle was a firecracker as well. Cordell hoped Randall could handle her.

"I had a light day at church so I was able to leave a
little early," Cordell replied to Gabrielle.

He smiled at Genevieve, glad to be in her presence
again. Since she and Gabrielle had left his office that
afternoon, he hadn't been able to concentrate on anything. He gave his undivided attention to the twin
seated next to him. "You look especially radiant this
evening, Genevieve. Did you change your hairstyle?"

Genevieve was impressed. "As a matter of fact, I
did."

"It's lovely on you."

Gabrielle couldn't take it. "It's just a ponytail."

Genevieve looked at her. "Don't hate."

Cordell moved his chair closer to Genevieve. "That's
an intoxicating aroma you're wearing. What is it?"

Gabrielle made a smacking noise with her lips. "That's
the pepperoni pizza the waiter just carried over your
head."

Genevieve was overwhelmed by Cordell's attention.
"It's Perry Ellis's Three Hundred Sixty Degrees. Does
it do anything for you?"

"Mmm hmm. It does a lot for me."

Gabrielle had never seen Cordell let his guard down
like this before. "Uh-oh, watch out there now, Pastor.
You're gonna be droppin' it like it's hot in a minute."

"I'm glad you like the scent," Genevieve said, smiling into Cordell's eyes.

Genevieve's teeth shined so bright, Cordell could see his own reflection. "You wear it well."

Gabrielle was fed up. "Oh, plllleeease. I wear the same scent and you've never complimented me."

Genevieve balled up her lips and looked at her sister. "Will you quit raining on my parade?"

"Will y'all quit tryin' to make me vomit?" Gabrielle placed her elbows on the table and her chin in her hands. "So, Cordell, have you talked to Randall today?"

"No, I haven't."

"Great, he knows Genny's in town for a visit, but he doesn't know she's my twin. He only said that we look a lot alike when he saw pictures of Genny. We're gonna have some fun with Randall when he gets here."

Cordell shook his head. "Uh-uh. No way. You're not gettin' me involved with twin games."

Genevieve leaned into Cordell and traced the rim of his ear with her finger. "Can't we have just a little bit of fun, Cor-Cor?"

How could he resist? Genevieve mesmerized him. Cordell giggled shyly. "Okay, but just a little."

Gabrielle stuck her finger to the back of her throat and gagged.

Randall arrived at the restaurant at 7:15, kissed Genevieve on the lips, then shook Cordell's hand. "Sorry I'm late. I had to help Joshua with his coloring. I love this daddy thing."

He looked at Genevieve. "How was your day, honey?"

"Fine. How was yours?"

"It was great. Is that a new shade of lipstick you're wearing?"

"No, it's Fashion Fair's Magenta Mist. I wear it all the time."

He noticed her hairstyle. "Didn't you tell me that you never wear your hair away from your face 'cause you thought your forehead was too big?"

"No, I don't remember telling you anything like that."

"Yes, you did."

"Randall, don't tell me what I've told you."

At Genevieve's response, Randall's eyebrows arched. He looked across the table and saw Cordell holding up the pizza menu to hide his face. "What's up with you, Cordell? Why are you hiding your face?"

Cordell lowered the menu just beneath his eyes and looked at Randall. "Huh? Uh, I'm just reading the menu." He raised the menu back up to where he had it.

The waiter came to the table to take their order. Randall did the honors as he always did when he, Gabrielle, and Cordell come to Giordano's. "We'll have a large stuffed sausage and a pitcher of root beer."

Genevieve spoke. "Uh, Randall honey, why would you order without consulting with me or Cordell?"

"Because I know what you like. The three of us always get the same thing whenever we come here."

"Well, I want a thin crust pepperoni pizza."

Randall frowned at her. "Gabby, you hate pepperoni."

"You're mistaken; I hate sausage."

Cordell was laughing behind the menu. Randall could see his shoulders shaking.

"Cordell, don't we always get the stuffed sausage, man?" Randall needed back-up.

"I don't know, Randall. I like everything," Cordell answered without lowering the menu.

Genevieve told the waiter to bring a large thin crust pepperoni pizza, then excused herself to the ladies room. When she was out of hearing range, Randall whispered to Cordell. "Man, did you see that mood swing?"

"I don't know what you're talkin' about."

"Put down that stupid menu. Gabby ordered already. And what's wrong with you?"

Cordell laid the menu on the table but wouldn't make eye contact with Randall for fear he'd laugh and spoil the fun. "Nothin's wrong with me. I'm cool."

"You can't tell that Gabby is p.o.'d about something? She darn near chewed my head off."

Just then, Gabrielle came and sat next to Randall. "Hey baby, how was your day?"

Her hair was flowing past her shoulders and her lipstick was darker. Randall looked at her in confusion. "I already told you my day was great. Why did you change your hair and make-up?"

"I didn't change anything."

Randall looked across the table at Cordell. "Wasn't she just sitting here with her hair pulled back and wearing red lipstick?"

"I don't know what you're talkin' about," Cordell replied.

Gabrielle patted his hand. "Are you feelin' all right, Randall?"

The waiter brought the pitcher of root beer and set it on the table. "Here's your soda. Your pepperoni pizza will be ready in twenty minutes."

Gabrielle looked at the waiter like he was insane. "What's the matter with you? We didn't order pepperoni. We ordered a large stuffed sausage."

Randall grabbed her hand. "Uh, Gabby, you just argued with me about this. You said you didn't like sausage, so you ordered the pepperoni."

"Randall, are you having a mid-life crisis or something? You know doggone well I don't eat pepperoni."

Randall became frustrated. He looked across the table at his friend. "Cordell, didn't she just order the pepperoni?"

Cordell could be nominated for best actor for his role tonight. "No Randall, she ordered the stuffed sausage. What's wrong with you, man?"

"Ain't nothing wrong with me. Something is wrong with y'all."

Gabrielle told the waiter to bring the stuffed sausage. Cordell poured each of them a glass of root beer. Gabrielle took a sip from her glass then spit it out onto the table.

"What is this?" she spat.

Randall was appalled that his fiancée could actually do something so ill-mannered as spit anything from her mouth in a restaurant. "It's root beer, Gabby. We always get a pitcher of root beer."

Gabrielle loved root beer, but she couldn't let on. "I'm allergic to root beer Randall, and you know it. Are you tryin' to make me catch the hives? You wanna see my face and throat swell up to look like the elephant man?"

Cordell could no longer restrain himself. He leaned down and pretended to tie his shoe under the table and laughed.

Randall didn't know if he was coming or going. "Gabby, everytime we come here we get root beer. You're the one who turned me and Cordell on to drinkin' it."

Gabrielle's neck rolled as she spoke. "Look Randall, I don't know what game you're playin,' but I don't like it. I'm going to the bathroom to rinse this nasty taste out of my mouth. Get that useless waiter to bring me a glass of Pepsi."

When Gabrielle walked away, Randall looked at Cordell. "Do you believe the way she's behavin'?"

"I don't know what you're talkin' about."

"I'm talkin' about the way she keeps changin' her mind and the attitude she has."

"I don't know what you're talkin' about."

"What, are you blind? You can't tell she's testy?"

"Look, Randall, Gabrielle is *your* woman. After the Amaryllis fiasco, I'm done with interfering in your love life. You decided that you wanna get married, so I suggest you become acquainted with that territory."

Genevieve came and sat down. Randall stared at the ponytail and bright lipstick. He threw his hands in the air. *Awe heck, here we go again.* "Gabby, why are you changing yourself back and forth?"

"What are you talking about, Randall?" she replied.

"First, you had the ponytail, then you let your hair down. Now you've got the ponytail again and you keep changing your makeup. What's going on?"

"Baby, I haven't changed a thing. Did you hit your head today?"

Randall looked at his friend. "Cordell, didn't she just have her hair down and a different lipstick on?"

"She looks the same to me. You're trippin', man," Cordell stated.

Randall's eyes went from Genevieve to Cordell, then from Cordell to Genevieve.

"It's something funky going on here, y'all."

Just then, the waiter told Genevieve that she had a telephone call at the front pick-up counter. "Excuse me, guys. I hope my sister isn't lost."

Randall watched her walk away and shook his head. Cordell saw the confusion on his face. "What's wrong, man?"

"I feel like I'm in a twilight zone. She's acting so weird. Can't you tell?"

Cordell stuck with his story. "I don't know what you're talkin' about."

Gabrielle came and sat down at the table with her hair flowing, wearing a darker shade of lipstick. Randall was too outdone. He inhaled and exhaled loud enough for the people at the next table to hear. "Why are you playing with me, Gabby?"

"Randall, what are you talking about now?"

Randall began to sweat. He shifted in his seat and looked at his friend. "Cordell, did she or did she not have a ponytail before she left this table?"

"I don't know what you're talkin' about."

The waiter placed a stuffed sausage pizza on the center of the table. Gabrielle looked up at him. "We didn't order this."

"Yes, ma'am, you did," the waiter replied.

"No, we didn't. I specifically ordered a thin pepperoni. Take this back and bring us a thin pepperoni, and you can forget about your tip." She stood up. "I'm going to the door to watch for my sister."

When she walked away, Randall apologized to the waiter. "I'm sorry about that, man."

"It's okay, sir. It was my mistake." The waiter took the pizza away.

Cordell spoke to Randall. "Why are you apologizing? It was his fault for bringing the wrong order."

"Cordell, she ordered the stuffed sausage."

"No, she didn't. She ordered the thin pepperoni."

Randall couldn't take it. "Man, am I crazy? I mean seriously, am I crazy?"

Genevieve came and sat very close to Cordell. Much too close for Randall's liking. "Ooh, you are so handsome tonight, Cordell."

Randall looked like a deer that had been caught in headlights. He quickly stood, knocking over his chair. *"What in the . . ."*

Cordell put his arm around Genevieve's shoulders.

"I'm sorry, Randall. We were gonna tell you, but we didn't know how to put it into words. We're in love."

Randall stood still with his mouth wide open. His lips were moving, but no words came forth. Gabrielle stepped out of nowhere and snapped his picture. "Gotcha."

Randall saw double. He couldn't say anything. He just stood with his mouth open.

Gabrielle stood by her sister. "Randall, meet my sister, Genevieve."

Still, Randall couldn't move or say anything. It hadn't registered that there were two Gabrielles before him. Cordell pushed his chin up to close his mouth. "Say something, man."

Randall looked at Gabrielle. "You said you had a younger sister."

"And two older brothers," Gabrielle stated. "Genny is eight minutes my junior."

Finally, Randall was able to unglue his feet. He smiled and sat down. "I knew I wasn't crazy. You two look exactly alike. I couldn't tell from the pictures. How did your parents know who was who?"

"When we were six years old, I got my ears pierced but Gabby didn't. So, a sure way to tell us apart was to see which twin wore clip-on earrings," Genevieve explained.

The waiter brought the stuffed sausage and thin pepperoni pizzas plus a pitcher of Pepsi. Gabrielle placed a fifty-dollar bill in his hand and thanked him for playing his part to perfection. For the next two hours, the couples laughed and ate.

New Years came and went like a flash. Before Cordell knew it, it was almost time for Genevieve to return to Dallas. She had only been in Chicago for five days, and already she had his heart gripped tightly in the palm of her hand. Not only was Cordell physically, emotionally, and mentally connected to Genevieve, but the two of them were divinely connected. Genevieve was like no other woman.

Beautiful, single women sat in Cordell's congregation Sunday after Sunday. Some had openly flirted with him and a few were bold enough to ask him out on a date. Being the hot blooded mammal that he was, it had been difficult for Cordell not to fall for the over-exposed cleavages or the slacks and short skirts that looked as though they had been painted on Coke-bottle frames. But he knew that as a pastor, he had to always keep his testosterone in check. The Bible says that it's a man who finds his wife, not the other way around. It was a turn off for Cordell when women threw themselves at his feet.

All week long, Genevieve and Gabrielle had been joined at the hip, forcing Cordell and Randall to tag along while the women went about their days shopping, dining, and getting facials.

The first Friday evening in January, Genevieve told Cordell that her vacation had come to an end and that she would be catching a plane back to Dallas on Sunday morning. They were all together in the great room of Randall's estate, watching Gabrielle and Randall toast marshmallows over the open fire.

"It saddens me that you have to leave so soon," Cordell told her.

Genevieve looked into Cordell's eyes. "*How* sad are you?"

"Extremely."

She smiled. "Why?"

Was she putting him on the spot? It wasn't that

Cordell didn't know how to express his feelings to her, but he'd only known Genevieve for a few days. He would sound foolish if he confessed what was in his heart. Already, he was in love with her. "I'm sad because I will miss your presence."

"Why would you miss my presence?" She was taunting Cordell, and he knew it.

"I love being in your company, and I love the way you smile. I hope what I'm about to say doesn't come out sounding arrogant, but women at church practically throw themselves at my feet. They outnumber the men ten to five. But honestly, I don't see my wife there."

"Single pastors have it hard. Gabby has mentioned that after morning service, you try to greet each member, and the women are lined up and ready to bat false eyelashes at you."

Cordell laughed. "It's crazy. I remember a time when a sister cut the line in front of another sister, and next thing I knew, weaves and wigs were being slung everywhere. The deacons had to clear the church."

"Well, that's what happens when you're as fine as you are," Genevieve flirted.

"Is that a compliment?"

"Absolutely."

"What are y'all over there whispering about?" Randall interrupted.

"Grown folks' business," Cordell and Genevieve said at the same time, and all four of them laughed out loud.

Genevieve sighed and rested her head on Cordell's shoulder. "I don't wanna think about work on Monday morning."

"Gabby mentioned you teach the third grade."

"Yes, I have thirty-five eight-year-olds going on twenty. But you know what's sad is that half of them have mothers and fathers only fifteen years older than they are."

"You've got to be kidding me. Really?"

Randall reclined in his La-Z-Boy and Gabrielle sat on his lap to feed him toasted marshmallows from a long thin silver stick. "Genny, tell Cordell about some of the parents when they come to get report cards."

"Uh-oh, this ought to be good," Cordell chuckled.

"I have sooooo many horror stories about parent/teacher conferences and report card nights, but there is one that I'll never forget. One of my students, a pretty girl named Alizé has . . ."

"Excuse me, Alizé as in . . . ?" Randall cut her off.

"Yes, Alizé as in red, blue, or gold."

"Wow, it's not hard to figure out what her parents were doing before she was conceived."

"You're right about that. Alizé lives with her twenty-one-year-old mother and grandmother, who isn't much older than I am, and she's got a flip mouth that runs a mile a minute. She's not a terrible child, but I believe she has a slight case of ADD because she can't keep still or stay quiet for more than two seconds. The week before Thanksgiving, I gave the kids a spelling test, and every word that I gave them, I used in a sentence. Well, I don't know if she was even aware that she was doing it, but Miss Alizé repeated the words and sentences aloud. And when she wrote the words on paper, she verbally spelled them."

"Well, was her spelling correct at least?" Cordell asked.

"Yes. Alizé is one of my brightest students, and I can tell she does her homework, but at the parent/teacher conference the following evening, I mentioned to her mother who can really pass for Alizé's older sister, that Alizé is extremely hyper and has a problem keeping quiet in class. This young chick placed her hand on her hip and shifted all of her weight onto one leg while chewing bubble gum *and* popping it. She said to me with a neck dance and much attitude, 'So, my child likes to express herself, what of it?' "

Gabrielle quickly sat up on Randall's lap. "No she didn't, girl."

"Oh, yes she did. My first instinct was to react to the attitude she was giving me, but I remembered that I was talking to a child about a child."

"So what did you do?" Cordell asked.

"I realized that talking to Alizé's mother would get me nowhere, so I ended the conversation because she looked like she was ready to whip my butt. I excused myself and tended to the other parents. But when I got home that night, I called Alize's home and thank God, the grandmother answered. I explained to her what was happening with Alizé and I mentioned how the parent teacher conference went with her daughter. For the sake of Alizé, she agreed to meet with me next week, after Christmas break. She went into great detail about how young she was when she had Brandy, Alizé's mother, and it was difficult because her own mother had put her out of the house and she went to live with Brandy's seventeen-year-old father and his family. Because of her pregnancy in her junior year, she couldn't finish high school, and even though she has her GED now, times are still rough. Because she didn't have the support of her mother while raising Brandy, she felt that she couldn't stop Brandy from following in her footsteps."

"Wow, that's deep," Randall said.

"It sure is," Cordell said.

Gabrielle stood to stretch her legs. "Well, hopefully, Alizé's grandmother can get her the help she needs."

"Yeah, I will keep Alizé and her family in my prayers and add all three of their names to the special prayer request list on the church programs."

Cordell's kindness touched Genevieve deeply. "Really, you'll do that for me?"

Before Cordell knew it, the words were out of his mouth. "I'll do anything for you, Genny. I care for you very deeply. Truth be told, I think I'm falling in love with you."

A hush fell upon the entire house. No one said a word. Gabrielle paused in the middle of her stretch. Randall was in the midst of bringing the recliner upright but paused. Genevieve sat next to Cordell with her tonsils on display. The kids could no longer be heard playing upstairs and everyone knew that Ma'Dear was on the other side of the house, excited to be on the telephone talking to her schoolmate, but her laughs came to a halt. The world was at a standstill.

"What did you say?" Genevieve asked Cordell after swallowing five times.

"Yeah, what did you say?" his best friend asked.

"Huh?" Gabrielle stood in the middle of the great room.

Ma'Dear appeared out of nowhere. "Can you repeat that, son?"

"What did you say, Uncle Cordell?" Tamika and Joshua were above them on the catwalk overlooking the great room.

There, he said it. He'd been wanting to say it since Gabrielle brought Genevieve to his office five days ago. Cordell was now a true believer in love at first sight. But now that his heart was exposed, what would happen? Only two things could unfold here, either Genevieve would think that he was coming on too strong too soon and change her flight plans to leave in the next hour, or God could answer his prayer and give him this woman.

"I'm not ashamed to say it," Cordell confessed. "When I first laid my eyes on you, it was love at first sight. It wasn't lust. It was true love. I know that sounds crazy. But I know what love is."

Genevieve didn't know she was crying until a single tear dripped from her chin. "Oh, my God, Cordell. I felt the same way too."

Cordell didn't care who was present. Yes, he was a pastor, but he was a man first. He pulled Genevieve into his arms and kissed her. They didn't break away until Randall spoke. "Ahem, uh, what happens now?"

"I don't know," Cordell as he stared into Genevieve's eyes.

"I think we should order Chinese. Who besides me wants beef fried rice?" Ma'Dear asked, already fumbling through the Yellow Pages.

Bright and early Saturday morning, before the rooster crowed somewhere in Beloit, Mississippi, Cordell was ringing the telephone in Gabrielle's apartment.

"Good morning, Gabby."

"Pastor, it's not even six o'clock, are you okay?"

"All is well. I'm calling because I know this is Genny's last day in Chicago and I was wondering if you had any plans with her?"

"Well, when Genny first told me she was coming for a visit, I bought tickets for Oprah's *The Color Purple* stage play. It's at the Cadillac Theatre. She is a huge fan of Oprah's and actually, *The Color Purple* is Genny's favorite movie. She mentioned a while ago that she really wanted to see the play. She doesn't know I have the tickets yet. I'm gonna surprise her with them while we're at breakfast. The play isn't until eight o'clock, tonight. Other than the play, we don't have any plans."

"Gabby, how much do you love your pastor?"

"It depends on what he wants me to do for him?"

Cordell chuckled. "I want you to let me have your sister today, *all* day."

"But what about the play? I already have the tickets, and I wouldn't want Genny to miss it."

"Will it be alright if I purchased the tickets from you and took Genny myself?"

Gabrielle was just as much a fan of Oprah and *The Color Purple* as her sister was, but knew Cordell really wanted to spend some alone time with Genevieve. And if Gabrielle could choose a man who would love Genevieve just as much as Randall loved her, she'd choose her pastor. "You didn't get any sleep at all last night, did you?"

"What can I say? I can't get her off of my mind."

"Pastor, Genny is my world. She deserves to be happy."

"I agree with you."

"I guess I won't be selfish. You can have her today."

"Thanks, Gabby. And please don't mention to Genny what my plans are for her."

Genevieve was up and dressed and knocking on Gabrielle's bedroom door at nine AM.

"Come on, Gabby. What's taking you so long?"

"Why are you in such a hurry to get to IHOP. They specialize in pancakes, Genny. I promise they won't run out."

Genevieve opened the door and peeked in. "Will you please get up and get dressed?"

Gabrielle pulled the sheets over her head. "It's Saturday and I don't know what y'all do in Dallas, but in Chi-town, we sleep 'til noon."

There was a knock on the front door. "Can you get that, please?" Gabrielle asked.

Genevieve opened the door and saw Cordell standing with a bouquet of the largest, fullest red roses she'd ever seen. "Oh, my God. What is this?"

"My name is Calgon and I've come to take you away."

She laughed. "That was very corny, but cute. Come in."

Cordell entered the living room and presented her with the roses. "These are for you, and I'm glad you're dressed and ready to go."

"Gabby didn't tell me you and Randall were coming to breakfast with us. If he's waiting in the car, you may as well tell him to come in, because Gabby is still in bed."

"There's been a change of plans. You and I are having breakfast alone."

"Oh, really?" She smiled.

"I've decided to kidnap you from the rest of the world. This entire day will only consist of you and me."

Since Genevieve had been raving about the buttermilk pancakes at the International House of Pancakes, Cordell decided to give her her heart's desire. "These pancakes are like Krispy Kreme donuts; they melt in your mouth," she said.

Cordell took pleasure in watching Genevieve moan as though she was enjoying a deep tissue body massage as she ate. "They're that good, huh?"

"Oh, my God. The pancake houses in Dallas don't even come close to this."

Cordell noticed a drop of syrup lingering on Genevieve's bottom lip and couldn't take his eyes off of it. She bit a piece of bacon, drank orange juice, and still the drop of syrup on her lips was calling his name.

"You want it?"

Cordell snapped out of his daydream and saw Genevieve extending a piece of bacon to him. "Excuse me?"

"You ate seven strips of bacon, obviously you're a bacon man. So I'm offering you the last bite of mine."

If she only knew that at that moment, Cordell was a lip-dripping-syrup-licking man. Cordell was trying, with every fiber of his being, to stay anointed, but the drop of syrup was making it extremely difficult. "No thanks, I can't eat another bite."

Genevieve drank all but one swallow of her orange juice and held the glass up for Cordell to see. "I've also noticed that you drank your entire glass of orange juice. Would you like the rest of mine?"

It amazed Cordell that after all of the eating, drinking, and talking Genevieve had done, that single drop of syrup was still present and taunting him. "Hmm? Oh, no thanks."

"Well, then, you wanna lick this drop of syrup from my bottom lip before it drips onto my blouse?"

Cordell laughed out loud. "You knew all along that drop of syrup was messing me up. You purposely let it dangle, didn't you?"

"I plead the fifth," she smiled.

"You don't think I'll do it, do you?"

"You haven't done it *yet*."

Cordell looked all around them to see if he recognized any familiar faces. "I'm not afraid to do it."

"Actions speak volumes, much louder than words."

Again, Cordell glanced around the restaurant, everyone was into their own conversations. No one paid him and Genevieve any attention. "I ain't a punk."

"You can show me better than you can tell me."

Cordell rose from his side of the booth, slid next to Genevieve, and kissed her bottom lip.

"Can I get you anything else, a hotel room perhaps?" a waitress appeared and asked.

Being a pastor, Cordell's first instinct was to apologize to the waitress for his behavior. Then again, people kiss in public all the time. It wasn't like he and Genevieve were naked on top of the table. "Just the bill."

Genevieve found herself wrapped in Cordell's arms as they enjoyed a horse and carriage ride along the streets of downtown Chicago in the bitter cold January weather. Snuggled under a quilted blanket, Cordell and Genevieve were in awe of the showcase windows along the magnificent mile, still adorned with Christmas decorations. Macy's, Saks Fifth Avenue, and Lord & Taylor all displayed mannequins wearing the latest fashions. But it was when the coachman strolled past Andrianna Furs on North Michigan Avenue that Genevieve sat up. In the window, a mannequin modeled a full-length black coat.

"Oh, my God. Would you look at that?" Her eyes were the size of golf balls. She'd never seen a more beautiful fur coat.

Cordell followed the point of Genevieve's finger. "You're talking about those fur coats?"

"I'm talking about that black one the mannequin on the left is wearing. It is beautiful."

"You wanna go in and try it on for size?"

"No, that would be a tease. The weather in Texas doesn't fall below sixty degrees very often. I would look foolish walking around with that on."

Before the horses pulled the carriage away from the showcase window, Cordell studied the fur coat.

Genevieve felt as though she was a teenager again. Who would've thought that on her last day in Chicago, she'd be sitting at the top of the largest Ferris wheel in the world at Navy Pier? "This view is amazing. Chicago has the absolute best skyline I've ever seen."

"Yeah, you can pretty much see everything from up here."

"Are all of these high rises office buildings?"

"Actually, more than half of the buildings facing Lake Michigan are condominiums. As a matter of fact, before Randall was blessed with his estate, he rented an apartment just one block north of where we are now. He was on the eighth floor, and in the summer time, the view from his place was awesome. The fireworks show on the eve of July Fourth, the air and water show, the yacht and boat show and even the Taste of Chicago could be seen from his living room windows."

"Taste of Chicago?"

"The Taste of Chicago, affectionately known as The Taste, is when every restaurant, from gourmet to fast food, shows off their best entrees in Grant Park. Booths are set up that stretch blocks and blocks long, with every bakery and ice cream shop in Chicago. We buy tickets to sample everything like barbeque ribs, steak, dressed up corn on the cob, all sorts of cake, ice cream, sno-cones, hamburgers, the best hotdogs, pizza from Giovanni's, Baraconi's, Giordano's and Beggar's and the list goes on and on. It's a feast that lasts for ten days, leading up to the Fourth of July."

"Wow, this event happens every year?"

"Every single year, and there are also blues, jazz and gospel festivals during The Taste. You'll have to come back this summer and allow me to show you what it's all about."

"It's a date, Pastor!"

By noontime, Cordell and Gabrielle had toured all of downtown Chicago, shopped at the Water Tower and worked up an appetite.

"Welcome to the Signature Room, Mr. Bryson." The host showed the couple to a table on the sixty-seventh floor of the John Hancock Building. Genevieve sat down and admired the silk curtains, floor-to-ceiling windows, and the Swarovski crystal chandeliers dangling from the trey ceiling. It was early afternoon, and the dining room was filled to capacity. She looked out of the window, at the view, and noticed that the Chicago skyline was slowly moving to the left.

"What in the world? Cordell, look at those buildings. They're actually moving."

Cordell laughed. "Those buildings aren't moving, we are."

Genevieve watched in awe as the Sears Tower disappeared from her sight. "Okay, I'm about to sound foolish, but I gotta ask anyway, is this building rotating?"

"This building isn't rotating, but this floor is. We're sitting in a revolving restaurant. I thought you might enjoy it."

She smiled at Cordell. "I am truly amazed at the lengths you've gone to make my last day in Chicago a memorable one. You're making it extremely difficult for me to get on that plane in the morning."

"I'm glad to know that my plan is working."

For the next hour and a half, Cordell and Gabrielle feasted on filet mignon and lobster tails.

Cordell escorted Genevieve to Gabrielle's door and told her that he had some business at the church to tend to, but he'd be back to pick her up at six PM sharp. "I'm taking you someplace special this evening."

Genevieve became excited. "Can I have a clue? I don't know how to dress."

"Hmm, let's see. How about wearing something warm? It's cold outside." Cordell quickly kissed her lips and ran to his car.

Once inside the apartment, Genevieve saw that Gabrielle was gone and called her cellular telephone. "Hi, sis, where are you?"

"I'm at Randall's. Tamika, Eboni and I are getting our hair braided. Did you have a good time at Navy Pier?"

"How did you know Cordell took me to Navy Pier."

Cordell had sworn Gabrielle to secrecy. Now she had to correct her mistake.

"Uh, I just assumed he'd take you to Navy Pier. It's a hot spot, and he's always talking about it."

"Oh, well, yes he did take me to Navy Pier, and I loved it. Gabby, you won't believe the morning and afternoon I had with your pastor."

Gabrielle could believe it, because she had Cordell's agenda for the entire day. "Tell me about it."

"The morning started at IHOP."

Gabrielle knew Cordell took her sister on a horse and carriage ride but had to ask Genevieve anyway. "What happened after breakfast?"

"After breakfast, I had my first horse and carriage ride in downtown Chicago. Then we walked and shopped at the Water Tower after that. Cordell took me to a rotating restaurant in the John Hancock Building and fed me lobster and filet mignon. Can you believe that, girl?"

"That's my pastor. Of course I can believe it. He's head over heels for you, and I bet Cordell is trying to get you to stay in Chi-town. So, you wanna come over and hang out with me and the girls at Randall's?"

"I can't. Cordell said that he's taking me someplace special this evening. He's coming back to pick me up at six, so I think I'll lie down and rest a while."

"Any idea where he's taking you?"

"He wouldn't give any hints, so I'm in the dark."

When Genevieve disconnected the call, Gabrielle said, "Enjoy the play, sis."

The ringing of the doorbell roused Genevieve at five o'clock PM. Looking through the peephole, she didn't recognize the man's face. "Who is it?"

"Special delivery for a Miss Genevieve Davis."

"What in the world . . . ?" was all she could say when she accepted a large garment bag with the Andrianna Furs logo displayed across the front. Genevieve laid the very heavy garment bag on the living room sofa and stared at the logo in shock. She remembered the fur coat she oohed and aahed over earlier in the show-case window of Andrianna Furs.

She also recalled Cordell asking her if she wanted to try it on for size. "Oh, my God. Cordell, you didn't."

Genevieve tore open the small white envelope the delivery man had given her and read what was inside.

'It's cold outside, this is a little something to keep you warm.'
Pastor Cordell

Genevieve squealed in delight as she unzipped the garment bag with shaky hands. The mannequin in the showcase window didn't do this coat justice. The beautiful black coat Genevieve held in her hands was magnificent. "Oh, my God."

She slipped into the coat and hurried into Gabrielle's

bedroom to look at herself in the full length mirror. "Oh, my God."

It was a perfect fit and draped to her ankles. Genevieve opened the coat and saw Genevieve Latrice embroidered in gold stitching. "Oh, my God."

Even before Genevieve rang her cellular telephone, Gabrielle already knew why she'd be calling and screaming. Cordell called Gabrielle hours ago for Genevieve's measurements and the correct spelling of her name.

"Genny, if you don't calm down and speak clearly, I won't understand what you're saying."

"Oh, my God. Gabby, he, Cordell, fur coat, my name in it, beautiful, unexpected. Oh, my God."

Gabrielle laughed. It's a good thing she already knew about Genevieve's fur coat or else she'd never understand what she was screaming about.

At exactly six o'clock PM, Cordell escorted Genevieve, wrapped in her black coat, from Gabrielle's apartment to a white stretch limousine. Once inside, Genevieve couldn't thank him enough for her gift. "I don't know what to say to you, Cordell. This is so unexpected and very appreciated. No man has ever given me a gift such as this."

"That's because no man has ever realized how special you are."

"How can I top this? What can I do for you?"

"You're already doing it. Just allowing me the pleasure of your company is all that I ask."

The chauffer drove them to the front entrance of Lawry's Steakhouse. Genevieve had never eaten so much in one day, but she wasn't about to complain. She relished in Cordell's attention.

After they placed their orders with the waiter, Cordell looked across the table into Genevieve's eyes. "You are absolutely breathtaking this evening. I've never been on a date with a more beautiful woman. I can't take my eyes off you."

Genevieve's smile lit up the dining room. "Then don't."

"I bet you're beautiful even while you're sleeping."

"Maybe one morning, real soon, you'll get a chance to see for yourself."

Cordell was praying for a response like that because the closer it got to the time for Genevieve's plane to leave Midway Airport, the more he wanted to ask her to stay in Chicago. His ultimate goal was for her to become his wife.

"A penny for your thoughts," she said to him.

"Oh, um, I was just thinking how perfect this entire day has been. I had a wonderful time hanging out with you, and I hate to see it come to an end."

"Who says it has to come to an end?"

This woman was working on Cordell's last nerve, but in a good way. Telling him that he'd get a chance to watch her sleep and saying that their time together didn't have to end, made Cordell believe that Genevieve wanted to stay in Chicago just as much as he wanted her to stay. All she needed was a reason.

During dinner, Genevieve noticed Cordell checking the time on his watch every fifteen minutes. "Do you have a curfew?"

"Excuse me?"

"You keep checking your watch. Is there someplace else you need to be?"

The Cadillac Theatre was twenty minutes away. Cordell knew that they needed to leave now in order to catch the beginning of the opening act. "As a matter of fact, there is."

Cordell quickly paid the bill and hurried Genevieve out to the waiting limousine.

"Okay, you said we didn't have time for dessert, so tell me where we're rushing to."

"And spoil the surprise? I would never do that."

As the driver pulled in front of the Cadillac theater, Genevieve's face was as bright as the neon lights that read, **Oprah Winfrey Presents** *The Color Purple.* Genevieve squealed and jump onto Cordell's lap and began kissing his entire face.

A long distance courtship began. Genevieve returned to Dallas but she and Cordell talked by telephone and prayed together daily. They were also on their knees daily asking God to reveal to them if the other was the chosen mate He had for them. Every other weekend, Cordell sent Genenvieve a round trip plane ticket. Two months prior to Randall and Gabrielle's wedding, Cordell presented Genevieve with a three-carat, princess-cut platinum diamond ring. God had answered their prayers.

August 15th

It was Sunday, and a very special day in the Loomis household. Randall was awakened with a beautiful song. He opened his eyes, smiled, and sat up on the bed. It had been a year and a half since he last heard it and hadn't realized how much he missed hearing it. He got out of bed and walked to his window and saw three little birdies.

"How did y'all find me?" He stood and watched them fly away. He got on his knees and prayed. Today was his wedding day, and what better time to get married than a Sunday after morning service? He thanked God for what He'd done for him. The Lord took Randall to Proverbs 10:17.

*He who keeps instruction is in the way of life, but he
who refuses correction goes astray.*

That scripture reminded Randall of the day God led
him to Brandon, but he allowed sin to turn his back on
Him. Then the Lord took Randall to Luke 6:33.

*Give and it will be given to you: good measure,
pressed down, shaken together, and running over will
be put into your bosom. For with the same measure
that you use, it will be measured back to you.*

That scripture told Randall that he was highly favored by the Lord. *Good measure,* he got his brand new
car. *Pressed down,* he got his mansion. *Shaken together,* he got his kids. *And running over,* today God
was giving him a righteous woman. If God never did
anything else for Randall, what He had already done
was more than enough.

Apostle Donald Lawrence Alford gave the organist
the cue to start the music. Cordell was a pastor
but he himself was without a covering of his own. He
asked Apostle Alford to become his pastor and the
apostle agreed.

Randall stood at the altar facing the congregation
with his best man on his right. Cordell and Randall were
handsome in their white tuxedos.

Ma'Dear sat on the first pew with Eboni, who was
dressed in a little white lace gown identical to
Gabrielle's, on her lap. The doors to the sanctuary
opened and Donald Lawrence and the Tri-City Singers'
"Walk Into Your Season" filled the room. Joshua strolled
down the aisle with the rings on top of a white satin
pillow. Tamika followed, wearing a white lace gown
matching Gabrielle's and Eboni's. She decorated the aisle

with rose petals. Randall could hardly see as tears flooded his eyes.

Gabrielle appeared in the doorway. Apostle Alford asked everyone to stand. It took all that was within Randall not to run and meet his bride halfway. Gabrielle was beautiful. Her skin glowed as bright as her lace gown. Cordell couldn't take his eyes away from Genevieve. She was just as beautiful as Gabrielle, wearing a white satin gown, as they walked down the aisle together, arm in arm. Genevieve and Gabrielle had decided to share the same wedding day just as they had shared a womb.

"Dearly beloved, we're gathered here today to witness before God a glorious occasion. Do you, Randall Lamont Loomis, take Gabrielle LaShawn Davis to be your lawfully wedded wife?"

Randall answered, "I certainly do."

"Do you, Gabrielle LaShawn Davis, take Randall Lamont Loomis to be your lawfully wedded husband?"

Gabrielle answered, "Yes, I do."

"Do you, Cordell Joseph Bryson, take Genevieve Latrice Davis to be your lawfully wedded wife?"

Cordell looked at his bride. "Yes, I do."

"Do you, Genevieve Latrice Davis, take Cordell Joseph Bryson to be your lawfully wedded husband."

Genevieve answered, "I do."

The saints had good 'chuch' at this double wedding. Apostle Alford preached a short sermon entitled 'Equally Yoked.' Randall shouted and danced as if he'd lost his mind.

When Cordell saw his best friend lose himself in the Lord, he couldn't help but join in the praise with Randall.

They were at it again. Two peas in a pod, just like old times. When you saw one, you saw the other. Brothers in Christ celebrating Jesus—what a wonderful sight to see. As Apostle Alford pronounced the couples men and wives, Randall and Cordell danced down the aisle, out into the vestibule and left their wives standing at the altar.

Gabrielle looped her arm through Apostle Alford's right arm and Genevieve looped her arm through his left and he escorted them both out of the sanctuary.

There wasn't a formal reception downstairs in the fellowship hall. The kitchen staff baked two wedding cakes and served fried chicken, macaroni and cheese, a tossed salad, and fruit punch.

After many hugs and kisses from family and friends, Randall announced that he and his family had a plane to catch. Cordell and Genevieve walked them outside to their waiting limousine. Once everyone was seated, Randall shook his friend's hand. "Did you ever think this would happen to us?"

"You know what, Randall? I always knew God would bless us abundantly, but this is exceedingly above and beyond anything that we could ever asked for."

"I feel you, man."

"So, what's the plan?"

"You and Genny fly to Hawaii tomorrow. Me, Gabby, and the kids leave for Disney World tonight. In a week, we bring the kids home, then join you and Genny in Hawaii."

"Alright, man, we'll see you in seven days."

Before the limousine driver pulled away, Randall looked at his friend. "Hey, Cordell? Am I my brother's keeper?"

"Yes, you are. Am I?"

"Yes, you are."

Gabrielle stepped out of the limousine and stood next to Cordell as Genevieve took Gabrielle's place next to Randall inside the limousine. Both Cordell and Randall looked at each other then both their wives. Before anyone could say anything, the twins switched places again.

"What is going on?" Cordell asked.

"I don't know what's going on, or who is who, but if they switch again, I say you keep who you got and I'll keep who I got," Randall stated.

They shook hands again then the limousine pulled away from the curb. Cordell's attention was drawn across the street to a woman he thought he recognized. He watched her as she watched Randall's limousine drive away. She wore a neck brace, and her right arm was in a cast. It looked as though her left eye was blackened. He stepped to the curb to get a closer look at her. "Amaryllis?"

Amaryllis looked at Cordell, stuck her middle finger up at him, and limped down the street on crutches. Genevieve was curious. "Who's that?"

"Trust me, you don't wanna know." The pastor and first lady of Holy Deliverance Baptist Church went back to their reception.

That night, Cordell was lying in bed waiting for his wife to join him. Genevieve came from the bathroom dressed in a gorgeous white sheer gown. She took her robe off, got under the covers and snuggled next to him. Before he turned off the lamp, Cordell gently pulled on Genevieve's earring and was happy that it didn't come off. He turned off the lamp and enjoyed his wife.

Twelve hundred miles away in Orlando, Randall gently pulled on Gabrielle's earring and it fell into his hand. "Just checkin,' " he said.

Readers Group Guide Questions

1. Amaryllis wasn't saved when Randall met her. As a man of God, why do you think he was so willing to lose everything he had for her?

2. Would it have been wrong for Cordell to give up on Randall and allow him to live his own life? Was Cordell truly Randall's keeper?

3. What do you think were Amaryllis's intentions with Randall from the very beginning?

4. Explain Randall's mindset when he found out that Brandon lost his life after he didn't meet him at the church.

5. At what point in the book did Randall face the fact that Amaryllis was ruining his life? What do you think woke him up?

6. How did Gabrielle's character differ from Amaryllis's character?

7. Cordell fell for Genevieve in a matter of days when prior to that he hadn't even been seeking a woman to play a role in his life. Why do you think that was so?

8. Why did God give Randall back everything he lost and much more than he deserved (i.e. the

mansion, a saved woman, three children and a brand new car)?

9. Although Amaryllis's character is definitely one of the strongest and most engaging, the author established men as the main characters. What do you think is the overall message that men will receive after reading this book?

10. Amaryllis saw with her own eyes that Randall is a married man, what do you think she will do now? What is her fate?

Urban Christian His Glory Book Club!

Established January 2007, **UC His Glory Book Club** is another way by which to introduce to the literary world, Urban Book's much-anticipated new imprint, **Urban Christian** and its authors. We are an online book club supporting Urban Christian authors by purchasing, reading and providing written reviews of the authors' books that are read. *UC His Glory* welcomes both men and women of the literary world who have a passion for reading Christian based fiction.

UC His Glory is the brainchild of Joylynn Jossel, Author and Executive Editor of Urban Christian and Kendra Norman-Bellamy, Author and Director of Talent & Operations for Urban Christian. The book club will provide support, positive feedback, encouragement and a forum whereby members can openly discuss and review the literary works of Urban Christian authors. In the future, we anticipate broadening our spectrum of services to include: online author chats, author spotlights, interviews with your favorite Urban Christian author(s), special online groups for *UC Book Club* members, ability to post reviews on the website and amazon.com, membership ID cards, *UC His Glory* Yahoo Group and much more.

Even though there will be no membership fees attached to becoming a member of *UC His Glory Book Club*, we do expect our members to be active, committed and to follow the guidelines of the Book Club.

UC His Glory members pledge to:

- Follow the guidelines of *UC His Glory Book Club*.
- Provide input, opinions, and reviews that build up, rather than tear down.
- Commit to purchasing, reading and discussing featured book(s) of the month.
- Agree not to miss more than three consecutive online monthly meetings.
- Respect the Christian beliefs of *UC His Glory Book Club*.
- Believe that Jesus is the Christ, Son of the Living God

We look forward to the online fellowship.

Many Blessings to You!

Shelia E Lipsey
President
UC His Glory Book Club

**Visit the official Urban Christian Book Club website at *www.uchisglorybookclub.net*

Coming in April 2009:

Amaryllis by Nikita Lynnette Nichols

James opened the door to Michelle's office and was walking out when he stopped and turned around. From his pocket, he withdrew something large and squared that was wrapped in silver paper foil. He tossed it to Michelle. She caught it and gave James the widest grin when she saw what it was.

"Ooh, a Chunky. My baby knows what I like."

"There's more where that came from. I'll call you later." He shut Michelle's door behind him and completely ignored Amaryllis and went straight to the elevator and pressed the 'down' button.

Her eyes followed him and she admired the way his suit framed him. She'd give anything to see those biceps and triceps that were bulging through the linen. And tonight she may get her chance to do just that.

"Hey, Detective, you want to have a little fun with your handcuffs? We could play 'cops and robbers' and I'll let you lock me up," Amaryllis teased.

The elevator doors opened and James stepped inside. He turned to face Amaryllis. "You're sick, you know that?"

The elevator doors closed and she sat there hot and bothered. *Okay, James, you're playing hard to get real well, but that's okay, because tonight I'm gonna break you all the way down.*

Amaryllis looked at the piece of paper she had written information about James' apartment keys on, then folded it and put it in her purse. Just then, Michelle's office door opened again and Michelle came out.

"Hey, sis, I'm on my way to meet Daddy for brunch before heading to the courthouse. You ought to come with me," Michelle suggested. "You could see your big sister do her thang."

"Nope, don't feel like being bothered with Daddy today. He irks me," Amaryllis said nonchalantly.

Michelle exhaled. "Amaryllis, you and Daddy have got to get it together."

"Tell him that."

Michelle put her purse on her shoulder and walked to the elevator. "You know what? I'm not gonna let you two stress me today. I'll see you later."

As soon as Michelle was out of sight, Amaryllis hurried into her office to look for James's keys. She didn't see them on the desk so she frowned. She then walked around and opened Michelle's center drawer. There she saw one big key, a gold key, and a silver key. She snatched James's keys and grabbed her own keys and purse and walked to the elevator.

Fifteen minutes later, Amaryllis exited a hardware store with her own set of keys to James's apartment. She crossed the street and entered a beauty supply store. She found just what she was looking for on a shelf sitting on a Styrofoam head.

A sales lady approached her. "May I help you?"

"Yes, how much is that long blond wig?" Amaryllis asked.

Ten minutes later, Amaryllis walked into 'Snap To It' and approached the sales clerk standing behind the counter. "I want to purchase a small camera with a timer."

She had one more stop to make. From the moment Amaryllis walked into the pharmacy, it took a half hour for her name to be called. The pharmacist handed over Amaryllis's prescription.

"I'm sorry about the wait, Miss Price; we had to call Chicago to get your doctor's approval." The pharmacist smiled.

Amaryllis returned to the law firm with everything she needed. She placed James's original keys back in Michelle's center drawer and sat down and called Bridgette in Chicago.

"Parker & Parker Law Offices, Bridgette speaking."

"Hey girl, it's me. I called to tell you that I'm getting ready to get my man."

"You mean you're getting ready to get someone else's man."

"Whatever."

"When is this going to take place?"

"If I play my cards right, I could sneak in his place and set everything up before he gets home tonight."

"Set everything up? What are you gonna do, film a movie?"

"Something like that. I gotta wait for Michelle to do her thing first."

"Your sister, Michelle? What's she got to do with anything?"

"Oh, Bridgette, I didn't tell you. James is Michelle's man."

Bridgette was typing but she stopped and gave Amaryllis her full attention. "Say what?"

"You heard me."

"Amaryllis, is this the same man you told me about last week? The detective? The minister?"

"Yep."

"And he's your sister's fiancé?"

"One and the same."

"Okay, you've done some wild stuff in your day, Amaryllis, but this is totally off the chart, even for you. You didn't tell me this guy was your sister's man. What are you thinking?"

"I'm thinking about how good it's going to feel laying in his arms tonight."

"Do you hear yourself, girl? He's your sister's fiancé. *Hello?*" Bridgette couldn't believe Amaryllis's gall.

"And?"

"And what you're doing is wrong."

"Bridgette, you're the one who told me to do what I gotta do to get my man."

"That was before I knew he was marrying your sister. You left that part out when you told me about him."

"Well, now you know. I need to get off of this phone and plan my evening right."

"Don't you hang up on me, Amaryllis. This will destroy your relationship with Michelle. You do know that, don't you? She's your only sister, and she loves you. How can you live in her house, work for her, and do this behind her back?"

Amaryllis looked at James's photograph and traced his smile with her finger. "Easily."